PRAISE FO

"G.M. Ford is must reading."

—Harlan Coben

"Ford is a witty and spunky writer who not only knows his terrain but how to bring it vividly to the printed page."

—*West Coast Review of Books*

"G.M. Ford is a born storyteller."

—J.A. Jance

"He's well on his way to becoming the Raymond Chandler of Seattle."
—*Kirkus Reviews*

"G.M. Ford is, hands down, one of my favorite contemporary crime writers. Hilarious, provocative, and cool as a March night in Seattle, he may be the best-kept secret in mystery novels."

—Dennis Lehane

"G.M. Ford has a supercharged V-12 under the hood."

—Lee Child

"G.M. Ford writes the pants off most of his contemporaries."
—*Independent on Sunday*

HEAVY ON
THE DEAD

OTHER TITLES BY G.M. FORD

HEAVY ON THE DEAD

A LEO WATERMAN
MYSTERY

G.M. FORD

THOMAS & MERCER

Text copyright © 2019 by G.M. Ford
All rights reserved.

Published by Thomas & Mercer, Seattle

www.apub.com

Amazon, the Amazon logo, and Thomas & Mercer are trademarks of Amazon.com, Inc., or its affiliates.

ISBN-13: 9781542041300
ISBN-10: 1542041309

Cover design by Pete Garceau

Printed in the United States of America

HEAVY ON
THE DEAD

The door burst open and banged against the wall. Half a dozen men shuffled into the room, shaking rain from their coats as they jostled inside. The short man with the black rubber raincoat and Coke-bottle eyeglasses elbowed his way to the front.

"Show me," he said.

"Right there, Mr. Marshall." The technician pointed at his computer screen. He tapped a grainy image of a dozen or so men and women waiting in line inside what appeared to be some sort of public building. The man in question was considerably taller than the others in the line. Fishing charter T-shirt, shorts, flip-flops. Long hair and beard. Your basic *turista*. Extra-large variety.

"Quality's not very good," Marshall groused as he folded his coat inside out and draped it over his arm.

The technician shrugged his narrow shoulders. "Mexican equipment." He tapped the screen again with an ink-stained finger. "Just a second here," he said. "Wait till the line turns the corner."

The tape jumped ahead. The tall man was now in full profile. Everyone in the room leaned closer to the screen, like the folding of a flower.

Marshall nearly touched his nose to the screen. Then he slowly removed his glasses, sighed, and straightened up.

"He's about the right height, I suppose," Marshall said.

Everyone waited for him to say something else. When he remained silent, someone blurted out, "We need to be sure."

The little man hacked out a short, bitter laugh. "The understatement of the century." He waved a disgusted hand at the computer screen. "We can't have any more setbacks," he said, "and a guy about the right height, in the right place, at the right time isn't gonna cut it. That's the kind of sloppy work that very nearly . . ." He stopped himself and massaged the bridge of his nose.

"Gonna have to send some people down to Greaserville," the bald man in the corner said. "They can probably."

Marshall's voice rose a full octave. "Don't talk to me about probably. *Probably* cost us nearly a hundred men and all the material we'd collected." He slashed the air with his hand. "Years of work. Millions of dollars," he screeched. He gave his anger a moment to sink in. "From now on, you just tell me what we know for certain, and nothing else." He looked around the room. "Do you hear me?" he shouted.

Somebody cleared his throat. "There's been money going in and out of his American accounts. Some of it paying taxes on his old house . . . insurance bills . . . things like that . . . but the great majority of it ended up right there . . . the Tijuana Rio branch of the BanRegio bank. We also know that in order to open a bank account in Mexico you have to show up in person. We checked the bank CC camera footage for the two weeks before the first transfer of funds. What we've been looking at here is footage from the same day the account was opened."

The technician tapped the screen again. "Look at the person in line behind Waterman. It's that freak he hangs out with. Always right at his elbow, but since Waterman disappeared . . ." He snapped his fingers. "Gone. Nobody seen that pervert motherfucker for months now."

Marshall bent again and squinted at the screen. "We need absolute confirmation," he said finally. "And it needs to be completely under the radar. No public presence at all. We are in no position to attract further attention."

He started for the door. Stopped. Turned back around and wagged a stiff finger. "But . . . if that *is* that son of a bitch Leo Waterman, I want him dead and buried." He started for the door again.

"Heavy on the dead," he said.

Chapter 1

The ocean has a primal call. A voice, deep and resonant, that beckons everyone, almost on the cellular level. The rich, the poor, the homeowner, and the homeless, it called them all, and they all came, living an uneasy cheek-to-jowl existence in Ocean Beach.

The last of the ungentrified surfer towns in California, Ocean Beach was a place defined by the variety of its lifestyles and its good-natured acceptance of all. O.B. was the kind of place where nobody was gonna bat an eye at a couple of new people in town. Or ask any questions about them either. So for a laid-back guy who'd been forced to go underground, it had seemed like the perfect place to chill out and disappear for a while.

I'd been holed up in O.B. for a little over seven months and had only recently stopped checking the sidewalk behind me. Truth be told, I was thinking about staying forever. Not just because of the perfect weather, although I've gotta admit that was a major player. What really attracted me was the fact that, like me, O.B. was a perpetual outsider. The redheaded stepchild of San Diego. A onetime mudflat campground of the terminally adventurous, Ocean Beach had refused to move beyond the sixties. Gabe came down later, after months of physical therapy made it clear that the piece of shell casing that had shattered Gabe's calf had healed as much as it was gonna, which, unfortunately, wasn't enough for Gabe to function as full-time muscle anymore.

To a lesser degree, the same was true about me. Gabe and I had stumbled into something we weren't prepared for, and both of us had emerged quite a bit worse for the wear. Gabe moved with a perceptible limp, and three spinal surgeries later, I had all the fluid mobility of a backhoe.

We found a two-bedroom rental on Del Monte Avenue, a block and a half from the ocean, settled in, and then, for want of anything else to do, got involved with the community. Gabe was taking a couple of art classes at SDSU and had started a three-times-a-week women's karate class in Old Town. I volunteered for a beach cleanup crew and then joined the local citizens group that opposed any incursion of corporate culture into the otherwise homegrown commercial environment. Being around people who gave a shit about their town and their fellow citizens made me feel damn near as warm as the weather did. Life was slow and simple. Predictable. Just the way I liked it.

It was Thursday night. Beach cleanup night. Couple hours of daylight left when I wandered down Niagara to the foot of the pier and signed in. The crew had already started to fan out. I smiled and mumbled my way through the assembled multitude, picked up my bucket and my picker, and headed south, down toward Santa Cruz Cove.

In a good week, beach cleanup night was the only time I put on anything with shoelaces. You spend enough time wearing flip-flops and even sneakers make you feel like you're clomping around with paving stones wired to your feet.

The beach, not surprisingly, turned out to be a miniature model of society. You only had to participate in one beach cleanup to figure out that the two biggest problems facing O.B. were the waves of homeless folks, who quite literally had no place else to go, and the rising tide of opiate addiction that was shredding their ranks like a wood chipper.

The beach crew had taken one neck-craning look at me and asked if I'd mind working the south end of the cleanup, down at Santa Cruz Cove, where the piss stairs would get you down to a small beach where the homeless and the drug addled wedged themselves onto sand ledges forty feet above the roaring Pacific and hoped like hell it wasn't a plus tide, or worse yet, that the section of cliff they'd chosen didn't decide to peel off and fall into the ocean, which it did on a very regular basis.

That's also where you were most likely to run into the trolls. Those shuffling piles of rags and fury whose lives had spun perilously out of control, leaving them at the mercy of the sand, the sea, and the SDPD.

Because the stairs over at the Silver Spray Apartments were currently under reconstruction, I walked back to Bacon and took the sidewalk south. On the way I picked up a couple of beer cans and the remains of an empty pint of whiskey shattered on the sidewalk. Just before Del Monte I came upon a dead possum on the side of the road but decided that toting a stiff, malodorous marsupial around in my bucket was above and beyond the call of civic duty, so I left it there and kept walking.

My surgically repaired right knee hated going down stairs, so I paused at the top of the Santa Cruz stairs and reminded myself there was no hurry. Nobody was looking. I could short step it down the stairs like a gimpy geezer and nobody would be the weezer. A sudden onshore flow slapped my face with artisanal hints of piss and body odor, but I resisted the urge to hurry. Last thing in the world I needed was to take a tumble, so I kept my eyes focused on the stairs instead of all the little paths leading off into the undergrowth. I stopped a couple of times, shook out my balky knee, then moved on.

The exposed seabed on my right seethed with lime-green seaweed, swishing in and out with the tide, long and languid, like the floating hair of some long-submerged sea witch. Half a dozen beachcombers were spread along the largest crescent of sand. Couple more sitting on top of the tallest finger of rock. Right out in front of me, a kid in polka-dot board shorts had found a sand dollar and was yelling for his mom to come and have a look. A guy and a girl were snugged up under the lip of the cliff. He was scratching away at a guitar. She was staring into her phone as if the secrets of the ages were just a button push away.

Farther out, right at the tide line, somebody was seated in the full lotus position, becoming one with the sea. It happened nearly every night. Kind of an Ocean Beach tradition, watching the Technicolor sky sink into the Pacific until that final flash of ungodly green signaled the arrival of the night.

I started at the south end and worked my way north. Took me an hour to pick up all the crap. About halfway through, I had to find a flat rock and stomp all the beer and soda cans flat so's they'd fit in the bucket.

By the time I'd finished, the sun was hanging over the edge of the world, burning like a rocket engine, and I was alone on the beach.

I picked up my bucket and my picker and started for the stairs. Nobody, including me, wanted to be down there with the trolls when darkness arrived. Shrieking of gulls tore at my attention. I kept my eyes glued on my feet and kept climbing. I threw a quick glance to my right. Half a dozen of them were squawking and flapping over something farther up the cliff, in the bushes.

I wasn't looking for trouble, so I turned my face away and kept climbing the stairs, watching the waves tumble toward shore, zoning out to the sounds of the surf, when a pair of big California gulls came screaming and flapping across my field of vision. Fighting over a dangling scrap of food one of them was carrying in his beak.

Without wishing it so, I stopped climbing. I was watching the contentious gulls when a single word came to mind. *Meat,* my mind said. *Looks like a piece of meat they're quarreling over.*

I stood still and gave myself a pep talk about how bringing any kind of attention to myself was not a good idea. Maybe even suicidal. About how I needed to keep strictly under the radar. Then I set the bucket on the stairs, grabbed the picker, ducked through the steel railing, and started into the scrubby cliffside foliage.

The scuffling gulls saw me coming and veered off. I carefully made my way across the grade. I slipped past a couple of empty campsites—burned-out fires and a blue sleeping bag with a red flannel lining featuring images of the cow jumping over the moon. Hey diddle diddle.

Fifty feet farther on, my knees began to rise toward my chest as the little sandstone plateau lost its battle with gravity and turned back into a cliff. Two forced steps and I was nose to nose with a nearly perpendicular piece of sandstone. I leaned against the rock, heaved a couple of labored breaths, and looked around.

Didn't take a genius to see I had only two choices. I was either traversing back the way I'd come, making damn sure I didn't lose my footing and go rolling down the shit-covered embankment, or climbing straight up into the stubborn tangle of ground cover beneath the condos above.

I might have given up right then except the gulls came back, keening and swirling over the same piece of ground cover, feathers floating to the ground as they roughhoused ten feet above where I was standing.

A big California gull floated past my face. His bright-yellow beak dripping red. I dug my feet in, forced a bunch of onshore flow into my lungs, and peered up the embankment. No question. This was gonna take four-wheel drive, so I leaned the picker against the cliff, grabbed a couple of bushes, and used both hands to inch up the grade, wedging my sneakers at the rooted bases of the plants, hoping like hell the slope didn't come apart.

From this angle I could see the scrub was bent outward, as if supporting something of weight. Two more steps. My legs were screaming at me. I was looking down between my legs, focused on where I put my feet.

By the time I looked up again, I was face-to-face with the body. Could have kissed him on the lips. Upside down anyway. It was a kid. A boy maybe ten. Brown skinned. Wearing an impossibly white shirt. He was lying on his back with one leg twisted beneath him at an ungodly angle.

From where I hovered, he was looking right at me. Or at least he would have been if he'd had eyes in his sockets. I stifled a gag and turned my face away. Tried to take in all the oxygen in the world in a single breath but found only the rank remnants of human decay. I gagged again and slapped a hand over my mouth. Took me a couple of minutes to settle my stomach.

I hung there for a long minute and ran the situation through my circuits. Seemed like the only sane thing to do was to go back down to Niagara, sign out so's nobody would be looking for me, then go back home and call 911 on one of the burners I always used these days. Tell 'em where to find the kid and then lose the burner forever. Way I saw it, that was the only way I could do right by the boy without blowing my cover.

On my way back to the stairs, I cut a strip from the discarded sleeping bag and tied it around the steel stair rail about level with where the kid was to be found. I grabbed the bucket and hustled up the stairs a whole lot faster than I'd come down.

Wasn't till I got back to Niagara and nodded my way through signing out that I realized I didn't have the picker. A picture of me leaning it against the cliff flashed before my inner eye. I thought about going back for it, but all that would have accomplished was to bring more attention to myself. I silently cursed.

Ten minutes later, I was back at the apartment, rummaging around in the junk drawer until I came out with a pair of blue latex gloves, a claw hammer, and a brand-new burner. I took a couple of deep breaths while I wiggled into the gloves and then called 911. Years of working as a PI had taught me that the secret of leaving an anonymous tip was to keep it a one-way conversation. Short and sweet.

"There's a boy's body on the side of the hill at Santa Cruz Cove," I said. "There's a piece of blue cloth tied to the rail at about where the body is."

"Sir . . . what is your—"

Bang. Broke the connection. Waited a long second and powered off the phone and then took it out on the small balcony off the living room and pounded it to dust. Then pounded the dust to talc. In the spirit of tidiness, I then swept up the mess, poured it into a ziplock sandwich bag, and just to be safe, walked the block and a half over to the parking lot behind the Olive Tree Market and rifled it into the dumpster. On the way back to the apartment, I dropped the latex gloves into an apartment house trash bin and mamboed back home.

. . .

"Mr. Marshall."

The man behind the desk slipped his glasses from his narrow face and looked up at the young man peeping through a crack in the office door. He motioned with his hand. The younger man slipped through the opening like smoke sliding into the room.

"Tell me you finally have something," Marshall said.

"Yes sir."

"And it took five days for you people to come up with someone we can send down to Tijuana to check on this bank thing?"

The younger man swallowed hard and slid a manila folder onto the desk. "We needed people with valid passports and without criminal records, sir. Not many of our brothers qualify." He shrugged. "The Mexicans are making it harder and harder to get into the country . . . you know with all the immigration and building a wall stuff going on. There's a lot of hard feelings."

The man behind the desk made a waving motion with his fingers. Looked like he was flicking a fly. "So?"

"So . . . our contact at the bank won't come to us."

"And why is that?"

"He says he doesn't have the necessary paperwork to get back and forth across the border, but I think he's holding out with the information until he gets the money in his hand." The young man cleared his throat. "So . . . you said no phones, no internet, no nothing. That you wanted the information in person from whoever we sent to get it."

"No footprint whatsoever, electronic or otherwise. Not a goddamn thing!" He pounded his fist on the table.

Startled, the kid kept talking. "So some of the Brotherhood who are staying in the Tecate safe house are bringing the bank guy up there. Our guys are gonna meet him there, hand over the money, and come right back here to report in person."

"Our guys who?"

The young man reached out and opened the folder, removed the contents, and made two piles. Each with a color head shot paper clipped to the first page. He pointed to the big moon-faced guy on the right.

"This one is Chub Greenway. From the northern Florida chapter. His brother—"

The older man cut him off. "Randy Greenway."

"Yes sir. Killed up in Conway."

"What's Chub's real name?"

"Chub. That's what's on his birth certificate. I understand he was an unusually large baby. Over twelve pounds, if my information is correct."

"A most prodigious issue," Marshall mused.

"Came from a family of truck farmers in Marrinna, Florida. Way the hell up in the corner of the state. *Not quite Georgia, not quite Alabama,* they like to say. Lost their farm to taxes. Got evicted. The father . . ." He squinted down at the file on the desk. "Ah, Ewell Greenway . . . he met the sheriff's eviction crew in the driveway with a shotgun. Shots were exchanged, and the elder Greenway was pronounced dead at the scene."

"Losing a father and a brother to the race pigs. I'd say Chub is motivated." He mused over the thought for a moment and then asked, "The other one?"

The other man pointed at the pile of paperwork. "Lamar Pope," he said. "His parents were some sort of Holy Roller missionaries. They lived a couple of miles south of the U.S. border. Lamar speaks fluent Spanish."

"And what prompted Lamar to join our Brotherhood?"

"His parents got killed in a car accident down in Mexico. Only relative he had was an eighty-year-old aunt in Chicago, Illinois, so that's where they sent him. He was eight years old at the time. Problem was, the old lady died a year or so later, and Lamar ended up in the foster care system. Couple of professional foster parents from Gary, Indiana, took him in. From what I understand, it wasn't an altogether pleasant experience for Lamar."

"How so?"

The younger man hesitated. "Well . . . you know, sir, Gary, Indiana isn't exactly . . ." He cleared his throat.

"It's a cesspool of racial impurity," the older man said.

The kid nodded. "Also, several of the other foster kids claimed they'd suffered years of sexual abuse at the hands of their foster parents. The welfare system investigated and agreed. Took all the kids away from them."

"And Lamar. Did he . . ."

"We don't know, sir. He was sixteen at the time. Supposedly a hustler-type con man who thought he could talk his way out of anything. So anyway . . . while the state was looking for another foster family he apparently walked away. Doesn't show up on the radar again until four years later, when he was accused of beating a black man to death in Pineville, Arkansas."

"You said his record was clean."

"It is, sir. He was acquitted. In Arkansas, they expunge your record if you're acquitted."

The little man sat back in his chair and laced his fingers over his bony chest.

"Good folks in Arkansas," Marshall said.

The younger man kept talking. "We figured they'd make a good pair. Lamar is about as good a talker as we've got, and Chub can sure as hell handle anything physical that comes up."

"How long till we're fully operational?"

"A few more days."

"Why the delay?"

"We're still working on their paperwork. Making sure it's just right."

"It better be," the man behind the desk muttered.

"We're working on it, sir."

■ ■ ■

With me, it always starts with a single innocent-sounding self-deception. This time I told myself I was going to walk up to Santa Cruz and simply peek around the corner. See what in hell was going on. Nothing more. And then go straight home. A red aid car screamed up Bacon in the wake of the squad car. And then another.

Four minutes later I was standing behind the yellow cop tape, looking down into Santa Cruz Cove, doing the Lambada with all the other spaced-out gawkers milling around the top of the stairs. What can I say?

I'd been there a couple of minutes, standing at the end of Santa Cruz, looking at the action from a completely different angle, when I was inundated by a sudden spasm of lucidity.

First thing that backhanded me across the face was the question of how in hell the body got to the spot where I'd found it. From below, it had looked as if the condos up on the cliff hovered directly over the spot. From here, though, you could see how far the condos were set back from the edge. Hell, there was a pool and a patio between the closest condos and the edge of the cliff. No way had anybody thrown that body from one of the balconies. I don't care how big and strong that mofo was, there was no way anybody could throw a body that far without a medieval catapult.

I'd originally come up from below. Took everything I'd had to crimp and claw up that slope. No way was anybody carrying a body up from below either. I don't care if it was just a little boy.

Realistic alternatives refused to readily come to mind.

I craned my neck over the guy in front of me. Half a dozen EMTs and firemen were forcing a gurney through the undergrowth on pure muscle power. I watched as they plucked the kid from the bushes, wrapped him up in an oversize body bag, belted him down, and started passing him back across the slope. The body looked so small. I turned away. Looked out over the Pacific, listening to the roar of the tide. Half a dozen crows bounced around the phone lines, cawing and flapping as if to announce that the end was near.

A couple of beefy SDPD uniforms started pushing the crowd back. "Give 'em room," an Asian officer shouted into the gathering night. The assembled multitude shuffled backward about an inch and a half.

Couple minutes later, the first fireman came into view. A car-wreck rumble rose from the crowd as the men eased the body up the last of the stairs, popped the wheels of the gurney down, and rolled it over to the back of the aid car. Last cop up the stairs was carrying the picker. I silently cursed again.

That's when I noticed how one of the cops had parked his cruiser across the street pointing directly at the collection of gawkers at the top of the stairs. The blinking red light in the windshield suggested that we were being recorded for posterity and that all of us might be expecting a visit from the SDPD if they didn't come up with something better to go on.

I gave myself a mental kick in the ass for being such a careless jerk and then checked the street. The police had barricaded the last block of Santa Cruz. I watched as they moved one of the cruisers so the aid car could get out. I wanted to get the hell out of there too but didn't want to be the first one to leave. Overhead, the crows got louder. The aid car disappeared around the corner.

I waited until the crowd began to thin and then walked off behind a couple of girls wearing wet suits and carrying boogie boards, hoping it would look to the camera as if we were together.

"I wonder how many people fall off Sunset Cliffs every year," I said to their backs. In unison they both looked over their shoulders and scowled at me. "As if," the taller of the two said as they hurried off down the street.

So much for subterfuge.

Chapter 2

"We're lookin' for row D, number 107," Lamar said.

Chub pointed off to the right. "D row," he rumbled. The guy's hand was the size of a fucking waffle iron. Lamar, who was a little over six feet two himself and considered by most to be a damn tough hombre, felt pretty sure he'd never seen a human being quite as large as Chub Greenway. They'd only met an hour ago. When Lamar had gotten off his plane from Tucson, Chub had been standing by the terminal door blotting out the sun.

They'd exchanged a series of mumbles and manly nods and started off through the terminal, following the signs to the long-term parking lot in search of their ride. Chub was half a dozen steps ahead of Lamar when he suddenly skidded to a halt on the asphalt. The big duffel bag dropped from his hand. Lamar stopped walking and tried to peer around Chub, which was a lot like trying to see around Arizona.

"What the fuck is this?" Chub demanded.

Lamar stepped around his companion. D 107 was indeed painted on the pavement. He pulled a set of keys from his pants pocket.

"That's not a car," Chub said.

The noncar was yellow and white.

"I believe it's called a Smart car," Lamar said.

"Who the fuck rented this piece of shit?"

"They bought it," Lamar said.

Chub's barn door forehead wrinkled. "What the fuck for?"

"Supply told me they bought it in case . . . they figured, you know, we might have to ditch it down there, and they didn't want some rental company looking for the car. They said if we needed to ditch the car all we had to do was leave it at the curb with the keys in it. The beaners would be all over it like white on rice, and that way there wouldn't be nobody lookin' for it neither."

"I ain't gonna fit in there." Chub Greenway turned in Lamar's direction. His furled fists hung from the ends of his arms like cannonballs.

"Hey, man . . . ," Lamar said. "I didn't have nothing to do with this. I'm just doin' like I was told." He walked over to the front bumper of the little car.

"You wanna drive?" he asked his humongous companion.

Chub snatched the keys from Lamar's fingers, unlocked the door, and jerked the driver's seat back as far as it would go. He made a rude noise with his lips and then slammed the door. "It's a fucking clown car," he growled.

"It's only about sixty miles to Tecate," Lamar said.

By the time Lamar got their duffel bags tamped in behind the seats, Chub had folded himself nearly double into the passenger seat. With his eyes squeezed shut, he appeared to be praying for salvation. "Open the fucking sunroof," he growled as Lamar got into the driver's seat.

Lamar reached up and began to twist the handle. The plastic panel slid back. And then stopped. Lamar stretched up a bit in the seat. A part of Chub's jacket was caught in the mechanism.

"Stuck," Lamar said to nobody in particular.

Not for long. Chub reached up, grabbed the edge of the sunroof, and with a muffled grunt, ripped it the rest of the way open. Mechanism notwithstanding.

Lamar watched in silence as he folded his arms back against his sides, wiggled his ass deeper into the seat, then stuck his head out the sunroof.

"Let's get the fuck outta here," Chub said.

Lamar stifled a grin. "Less than sixty miles," he said again. "And what the hell, man . . . it never rains in California."

• • •

Took 'em three days to get around to me. By Sunday I was beginning to think that the cops might have missed the discrepancy with the picker. But no such luck. Gabe and I were working our way through a bale of cilantro-garlic naan and some lamb dish from the Indian joint around the corner when somebody began to knock on the security door.

Gabe wandered over to the front window and peeked out through the vertical blinds. I watched a smile settle in.

"You want the good news or the bad news?" Gabe asked, letting the slat slide back within the others.

"Good."

"One of 'em's a cute little dish."

"What's the bad news?"

"They're both sure as hell cops." Gabe waved a diffident hand. "You know that heady mix of institutional arrogance and primal fear they emit."

I couldn't help but return the smile.

"Should I let 'em in?" Gabe asked.

"No," I said quickly. I jerked a thumb toward the back side of the apartment. "Let's not give 'em anything we don't have to."

Gabe lobbed the last of the naan onto a paper plate, picked it up, and headed for the back of the apartment. I wiped my lips with a paper towel and pushed myself to my feet. I started for the door but had a second thought. I walked back to the table, put Gabe's glass and silverware in the dishwasher, and quickly wiped off the table.

The apartment had a burglar bar security door that we kept double locked at all times, so I wasn't worried about one of them sticking a foot in the doorjamb as I pulled open the interior door.

One of each. And Gabe was right too. She was fortysomething, about five foot six or so, in a brown two-piece suit that looked like it was fresh from the cleaners. Mona Lisa face and big blue eyes. She had her hair pulled back hard enough to lift her eyebrows. Seemed to be in firm possession of all the requisite woman equipment too.

Her partner was about the same height, short brown hair, wearing one of those super skinny suits that clutched at his body like a sausage casing. His legs looked like pipe cleaners. One more tassel and his shoes would have been considered fringed. I was betting he regularly had himself waxed all over. Smooth as a billiard ball, I was guessing. Mr. Metrosexual.

"Mr. Marks?" she asked immediately.

"Who wants to know?"

It was a dumb question. I mean the woman was wearing her badge around her neck.

"I'm Sergeant Carolyn Saunders of the San Diego PD." She threw a hand in her partner's direction. "This is my associate, Detective Reynolds. We were wondering if we might ask you a few questions."

"Fire away," I said through the grates and bars.

"Perhaps we could come inside," she said.

"What can I help you with?" I asked.

They exchanged a glance. I was guessing I wasn't the first person to keep them out on the sidewalk. This was a real iconoclastic part of town. Lots of old hippies, free thinkers, and folks who weren't exactly big fans of the system.

Saunders took the lead. "Are you a member of the Thursday night beach cleanup crew?"

"Sure am."

"Did you sign out for picker number seventeen on Thursday night?"

"I signed out for a picker." I shrugged. "The number I couldn't tell you."

Mr. Metrosexual reached over to the side of the building and came back with an orange picker. It had a yellow evidence tag hanging from the handle.

"Is this the picker, Mr. Marks?" he wanted to know.

"Looks like it," I allowed.

"So this *is* the picker you were using on Thursday night," she said quickly.

"That's *not* what I said. I said it *looks* like the one I used. They all look alike to me," I said with a grin. Apparently humor is, as rumored, highly subjective.

Cops are professional contradiction collectors, so the secret to dealing with them isn't what you tell them. It's what you don't. *Don't* being the key concept here. "I don't know" is rather hard to dispute.

"Is this about the body they found down there?" I asked.

Another baleful glance was exchanged. You could hear boulders rolling in caves.

"What do you know about that, Mr. Marks?" she asked.

"Just that it happened."

"What was that, Mr. Marks?" her partner asked.

"They found a kid's body down there."

"How do you know it was a kid?" she asked.

"The body bag was only half-full," I said.

"So you were present when they brought it up?"

They already knew the answer to that one, so I confirmed it for them. Told them how I'd done my cleanup, walked back down to Niagara, dumped my junk, signed out, then realized I'd left my picker back at the cove and had gone back to fetch it, only to find the street full of cops and firemen, so naturally, like any curious primate, I'd walked up to the end of Santa Cruz to see what in hell was going on. I showed the ceiling my palms. "That's it. End o' story."

I'd just pissed all over their follow-up questions, so it took her a few seconds to regroup and decide what to ask me next.

"Were you the last one on the beach, Mr. Marks?" she asked me.

"I believe I was. They find out who the kid was?" I asked, before she could dredge up another query.

"It's an ongoing investigation," Marvin Metrosexual sneered.

"Well, if there's anything else I can do, be sure to let me know."

I started to swing the inside door closed. She stepped right up to the security door. "And when you left . . . you had no idea the body was there?"

"None whatsoever."

She locked onto my eyes like we were magnetized. It was supposed to scare the pants off me. Under different circumstances, I would have gratefully let it happen.

Another ten seconds of glowering and they turned and walked away. Metroman led the way toward the stairs, twirling the picker like a majorette's baton. I snapped the locks open, pushed the security door open, then poked my head out into the walkway. She heard the door squeak, turned her head as she started down the stairs, and caught me looking at her ass. Pretty sure I was supposed to look contrite.

. . .

It didn't start to rain in earnest until they'd been waiting at the border for about a half hour. Chub pulled his plaid hat down over his ears and gutted it out in silence. The closer they inched toward the checkpoint, the harder it rained, until, as they finally pulled up under the border arch, the hammering downpour could only have been described as biblical in its ferocity.

An hour later, as they pulled into Tecate, Mexico, six inches of water was sloshing back and forth along the floor of the little car. A steady stream of discolored water dripped from the bill of Chub's cap. Lamar's right side was soaking wet. It was like driving a bathtub.

Lamar pulled the car to the curb and doused the lights. A sudden gust of wind off the Pacific rocked the car on its springs. Lamar unfastened his seat belt and watched as the wind gathered parts of palm fronds from the ground and swirled the pieces into the air like a mini twister.

HEAVY ON THE DEAD

"I can't reach the handle," Chub said. Lamar got out, leaving the driver's door open, and walked around to the passenger side, where he grabbed the handle and yanked open the passenger door.

Chub oozed out in sections. Took him several minutes of stretching and bending to work out the kinks, at which point he jammed a Herford-size shoulder through the open window and, with a muffled groan, tilted the car up onto its side, all the way up until the driver's door hit the ground. What looked to be a hundred gallons of water sloshed out the driver's side, creating a puddle that nearly surrounded the car.

After dropping the car back to earth, Chub groaned and rolled his shoulders. Lamar hustled over to the car and leaned inside to roll up the passenger window. The sunroof mechanism was, however, history. Annoyed, he slapped the windup handle. It spun like a pinwheel. He sighed, slammed the door, and locked it.

The rain hissed down like Phil Spector's wall of sound. Out in Sonora Street, a pickup truck rolled by and then another, second one booming hip-hop loud enough to rattle the car windows. "Hate that rap shit," Chub growled.

"Ain't music at all," Lamar agreed. "Just a buncha idiots yellin' at each other."

"Where we goin'?" Chub wanted to know.

Lamar nodded toward the street. "Other side of the street there. We got a buncha brothers hiding out down here. You know . . . since the thing up in Conway. Lotta guys had to get lost for a while." Chub nodded silently.

Lamar had taken one look at Chub in the airport and decided he wasn't gonna mention the guy's dead brother. Not as big as that mofo was. Uh-uh. Not unless Chub did, and even then, he was gonna keep it real cagey and sympathetic. None of that *blaming the victims* shit, like a buncha members of the Brotherhood were doing these days. Sayin' the guys up there in Washington had just plain fucked up and brought it on themselves. That if it wasn't for that sloppy shit, they'd have had white America back under control by now. He was keeping out of that political shit. Whatever Chub said . . . agree with him. That was the way to go.

Lamar checked the street. Nada. The rain had slackened to a drizzle. From the corner of his eye, he watched as Chub wrung half a gallon of water out of his checkered cap. Lamar pulled out his phone and thumbed in a number.

"We're here," was all he said.

Five seconds passed before the lights of one of the houses across the street blinked three times. "Let's go," Lamar said.

The wind whispered behind their backs as they sloshed across the street. In the eerie glow of the streetlight, the red bougainvillea took on an ungodly purple hue. Couple of houses up the street, an SUV pulled out of one of the driveways, hesitated at the curb, then turned off in the opposite direction. Lamar and Chub stood still and watched until the taillights disappeared around the corner.

Lamar pushed the lighted button on the gatepost. The place lit up like a ballpark at night. Chub pulled his hat low over his eyes. Lamar shielded his face with his forearm. The gate eased open. "Come on," a gruff voice said from inside the glare.

• • •

"What then? Somebody dropped him out of an airplane or something?" Gabe asked.

I shook my head. "The body wasn't fucked up like that. From what I could see, other than what the birds had done to him, he was pretty much intact. Yeah, the ground cover would have softened the blow a bit, but you fall out of the sky, there's a whole lot of impact damage."

"You sure? . . . Maybe . . ."

I waved Gabe off. "Saw a guy one time whose parachute didn't open. They had to slide a sheet of plywood under the body to pick it up. What was left of the guy quivered like cherry Jell-O when they carried it to the ambulance."

Gabe turned off the sink water and dried off with a dish towel. "Let's go."

"Go where?" I asked.

"Let's go figure out how the kid got to where you found him. Otherwise you're going to worry this friggin' thing like a terrier until you maybe get both of us killed or we have to move to fucking Iowa or something." Gabe put on a red SDSU sweatshirt and started for the door. "Come on. I ain't got Iowa in me."

I wanted to argue but instead grabbed a gray O.B. hoodie from the hook by the door and followed along, trailing Gabe through the alley and between buildings until we were both standing on Santa Cruz Avenue. Up at the end of the street, everything was quiet. No squad cars. No gawkers either.

Gabe slid to a stop at the corner. "This thing takes up the whole damn block."

Yeah . . . it was true. I'd walked by it a hundred times but had never taken notice before. The condo building was a block in length. All the way up to the yellow arrows lined along the fence at the end of Bacon, telling you that if you kept driving straight, you were about to experience a sodden sinking sensation.

Gabe's limp was more perceptible going uphill but didn't affect our speed. By the time we got to the end of the building, a couple of things were clear. First off, the building formed a complete barrier between Bacon Street and the ocean. No gaps. No doorways. No nothing. Unless you could get into the building itself, there was no getting to the cliffs and certainly no way of getting to the spot where I'd found the body. So, secondly and therefore, the answer to our little problem must have been either on a side street or on the ocean side of the building.

Gabe took off back down the hill, round the corner, and to the top of the Santa Cruz stairs. Santa Cruz Cove consisted of a series of rock fingers sticking out into the ocean. The two central fingers formed a U-shaped expanse with a little beach and collection of nice perches to commune with the ocean, especially suited for those not enamored with the controlled mayhem of the town's regular beaches.

The tide was in and so were the fish. A dozen brown pelicans were working the water about a quarter mile out from the cliffs. Gliding effortlessly, wheeling in slowly descending circles until, at about six feet above the tops of the waves, zeroing in on an underwater morsel, they folded their wings and dropped into the water like dark feathered darts.

"See where it's all mushed down?"

Gabe nodded and silently began to peruse the cove. A couple of minutes passed.

"The kid had to get put up there from below," Gabe announced, pointing a thick finger north along the face of the cliff. "They came up from the walking path. Someplace between here and the pier."

"They?"

"Much as I hate to admit it, Leo, you were right. No way one person could climb up that grade carrying anything, but you and I could do it together. You know, bucket-brigade style. One of us climbs up, the other one passes the body up to the guy who's already up there, who lobs it up into the ground cover."

"So . . . exactly who is it you ask to help you with something like that?" I cupped a hand around my mouth. "Hey, Larry, a little help here," I mock shouted. "Got me a kid's body to get rid of here." I pinned Gabe with a stare. "Would you do it for me?" I asked.

Gabe's lips pressed together hard. "A kid?" The broad face said Gabe didn't think so. "You'd have to have one hell of a story."

"Or?"

"Or I just might shoot you myself."

My turn to point. "You know . . . all in all, it was a pretty good place to stash it," I said. "It's not visible from the beach, and it's probably too close to the fence for anybody in the building to see it from above either." I waved at the path below. "Anyplace else down there's nothing but rocks. Somebody's gonna find it first thing in the morning and, even if you get lucky and the body washes out to sea, either some surfer's gonna find it or it's just gonna wash back in on the next tide."

"Let's take . . ."

That was as far as Gabe got when the garage door of the condo closest to us began to squeak its way upward. Without thinking, I moved over close to the building, putting a good-size bougainvillea between me and the garage.

A red Kia nosed out into the street, turned right, and bounced away from us. I made a dash for the closing door. Behind me I heard Gabe. "Goddamn it, Leo . . ."

I did a clumsy barrel roll under the descending door. Felt like I'd fallen off the roof, but I made it. I took stock of myself, making sure no body parts had dropped off, then grunted and groaned my way into the full upright position. Once afoot I walked over to the right side of the garage door and pushed the green button. The door began to rise again.

Gabe wasn't happy. "You're out of your fucking mind."

"Let's just see what this place looks like from the front yard," I whispered.

Reluctantly, Gabe stepped inside the garage. The overhead door rattled closed.

As my eyes began to adapt to the low light, I could make out a doorway in the garage wall. I headed that way, turned the knob, and bingo . . . Gabe stepped out beside me. We were in the building's front yard, looking out over the Pacific Ocean. The pool was closed. Big dirty blue tarp floating above pea-soup water. Buncha lawn furniture folded along the wall behind the flower beds.

I hustled over to the fence. Gabe reached up and grabbed the top of the fence, which was right up at the limit of Gabe's reach.

"Boost me up."

I laced my fingers together. Gabe stepped in, and I muscled two-hundred-plus pounds up a couple of feet. Gabe nodded and then looked down at me.

"Take a look."

Gabe got down and we swapped positions. No way was anybody going to see the spot where I'd found the kid from up here. Whatever happened had happened from down below. No doubt about it.

I was still running that fact through my circuits when a shout split the air.

"Hey . . . you two . . ."

Guy carrying a mop. Big thick bastard. Spent a lot of time on the weight bench in his younger days but was beginning to spill over his belt buckle now. Blond curls turned the color of dirty chrome. Maybe five-ten but a good two forty or so. Wearing a janitorial work shirt . . . said RUSSELL on the patch. Waddling hard in our direction. Puffing himself up like an adder as he walked. Making sure we noticed all that time he'd spent in the weight room.

"What you doin' in here?" he demanded. "You got no business in here. Get the fuck out before I kick both your asses."

He grabbed the mop in both hands as if he were going to use it as a weapon. From the corner of my eye, I saw Gabe turn sideways and load up, which I knew from past experience meant that either this guy was going to stop threatening us, or he was going to have to go on to Craigslist and find himself a new sternum after Gabe busted his present model in half.

I stepped between Gabe and the approaching janitor. "Sorry, man," I said. "We musta taken a wrong turn somewhere." Big smile.

I watched as he slowed down and then stopped, still brandishing the mop like a weapon. I also saw doubt in his eyes. Something in his alpha-male survival instinct was telling him he needed to be careful here. Bullies are generally cowards, and since neither of us had gotten the Hershey squirts at first sight of his muscles, he was beginning to have some serious and well-founded reservations. This wasn't the way it usually went. We were supposed to be way more scared than this. Something was wrong. He could tell.

"I'm callin' the cops," he said.

I laughed out loud. "Come on, man," I said. "You know the cops ain't comin' down here for that kind of petty shit. You could get Chinese food delivered first."

He frowned and took another menacing step forward. When neither of us developed an impromptu facial tic, he shuffled to a stop again. I heard Gabe shift weight and sidestep forward twice. I watched Russell's face. He was having the same problem with Gabe that most people do. One of the first categories we stuff people into is gender. Male or female. With Gabe that wasn't so easy. The army of scientists who had parsed out Gabe's genetic material over the years had all agreed. Gabe could be male, female, neither, or both.

The uncertainty that always engenders was painted all over Russell's face.

"What you think you got?" he demanded.

"Way more than you're lookin' for, asshole," Gabe said.

Maalox minute. Last thing we needed was to bring any more attention to ourselves, so I opted to break the tension before we got to the point of Gabe beating the shit out of this guy. "Sorry . . . ," I threw in. "We'll be on our way."

I put my hand on Gabe's arm and started sliding toward the door. Reluctantly, Gabe scuffed along in my wake. I opened the pedestrian door and stepped out onto the sidewalk. Gabe followed me out, then pulled the door closed behind us.

"Asshole," Gabe muttered as the door snicked. "All he had to do was ask us to leave. No need for all that hard-guy shit."

"Takes his job seriously, I guess."

Gabe was still pissed. "Motherfucker thinks he's a way bigger badass than he is. Must be accustomed to pushing around kids and drunks and junkies."

"I think maybe we were supposed to cower and beg for our lives or something," I said as Gabe wandered over to the top of the stairs and leaned against the railing.

What was left of the sun hung on the horizon like a giant yellow eye that never blinked. Gabe immediately began to wave me over. I loped over to Gabe's side.

Down on the walking path, a bedraggled troll was stumbling toward the bottom of the stairs, ragged sleeping bag leaking out from under his arm, huge hiker backpack hanging from the opposite shoulder. And two uniformed cops coming around the corner in tepid pursuit.

From the look of it, he must have been wasted. The way he kept bouncing off the railings, pinballing his way down the path, falling occasionally, climbing back to his feet, gathering anything that had shaken loose and then scrambling onward again.

I could hear his frantic breathing. Sounded almost like he was singing to himself as he panted toward the lower landing. The frayed bottoms of his pants waved like pennants in the wind as he began to struggle up the concrete stairs.

Instinctively, Gabe and I faded into the bougainvillea as the kid labored up the stairs. Seemed like the cops were herding him, rather than actually trying to apprehend his ass. I was guessing they'd had a complaint from one of the movers and shakers along the cliff face and were mostly interested in sending him someplace else. Someplace with considerably less political clout.

He tried to throw his sleeping bag up to the first landing, but it fell short and then began to unroll as it bounced back toward him. Using both his hands and feet, he bear crawled up the concrete stairs in pursuit, gathering the bag in sections as he went.

The cops reached the bottom of the stairs. The tweaker was scrambling up the last flight of steps. The nearest cop pointed at me, as if he wanted me to stop their quarry for them. I shook my head and turned my face away.

The tweaker might not be somebody I'd invite for lunch, but that didn't mean I was gonna help the cops arrest his filthy ass either. A man's gotta draw the line somewhere, and mine stopped considerably short of helping the cops round up the wretched refuse of our teeming shores.

Gabe and I stayed plastered to the side of the building as he crawled up the final flight of stairs. He was breathing hard by the time he came into view. From a distance, it had looked as if he were wearing a Lone Ranger mask. Up close, however, I could see he had a bar code tattooed across his forehead. Part of me wanted to run him through the scanner and see what it read. Succotash, maybe.

The scuff of shoes on concrete pulled my eyes toward the beach. The cops were coming up the stairs now. He heard it too. Sucked in a great mouthful of air and wobbled, wild eyed, to his feet.

For about half a second, I thought he was gonna make it to the promised land. He was three steps from the street when he tripped over the unrolled sleeping bag and went down flat on his face. I winced as he began to slide, his teeth clicking cadence as his chin bounced off the stairs. A high-pitched wail rose from his throat as he struggled to his feet, grabbed the rail, and began hauling himself upward again, the sleeping bag dragging behind him like a giant plaid tongue as he scratched his way up onto the upper landing.

At which point he did a couple of things that while singularly harmless should generally not be attempted at the same time. He looked back over his shoulder at the rapidly closing cops and then took off running at warp speed. Bang. Right into the passenger side of a blue Honda Civic parked at the curb. Needless to say, the car got the better of it.

The cops were on him before he could regain his footing. He kicked at them from the sitting position. They kept screaming at him to roll over and put his hands on top of his head.

Instead, he rose to his feet, dragging his back along the side of the parked car as he staggered downhill. The closest cop reached for him. He dodged to the right, reached into his pants pocket, and swung something at the cop, who dodged backward out of range, just in time for his partner to plant a size 13 brogan in the middle of the tweaker's back and send him staggering forward.

He banged into me. I felt a sudden pain in my neck as he bounced off my chest, wild eyed and flailing. I got both hands between us and shot putted him back in the other direction at considerably greater velocity than he'd arrived.

Things went downhill for him from there. Took the pair of cops all of ten seconds to get him trussed up like a holiday turkey and haul him to his feet. And then, when they looked over to make sure I was okay, it was like the world suddenly froze. They just stood there. One of them holding each of the tweaker's elbows, staring at me like I'd suddenly grown an extra head.

Gabe stepped out onto the sidewalk. "Aw Jesus, Leo," Gabe said.

"What?"

Gabe nodded. I reached for the burning place on my neck. My hand came away bloody. Son of a bitch bit me. My heart tied itself into a knot. I was still standing silent and slack-jawed when one of the cops started shouting into his shoulder radio. "I need an aid car . . . Santa Cruz Cove . . . stat . . . Repeat . . ."

I'd say that the rest is history, but, at that moment, I wasn't sure I had one. A siren moaned in the distance. I moaned back.

Chapter 3

"Way I hear it, the fuckin' place went off like a cherry bomb," the guy named Robbie said. "Some brother from Arizona told me they heard the bang thirty miles from Conway."

"Half a dozen guys I known all my life ended up blown to shit," the drunk in the corner slurred. "And all because those stupid fuckers got sloppy."

There were four of them, and these guys were not all that happy about being forced to hide out south of the border. Weren't much on housekeeping neither. There was no flat surface not covered with empty cans and bottles. The place smelled like a stable where all the horses smoked cheap cigars.

Chub's nose was twitching like the Easter bunny.

"Where's the guy?" he asked.

"Pete's bringin' him over. Be a coupla minutes," a third guy said.

Lamar was keeping track of Chub from the corner of his eye. Things were not going well. These guys here were of the *those assholes up in Conway got what they deserved* school of thought and didn't seem to be aware that one of those dearly departed rectums was Chub's older brother. The longer these guys talked, the slittier Chub's eyes got, a look Lamar was guessing didn't bode well for the furniture.

About the time the drunk in the corner started blabbing again, Chub started inching in his direction. "Ain't spending the rest of my fuckin' life down here in Greaserville just 'cause one of those assholes . . ."

"My brother was one of them got killed up there in Conway," Chub growled.

The guy in the corner looked up. Under normal circumstances, a confrontation such as this would have sent Lamar scurrying for the door, because Lamar was highly disinclined to be around when the shooting started if he could help it. But this time things were different. Lamar was pretty sure nobody in the room had a gun.

Getting caught with a firearm in Mexico would get you more time in a Mexican prison than anybody even wanted to think about. The *Federales* had gone through their little car like ants at a friggin' picnic. Over . . . under . . . everywhere. If either of them had been packing so much as a nail clipper, the Federales surely would have found it, and they'd have been hell bound by now.

"You know what they sent my mama?" Chub wanted to know.

Lamar groaned inwardly.

The drunk wobbled to his feet. Wasn't till he'd stood all the way up and blinked a couple of times that he realized how big Chub was. Lamar could see doubt crawl into his bloodshot eyes.

"What?" he slurred.

"A shoebox," Chub whispered.

He brought a fist up to stifle a belch. "Yeah?"

"I weighed it," Chub said.

The drunk frowned and then swallowed hard.

"Just under a pound and a half," Chub went on. "That was as much of the stuff as they could positively identify as being parts of my big brother Randy. The rest of him was vaporized, they said." Chub leaned right over into the drunk's face. "So . . . you keep runnin' your lips like you been doing, I'm gonna tear off your head and shit down your neck."

Lamar cleared his throat. And then again louder. Nobody seemed to notice. The scent of new piss and old cigars hung in the air like cannon smoke.

This wasn't the kind of crowd where backing down was an option neither. A mumbled apology and a shit-eating grin weren't gonna float with this bunch. You pussied out in front of these kinda rednecks, you were gonna start waking up in the morning with your boxers on backward. Lamar swallowed a chest full of air and spread his feet for balance as Chub grabbed the drunk by the throat, hoisted him from the floor, and began waving him like a Fourth of July flag. The drunk flailed with his arms and began making noises like a downed high-tension wire.

"Chub . . . dammit," Lamar growled.

The front door suddenly clicked open. A guy in a robin's egg–blue suit came stumbling into the room with a laptop under his arm, followed by a biker-type guy who must have been the aforementioned Pete. Chub set the twitching drunk back on the floor, but by that time the guy's legs were so far gone he just plopped down onto his butt, massaging his throat with both hands and rocking back and forth like a hobbyhorse.

"We got trouble here?" Pete asked, nudging Blue Suit forward with a shoulder.

Lamar saw his chance and stepped forward. "No . . . no trouble, man. Just gotta do a little business with this guy here"—indicating Blue Suit—"and we'll be on our way."

"And we're all supposed to get lost while you guys do whatever the fuck it is?"

"That's what they told me too," Lamar said. "You know, man . . . loose lips and all that kinda shit. The less people know . . ." He shrugged. "I'm just doin' like they told me, man. Getting the info they want and then gettin' our butts right back to HQ with whatever this guy tells us." Lamar snapped his fingers. "Over . . . done . . . just like that."

"What the fuck you talking about?" Chub said from the far side of the room.

"About doin' what the brass sent us down here to do."

"What's that?"

"Find out what this guy's got to say and bring the info back to them. We're just messenger boys. That way there ain't no electronic trail to follow."

"That ain't what they told me," Chub grumbled.

Pete started waving an angry hand. "You motherfuckers work this crap out between yourselves." He looked over at his housemates. "Let's go down and shoot a little pool while the secret agents here get out their decoder rings."

They managed to scrape the drunk off the floor and dribble him down the stairs. His grunts and groans hung in the air after the cellar door closed.

Lamar looked at the guy in the blue suit. "They told me to tell you to check your bank account online." The guy hesitated and then slowly eased the laptop out from under his arm. His eyes kept flicking up and down, from the screen to Chub and Lamar and back again. Couple of minutes later, he closed the laptop.

"You get your money?" Lamar asked.

The guy nodded and loosened his tie.

"You speak English."

The guy nodded again.

"What you got for us?"

He checked the room. "I work IT security for BanRegio bank. You know, mostly lookin' out for cartel money laundering, that kind of stuff. You notice . . . you know what I mean. Somebody gets fifty grand transferred into his account whenever he wants it, tends to come up on our scans. Always a wire transfer from a bank in Washington State to our branch in Tijuana. Don't happen every day. So . . . you know . . . I did a little snooping around . . . you know, checking the accounts and such . . . And then . . . somebody starts asking questions about this same guy, so I figure . . ." He shrugged. "He's using the name Leon Marks."

"You know where that fucker is?" Chub asked.

The guy stared up at Chub for half a minute and then nodded again.

"Where?" Chub demanded.

"The money always ends up in the Point Loma Credit Union."

"Where the fuck is that?" Chub inquired.

"San Diego," the guy said. "On Sports Arena Boulevard."

"You're sure?" Lamar asked.

"We got a way of tracing money flow. It's what we do."

"That all?" Chub growled.

The guy looked at his shoes and then up at Chub. "My cousin Arturo . . ."

"What about him?"

"He lives in Mission Valley . . . he gets his kids every other weekend. Mostly takes them to the beach." He could sense he was coming to the end of Chub's patience, so he spit the rest of it out in a rush. "Arturo saw the picture of the guy in the bank . . . this Waterman guy . . . swears on his mother he's seen that guy in Ocean Beach a couple of times."

A long quiet minute passed.

"I'll find you a ride back," Lamar said finally.

The guy rose from the chair. "You don't mind, think I'll just find my own way out," he said and started triple-timing it for the door.

Lamar and Chub stood silently as he threw the door open and began to sprint down the front walk. "A wise man," Lamar noted with a grin. "Didn't get the feeling that our brothers here were much into nurturing." When Chub didn't say anything, Lamar said, "Maybe we ought to get the hell out of here too."

Chub didn't move, just stood there glowering.

"Let's went," Lamar tried.

"That ain't what they told me," Chub said again. "I ain't no god-damn messenger boy. Only errands I run are for my mama."

"What'd they tell you?" Lamar felt obliged to ask.

"Told me I was gonna be able to take care of this motherfucker Waterman myself."

Lamar was waving him off before he finished the sentence.

"Uh-uh," he intoned. "All we do now is get back home quick as we can."

Chub was shaking his hay-bale head. "Ain't gonna happen," he said. "Gimme the damn car keys."

If he'd had the space to run, Lamar surely would have, but as things stood, Chub was between him and the door, so the way he saw things, his choices were real limited.

He tossed the keys at Chub, who snatched them in midair, did a crisp left face, and strode out the front door. By the time the metal front gate banged closed, Lamar had found the phone in his inside jacket pocket and was autodialing the preprogrammed number.

"Yes."

"I'm . . . ah . . . ah, one of the guys y'all sent down to Mexico."

"Weren't you told not to—"

"We got us an emergency here," Lamar blurted. He got about half-way through explaining the situation when whoever was on the other end started to yell.

"Don't let him out of your sight. You hear me? You stick to him like ugly on an ape. Don't let that motherfucker do anything stupid. You better—"

Lamar broke the connection and sprinted for the door. The wind in his face smelled of rotting kelp as he ran for the street. He jammed the burner phone into his pants pocket and pumped his arms like he was trying to take flight.

It was the laws of physics that saved the situation. Just like you couldn't stuff ten pounds of sand into a five-pound bag, there was no way to stuff Chub Greenway behind the wheel of a Smart car. He was trying to tear the roof off when Lamar skidded to a stop next to the car. "Okay . . . okay," he panted. "I'll drive."

. . .

When I butt bumped the swinging ER door open and stepped out into the waiting room, Sergeant Carolyn Saunders was sitting in a worn leather chair chatting quietly with Gabe. They both got to their feet at the sight of me walking their way.

"So?" Gabe said.

"Either I'm gonna die or I'm not," I said with a shrug.

"That's it?"

"They've gotta run a bunch of tests. Took enough of my fluids to float a paddleboard and said they'd give me a call as the results come back from the lab. They're telling me they don't know how long it will take to find out whether or not I've got anything. Months . . . maybe years."

Gabe pointed down at my hand. "Meds?"

I'd totally forgotten I was carrying a handful of prescriptions. I brought them up to eye level and began to read: "Tenofovir 300 mg a day." I shuffled the pages. "Emtricitabine 200 mg daily and raltegravir 400 twice a day. It's a twenty-eight-day program. The doctor already phoned them in to the Rite Aid on Sunset Cliffs." I shook the papers in the air. "These are just in case."

I looked over at Sergeant Saunders. "They're telling me what I really need to know is the medical status of the guy who bit me."

"I'll see what I can find out," she said. "But you're going to need to come down and look at the mug shots."

"Okay."

"I want to know what you were doing at Santa Cruz Cove when this happened."

I thought about lying to her but decided to just spit it out.

"I was being a nosy bastard. Trying to figure out how the body got to where you found it."

She gave me the fish eye.

"We been wondering about that ourselves," she said. "You got any ideas?"

I nodded Gabe's way. "We're thinkin' it had to be more than one person."

She looked at me hard. "You sure you don't have something you'd like to tell me?"

I met her gaze. "Sergeant . . . if I had anything at all that would help you with this kid's case, I'd have told you to begin with."

"They do a postmortem on the kid yet?" Gabe asked, before she could press me.

She looked over at Gabe and then back to me, trying to decide whether or not to tell us. "He died of the flu," she said finally.

"What?" I blurted.

She waved a scout's honor hand. "That's what we thought too. It's also why the case has been turned over to missing persons. Other than the illegal dumping of the body, as near as any of us can tell, there was no crime involved."

She pulled a small spiral-bound notebook from her back pocket and thumbed through it. "ME's office says the shirt he was wearing was of Mexican manufacture. He'd had a bunch of low-rent Mexican dental work lately. Cosmetic stuff . . . like somebody was trying to pretty him up a bit."

"Why would he need dental work that young?" Gabe asked.

"Malnutrition. ME said he'd been malnourished most of his life." She flipped another page. "No reports of a missing Mexican child that meets his description either." She closed the notebook and jammed it back from whence it came.

"Experience tells me that we're probably looking at some sort of human trafficking thing here," she said. "Lots of times they gussy the kids up a bit before they sell 'em, but like I told you, it's not my case anymore. I just came down to see if you were okay."

"That seems to be the sixty-four-thousand-dollar question," I said.

"I'm on duty at nine in the morning," she said. "Can you make it down to look at the mug books? Things are quieter in the A.M."

"I'll be there."

I watched in silent awe as she sashayed up the hall and out the door.

Gabe chuckled. "I don't think the specter of AIDS is much gonna enhance your prospects for gettin' any of that."

"Me neither."

"What now?"

"Let's go down to Newport and get drunk."

"Sounds like a helluva good idea."

■ ■ ■

Chub pulled the Chevy Blazer to a stop in the Red Lobster lot and pointed to the other side of Sports Arena Boulevard.

"There it is," he said. "Point Loma Credit Union."

They'd ditched the Smart car about a mile south of the U.S. border, left the keys in the ignition, and walked across the border at Otay Mesa, where they'd rented an SUV about the size of a Bradley fighting vehicle and driven north.

"So this is where the money goes. So what? They ain't tellin' us shit," Lamar said. "Banks are cinched up tighter than a frog's ass." He cut the air with the side of his hand. "I mean . . . what we gonna do, sit out here in the parking lot for a coupla weeks hoping this Waterman guy shows up?"

Chub just sat there behind the wheel, glowering out through the windshield. Traffic whizzed by on Sports Arena Boulevard.

"It's like I been sayin', man . . ."

"Where's this Ocean Beach place? The banker's cousin said he seen this Waterman guy there."

Lamar sighed and touched the GPS navigation device in the middle of the dashboard. He tapped several other buttons and then sat back on the seat.

"Looks like it's straight ahead, man. Not very far neither . . . but, man, listen to me . . . this ain't what we're supposed to be doing here . . . we're just supposed to . . ."

Chub turned his head slowly. "You wanna leave . . . leave. I'll drive ya to the friggin' airport, but I'm gonna settle up with this Waterman guy myself."

"But the Brotherhood—" Lamar began.

"Don't give a rat's ass about no Brotherhood," Chub drawled. "That was Randy's thing, not mine. For me this is about my family. About doing right by them. That's why I said I'd go along with this dumb-ass thing. Government's been cheating my family for as long as anybody can remember. They killed my father. They killed my brother. And since I can't kill all of 'em, I'm gonna kill this guy Waterman." The seat belt groaned as Chub leaned hard in Lamar's direction. "My family ain't never had nothin'. We always been dirt poor," he said in a low voice. "We worked the land in North Carolina for ten generations only to find out we didn't own the land and that land we did have title to, we didn't own the mineral rights, and when the mineral is coal, there ain't no land left when they get done with it. We moved from place to place ever since, always on the outside, struggling to keep body and soul together, never getting any of the good stuff, makin' tires in Akron, Ohio, cars in Detroit, makin' steel in Pittsburgh, workin' farms from Wyoming to Wisconsin. It's like somewhere way back somebody decided people like us didn't matter anymore, so they just walked off and left us behind. So if you wanna leave . . . leave . . . it's okay with me . . . just go."

Lamar could still hear the guy on the phone's voice, telling him to not let Chub go it alone. And these bastards were just crazy enough to come after him if he fucked this up too bad. Spending the rest of his days looking over his shoulder, waiting for a couple of Brotherhood banditos to put out his lights, didn't appeal to Lamar one bit.

"Okay," he said. "Let's go." He pointed west. "That way."

Chapter 4

Just before eight in the A.M., Mrs. Google navigated us to the SDPD's cop house on Gaines Street. The Western Division of the SDPD was a windowless stone building on the corner of Gaines and Friars Road. Gabe and I parked in the visitors' lot, followed the signs to the front desk, and asked for Sergeant Saunders.

Gabe knew something was up the minute two uniforms appeared from behind the desk . . .

"Won't you, er . . . you two come this way," the older of the two cops said.

We followed them down a long hall, turned left, and stopped in front of what the plastic sign said was **INTERVIEW ROOM FOUR**. One of the cops opened the door and gestured for us to step inside. "Sergeant Saunders will be along in a sec," he assured us.

We walked into the room only to find a couple more uniforms already in attendance. When Gabe hesitated, the first set of cops bellied into the room behind us, bumping both of us forward a couple of steps so's they could close the door.

"Put your hands on your heads," one of them said.

Gabe and I shot each other a disgusted glance and complied. Two of the cops patted us down. "Have a seat," another one said after they'd satisfied themselves we weren't heeled.

About three minutes later, Sergeant Saunders opened the locked door and stepped inside the room.

"You want to give me a hint as to what's going on?" I asked as she closed the door.

She didn't waste any time or energy. "You two don't check out," she said.

"What's that supposed to mean?" Gabe asked.

"My IT techs say neither Leon Marks nor Gene DeGrazia exist prior to five or six years ago. They say it's like you were created straight out of the ozone. They also say it's one of the finest hacking jobs they've ever seen, and that nobody without the kind of resources police departments have these days could possibly have found you out." She showed her palms to the ceiling. "Tell me how they're wrong about this. How it's all just some crazy mistake."

Pin-drop moment.

"Can I borrow your pocket pad and something to write with?" I asked.

She hesitated. Threw a look around the room at the other four cops and then reached gingerly for her back pocket. She came over to the table and put a small red notebook and a ballpoint pen in front of me.

As I picked them up, one of the cops started to sidle over so he could see what I was writing. Gabe stood up and got in the way.

"Goin' someplace?" Gabe asked the cop.

"It's all right, Officer Phelps," Saunders said.

Nobody moved an inch. I pulled the pad up tight to my chest and began to scribble. Took me a minute or so to write it all down, at which point I closed the pad and handed it and the pen back to Sergeant Saunders, who sauntered over into the corner of the room, thumbed her way back to the page, and began to read.

We watched as she read it a second time and then a third before she tore out the page, balled it into her fist, and turned to the uniforms. "Officers Roman, Sutter, and Dryscol, you can report back to regular duty. Officer Phelps, you will remain here," she said as she followed the uniforms out the door.

Twenty-eight minutes went by before she poked her head back into the room.

"Thank you, Officer Phelps," she said. "That will be all."

We all waited for the sound of his heels to fade to nothing. She looked from one of us to the other. "Let's take a walk," she said.

Gabe and I followed her out to the parking lot and then out onto Gaines Street, past the Resolution Church, where we crossed the street. We walked up Gaines for another couple of blocks before she stopped under a eucalyptus tree and said, "These days there's so much technology I can't say for sure whether or not we're being recorded at any given moment."

"Nothing's private anymore," Gabe offered.

"Captain Eagen of the Seattle PD explained the situation to me," she said in a low voice. "According to the captain, you two are your own personal witness protection program. Why's that? The Feds usually handle that sort of thing."

"You know the Feds," I said. "They don't end up with the glory, they get all pissy about it."

"So they decided to use us as bait," Gabe threw in.

"They put out a press release with our names in it," I said.

"Sounds just like 'em," she said with a wan smile.

She looked over at me. "You used to be a private investigator."

"Yep," I said. "I quit a while back."

She threw a hard glance Gabe's way. "And you . . . Gabriella Funicello. I pulled your file. I'd have brought it along, but I would have needed an officer to carry it for me."

"No felony convictions," Gabe said quickly.

"You're a professional leg breaker."

"Security consultant."

Saunders put her hands on her hips and looked at us hard. "And you two were the ones who took that whole Conway, Washington, white supremacist thing down?"

"Feds had been working on it for a couple of years when we just . . . sort of . . ." I searched for the right word.

"Bumbled in . . . ," Gabe filled in. "And then were stretchered out."

I gave Saunders the *Reader's Digest* version of the Matthew Hardaway story. "We were expecting to find a bunch of hayseeds yelling *yee-ha* and shooting ARs at tin cans out in the woods. Turned out to be a bunch of dangerous white supremacist assholes looking to start a race war."

"Forty some-odd dead," Saunders said. "Over a hundred people arrested and charged, as I recall."

"They'd been stockpiling military munitions for a couple of years. Had guys working in armories all over the West Coast, stealing a little here and a little there, shipping it all up to Conway, waiting for the big day to arrive."

"He said they burned down your house?"

"With a handheld missile," I said.

She paced around in a tight circle.

"The captain says you guys probably saved hundreds, maybe even thousands of lives . . . so how come this Ben Forrester kid ended up getting all the credit?"

Gabe and I passed a painful look back and forth a couple of times.

"Ben didn't make it out," I said quietly.

"Which was totally our fault," Gabe added.

"How so?" Saunders asked.

"We got sloppy. He was an amateur. We were professionals. We should never have taken him in there with us," Gabe said.

A red-and-white Metro bus roared by. Gabe patted my shoulder.

"And how in God's name did you manage to get yourself officially declared dead?" Saunders asked me.

"My former girlfriend is the King County medical examiner. She and Tim Eagen thought maybe it would be better—at least for the time being—if I was officially dead."

She pursed her lips and whistled. "That's one hell of a chance for a big-time county medical examiner and a high-ranking police officer to take."

I shrugged. "They must have thought I was worth it."

Her face said she wasn't altogether sure they'd been right.

"How do you know Eagen?"

"He was in love with my girlfriend too."

"The medical examiner?"

I nodded. She nearly smiled.

"And *that* brought you two together?"

"Yeah . . . ," Gabe said. "Right after she dumped the both of them."

I smiled. "I seem to remember a line about how those who suffer together end up having stronger connections than those who should be most content."

She thought it over. "Captain Eagen wants you to call him at what he called the usual time and the usual number. I assume you know what that means."

I nodded.

"Okay," she said with a sigh. "Let's go look at some mug shots."

• • •

Lamar plopped down into the plastic chair and watched Chub lumber up the sidewalk in search of a place to take a dump. The homeless onslaught had made Ocean Beach one tough place to find a communal commode. RESTROOMS FOR CUSTOMERS ONLY signs adorned nearly every window like merit badges. Lamar knew from personal experience that it was like the old song said: *nobody loves you when you're down and out.*

That's when he set his hands down on his lap, fingered the bump in his pocket, and knew right away what it was. The burner phone from Tecate. Without hesitation, he dialed the preprogrammed number. Same voice answered.

"Don't be givin' me no damn lectures," Lamar rasped into the phone before the guy could say anything. "I got me a serious problem here."

.M. FORD

He checked the street in both directions. "That Chub Greenway motherfucker is bound and determined to off this Waterman guy on his own . . ." He waved his free hand in the air. "And don't tell me how I oughta talk him out of it neither. That motherfucker's the size of a porta-potty."

Two clicks and a new voice. Pinched and high, like he had real clean nasal passages. "You must not let him do that."

"What in hell am I supposed to do about it?" Lamar's rising voice echoed off nearby buildings. He stood up and checked the street again. "That asshole from the Mexican bank says he's usin' the name Leon Marks and is living in Ocean Beach."

"You may have to neutralize him," the voice said.

"Waterman?"

"No, Greenway."

Lamar's lower jaw headed south. "What? . . . You gotta be . . . Yeah, man," he said sarcastically, "I'll get my ray gun and get right with the program."

"You don't want us as enemies, Mr. Pope."

"What's that supposed to mean?"

"Just what I said. Our reach is long, and our hour has come round at last. You don't want to be the enemy of a white America. Do your duty. Mr. Greenway cannot be allowed to bring attention to us. By whatever means necessary, you must not allow that to happen. We're depending on you, Mr. Pope."

"And how in shit's sake am I supposed to do that, man?"

"I believe we can provide you with the resources you'll require."

"I'm not a killer, man. That ain't what I signed on for. I'm more of an idea guy. You want to kill that motherfucker Greenway, you better find some other motherfucker to do it for ya, 'cause I ain't no killer."

"As I said, Mr. Pope. Our reach is long."

"Yeah . . . I got something that's long too."

"Call back on this number in an hour."

Lamar stood up again. He could see Chub now. Block and a half up the street. Head and shoulders bobbing above the rest of the crowd. Walking his way. Looked like he was walking quite a bit easier too.

When Lamar brought the phone back up to his ear, the line was dead.

● ● ●

Now you'd think identifying a homeless guy with an Afro the size of a beach ball and a bar code tattooed across his forehead would be easy. Not so. We stayed at it for the better part of three hours but came up dry.

The old uniform who'd kept supplying us with mug books came shuffling back to the room. "They're highly transient; most of 'em aren't in the books," he said after we'd thrown in the towel.

"I worked Mission Beach for eighteen years, and I'm tellin' you, patrol doesn't like riding in the car with them. They stink to high heaven, they piss and puke and try to kick out your car's windows. And, most of the time, the paperwork you gotta file isn't worth what they end up being charged with, so mostly patrol just takes 'em from wherever they're making a pain in the ass of themselves and leaves them someplace else where they ain't bothering nobody. In O.B. it's up the north end of town by the dog beach. Along the river there. Long as they don't cause no trouble for the local merchants, we try to be as accommodating as we can."

Sergeant Saunders got to her feet and stretched. "I'll put a BOLO out for him," she said. "He'll turn up again. Those guys always do. O.B.'s the only place that'll put up with them, so sooner or later patrol will come into contact with him and . . . you know, we'll see."

"See what?" I asked.

She eyed me hard. "See whether or not he's willing to be tested . . . because short of a formal complaint of some kind, nobody can legally be forced to have an HIV test."

"We'll make him an offer he can't refuse," Gabe assured her. She looked like she believed it.

• • •

Chub slammed the photocopy down onto the plastic table.

"Goddamn picture ain't no good. That's how come we're not gettin' anywhere."

"Shit," Lamar said. "Most of these folks I showed it to were so fucking stoned they wouldn't recognize Bugs Bunny if he came hopping up with a carrot."

"We need a better picture of this guy," Chub insisted.

"Ain't no such thing," Lamar said. "That's the only picture there is. And like I keep tryin' to tell you—ain't no one guy responsible for what happened up in Conway. This Waterman guy is just a symbol. Either the brass has gotta fess up about how they blew it, or they gotta find somebody else's ass to blame it on. They're just using Waterman to focus everybody's attention someplace other than at them." He spread his hands. "It's just human nature, man—when in doubt, blame some other motherfucker."

Chub wasn't buying it. He stomped around the sidewalk in a rage, forcing the constant flow of locals and tourists to navigate around him. Across the street, half a dozen Harleys filled the air with roars as they angled their machines to the curb, backing in, dismounting in front of Cheswick's, the two-wheeled leather set's preferred watering hole. Above the deep throb of the engines, the scrape and grind of skateboards suddenly rose above the rumble as a couple of locals came shredding by on the sidewalk, the first just barely managing to avoid Chub on the way by. Chub threw out an enraged arm, trying to clothesline the second skateboarder to the sidewalk, but the second guy squatted on the board, allowing Chub's massive limb to slide harmlessly over his back.

"Hey, man . . . chill," the guy shouted back over his shoulder.

For a long second Lamar thought Chub was going to start running down the street after the guy. Looked like lightning bolts were about to erupt from his head.

Lamar rose from the chair. "Hey, man . . . hey, man . . . take it easy. We ain't done yet. Let's keep on trying here." Lamar grabbed the picture of Waterman in the bank and shook it in the air. "We covered most of this street here. We could probably cover more ground if we split up."

Took a few minutes but eventually Chub came around. They'd do the streets together. Opposite sides. Working south to north. Then do it again and again till they got up to the far end of Ocean Beach, someplace up by that Voltaire Street. And then they'd see if anybody in that big park knew this guy.

Lamar watched as Chub tromped up the stairs in front of the O.B. Surf Club and disappeared inside.

Rather than step into the bikini store on the corner of Santa Monica and Abbott, Lamar hustled half a dozen steps east and slid into a narrow alley between private houses. He craned his neck out over the sidewalk and checked the street. No Chub.

He pulled the phone from his pocket, checked the street again, and pushed the button. Not a person. Just a recording this time. Giving him an address. Forty-four seventeen Muir. The electronic voice repeated the address three times and then broke the connection.

Lamar was incensed. His hands were shaking. He jabbed the button and missed. Again. Hit it. Same electronic voice. Mailbox is full. Not taking messages at this time. Lamar brought the phone up high, as if to dash it to pieces on the ground, but changed his mind and stuffed the burner back into his pants pocket.

"Forty-four seventeen Muir," Lamar murmured to himself. "Forty-four seventeen Muir."

. . .

The phone rang three times before he answered. "Yeah," was all Tim Eagen said.

I could hear the frigid Washington wind hissing like cold static. "It's me."

"Sergeant Saunders told me what happened. You okay?"

"I'd be okayer if people stopped asking me how I'm feeling every ten minutes."

I heard him sigh. "Not to add fuel to the fire, but I've got some bad news."

"Like what?" I asked.

"You know, Leo . . . ever since Conway, we've had those Brotherhood assholes under some serious-ass surveillance. For once everybody's on board with this thing. Local, state, federal, all of 'em. I mean judges are standing in line to sign the warrants for us. We've tapped into every computer and phone line they own. We're listening to their families. They fart, we hear it."

"So?"

"So . . . it's been real quiet; these guys have more or less gone underground—mostly—until lately."

"Uh-huh."

"So three days ago, one of their supposedly covert numbers gets a call from Tecate, Mexico. Your name comes up on the tape. Seems the IT guy at that Mexican bank you use . . . seems he flagged your account for potential money laundering activity, and just about the time he was wondering who this gringo with seemingly unlimited access to cash was, the bank gets an under-the-table inquiry about this same guy—this guy being you. Anyway, he puts two and two together and starts to think there might be some money to be made here, so he contacts the inquirer and says he's got some info and wants to sell it." The cold Washington wind hissed louder. "He won't come over the border, so they send a couple of guys down to Tecate to pay him and get the info."

"Okay."

"Well, one of the guys they sent apparently lost a brother up in Conway and is batshit crazy over it. Decides he's gonna find you and kill you himself. One of 'em calls in from Mexico, tells them what the other guy wants to do. They tell him to keep the other guy in sight and not let him do anything stupid, anything that could further endanger the movement."

"That won't get 'em to me," I said.

"We recorded another call. Hour and a half or so ago. Same guy tells them that the other guy, guy named Greenway, is still determined to kill your big ass. They tell the first guy he's gonna have to do his duty and kill this Greenway guy before he brings down the house. First guy don't like the sound of that at all. Claims he's a lover not a shooter. They tell him to call back in an hour."

"Okay," I said again.

"The second call came from San Diego County . . . from somewhere in Ocean Beach."

$$\bullet \ \bullet \ \bullet$$

Forty-four seventeen Muir was like the rest of the houses in this part of town. Little tiny joint, couldn't have been more than five hundred square feet. Mottled Spanish tile roof. Had a little masonry wall around the street side and about a thousand bright plastic toys strewn all over the front yard like confetti.

Lamar had managed to ditch Chub about six blocks south. He figured he had maybe ten minutes at best before Chub noticed he was gone and went into his Godzilla Unchained routine.

He moved the broken metal gate aside, stepped over a red-and-yellow Big Wheel bike, and mounted the slab of concrete masquerading as a front porch. He knocked on the door. A dog started barking. He could hear the squeal of kids. The door cracked. The barking and squealing got louder.

A heavily made-up eye appeared in the opening. Blinked.

"Somebody give you a call?" Lamar asked.

She didn't answer. Just used her foot to swing the door open and took a couple of steps backward. Lamar stepped inside. She was tall and had green hair. Pierced eyebrow and a big silver stud in her tongue. She had a tear-streaked baby balanced on her narrow hip and another little girl, maybe three or four, hiding behind her legs. The rest of the joint looked like a swap meet gone wrong. There was shit everywhere. Lamar could feel the carpet under his feet but couldn't actually see it. He shuffled to avoid stepping on anything. Behind her, in the archway, the dog—looked like some sort of border collie—stalked back and forth, barking every time it reversed course, like an old-time arcade bear.

"Jimmy's friends called," she said suddenly. "They said I should give you one of his guns."

"Where's Jimmy?" Lamar asked.

"Salinas Valley."

"What's in Salinas Valley?" he asked conversationally.

"The state prison," she answered.

"Oh . . . aah . . . ," Lamar stammered. "Sorry . . . didn't mean to . . ."

She waved him off. "Ain't none of it your fault. That dumb shit done it to himself," she said. "Him and them other white-power asshole friends of his." She swung her free arm in a slashing arc. "Out there playacting like they're soldiers or some such shit. Pretending they're not just another bunch of low-life losers who can't hold a job."

"Sorry . . . I didn't . . . ," was as far as he got.

"So now what?" She stood still for a moment, as if waiting for an answer from the skies. "I'm alone here. Two kids. No damn money. Working three jobs. My mom's in a nursing home that smells like piss. What the hell am I supposed to do now?" The baby on her hip began to squall and squirm. She bent at the waist and set it gently on the floor, where it immediately grabbed a discarded yellow hamburger wrapper and stuffed it into its wet mouth.

Her narrow eyes looked as if they were trying to burn a hole all the way through Lamar's head. Lamar blinked uneasily.

"I know what it's like to be the one left behind," Lamar blurted. "All my life I know what that shit feels like. Like there's really no place you're supposed to be. No place you belong. Like you're just wherever the hell you are, waiting to see what happens to you next. It ain't right."

"I'll bet you do," she said after a while.

"The gun?" Lamar said.

She pulled the hamburger wrapper away from the baby, who immediately began to voice its indignation. She ignored the siren sounds, walked over to the hall closet, opened the door, and pulled a ratty crocheted afghan down from the overhead shelf.

Lamar walked over, reached up, and came out with a green gym bag. He set it on the floor. Inside was a Browning Black Label Pro. Custom grips. Eight rounds of fury. Nice gun. Brand spanking new. Two full boxes of shells, one of which he opened and then carefully loaded into the semi, finally sliding one shell into the chamber before stashing the weapon in the back of his belt. He put the rest of the ammo back in the gym bag and then returned it to the closet shelf.

"Thanks," he told her.

"Just take it and go," was the best she could manage as she stepped over and separated the baby from a pink Styrofoam cup.

# Chapter 5

Gabe snapped a round into the chamber, thumbed the safety to "On," and stuffed the gun into a small leather holster hidden beneath the waistband of the Nike running shorts.

"Can you see it?" Gabe asked.

"Looks like you've got a dick."

"That makes one of us," Gabe said, smoothing the tank top down over the rest of it. I opened my mouth to speak, but Gabe beat me to it. "I'm thinkin' you maybe ought to break out that little Smith & Wesson you've got stashed around here someplace. If Supercop says there's a couple white-power assholes here in town looking for us—and much as I hate cops, I'm guessing he's probably right—then I think we probably oughta be carrying until further notice."

Wasn't until that moment that I realized how much I'd been enjoying my newfound freedom. How much being unarmed and unknown had saved my soul and my sanity. Probably explains why I said something so stupid:

"Neither of us has a California gun license."

It was hard to argue with a derisive snort, so I didn't bother. Instead, for once in my life, I followed directions. I found a plastic shoulder harness in the bottom dresser drawer, put on a Hawaiian shirt big enough to hide a lawn tractor, and slid the Smith & Wesson into place and snapped it in.

"So what now?" Gabe wanted to know when I came back out. "We just gonna sit around the apartment here and wait for these guys to figure out where we live and show up to put our lights out?"

I thought it over. "I guess I'm gonna go out and start looking for the guy who bit me," I said after a minute. "Nothing else seems to matter to me right now. It's like my life is on hold until I find out whether I'm gonna live or die."

"Yeah . . . I'm guessing that'd be a real attention getter."

I was feeling kinda pensive today, so I mulled that one over too. "In a way, it's liberating," I said after a while. "It's like all the other stuff in your life just sort of fades to black and then burns from the edges in, until there's nothing left in the room except you and the prospect of dying."

Gabe nodded. "I don't remember who said it—somebody famous, I'm thinkin'—but somebody I read once said that death is the *only* enemy."

"Sounds to me like whoever it was knew what they was talking about," I said.

"Where we gonna start?"

"Up by the river."

"Let's go."

. . .

You sail into the mouth of the San Diego River, you damn well better be on the north side of the breakwater so's you can hook a hard left into Mission Bay. Either that or you will immediately run aground in the river. That's because the present mouth of the river is not in its original location. Back in the late 1870s, the river got in the way of progress, so they moved it over here into the mudflats and sloughs of north O.B., where it wouldn't bother anybody 'cause there was nobody over here to bother.

We started up under the bridge at Sea World Drive by the skate park, about as far to the northeast of downtown O.B. as a body could get, and then zigzagged our way between camps on the banks of the river and those of the extended-stay folks who were living down in the park.

I've never been homeless, but personally speaking, it seemed to me that the banks of the river were a better place than the beach to pitch camp if you were living outdoors. You could find a little privacy amid the dense undergrowth. The river had your back, and you were far enough from the commercial zone so that the cops were inclined to leave your ass alone, unless the river was about to flood and they came down here and rousted everybody out so they wouldn't drown in their sleeping bags, or the once a year they sent the cleanup crews out to round up a couple thousand stolen bicycles and something like five hundred tons of loose garbage scattered and left about by our erstwhile urban campers.

If you didn't count the guy with the machete, things went well. We followed each well-worn path we came upon. Some of the campsites were empty. Most were not. You could tell right away how territorial people were regarding their chosen ground.

The first river camper we encountered met us about halfway down the bank. This guy was ready. He was holding a piece of lumber, with several rusty nails hammered through one end, above one shoulder like a sledgehammer.

Gabe raised a moderating hand. "Not here to give you a hard time, man," Gabe said. "We're not the cops. Just lookin' for somebody. That's all."

The guy was real nervous. He kept shifting his weight from foot to foot, almost like he was dancing. "Gwan get outta here," he chanted. "Go."

I stepped up next to Gabe. "Guy with a great big Afro and a bar code tattooed on his forehead."

He stopped dancing. Frowned at me. "Yeah . . . I seen him. Everybody seen him."

"You know his name?" I asked.

"Creamed spinach."

"What?" I croaked out.

"I asked him what the bar code was for one time. You know, what it would read if you ran it through the machine. He told me it was for creamed spinach."

Our stunned silence spurred him on. "Swear to God," he said as he pulled one hand loose from the cudgel and shot us a peace sign. "Creamed spinach."

Gabe looked my way. "You know, my man . . . you know how I am . . . we catch this motherfucker . . . I'm gonna have to run him through the machine and see what it says."

"What say we just use the wand," I said. "Like the checkers do when you've got heavy shit in the cart. That way we don't have to hoist him up onto the conveyor belt."

"That'll work," Gabe conceded.

We climbed back onto the bike path and then slalomed down the other side of the berm onto Robb Field, a massive athletic complex that comprised the northwestern boundary of Ocean Beach. In addition to fields for all known sports and hobbies, the vast area was ringed with concrete picnic tables and benches originally intended as an amenity for a nice family respite in the park but which, if you were living in the streets, were a definite step up from the au naturel end of the local housing market.

Most of the picnic table ensembles had morphed into something roughly akin to those blanket forts I used to build in my bedroom when I was a kid. Tents, parts of tents, big sheets of blue plastic, lean-tos, scrap roofing, you name it and somebody had found a way to make it work for a shelter.

It didn't take long for us to figure out that the working plan for the tables was gonna have to be different than it was for the riverbank, where a certain amount of stealth was called for so's to keep from getting your head bashed in by some paranoid lunatic.

Out here in the flatlands, things were a little different. We tried to make a lot of conversational noise as we walked around, making sure they heard us coming from a long way off so we didn't freak anybody out.

Also didn't take long to discover the underlying hierarchy of homelessness. The screaming crazies—those poor souls who simply weren't watching the same TV channel as the rest of us—they were the riverbank people. The better adjusted, but likewise domestically challenged, were most likely to be found in the park. Couples, small families, and single mothers with children preferred the more suburban, lawn-like ambience of Robb Field.

We'd been at it for an hour and a half or so. Lots of people knew who we were looking for but couldn't be of any help in finding him. The best any of them could come up with was that he must live around there someplace because they saw him all the time. The only real trouble we'd come across was a guy who came charging through the brush at us waving a machete, spittle bursting from his mouth as he screamed and shrieked around the shrubbery like a deranged weed whacker. Gabe and I didn't need to talk about it. We'd just turned around and walked away.

It was the Native American woman with the two long-haired little boys who finally got us pointed in the right direction. Despite the warm weather, she had a little fire going in the firepit. Sleeping bags were airing on a rope tied between trees. A couple of Coleman lanterns, a pair of kids' bikes chained to a tree. The place looked picked clean, like it had been used for quite a while.

At the sight of Gabe and me heading her way, she got to her feet, looking around on the ground as if she were trying to find something she'd dropped. Gabe put a sideways hand on my chest, silently telling me to hang back so we didn't scare the woman any more than necessary. I stopped walking. Waited.

I stood thirty yards away and watched as the woman traded strained pleasantries with Gabe. Two minutes later, the woman turned her back on me and pointed in the direction of the river. Gabe was nodding and listening to what she had to say.

I watched Gabe pull a handful of folding money out of the shorts and extend it in the woman's direction. She shook her head and turned away. Gabe tried again. The woman ducked inside the makeshift tent. As if connected to her by rubber bands, the two boys scuttled across the ground and followed her inside.

I could feel Gabe sigh from thirty yards away. Gabe crooked a finger in my direction. I walked over. Gabe shouldered me a few feet to my left.

"See the thicket over there with the yellow flowers?"

"Yeah," I said.

"She says she sees him goin' in and outta there all the time. That his camp's down on the river there behind the thicket."

"Let's go see if he's home," I suggested.

We took our time scouting the area. Real careful like. This section of underbrush was about thirty yards long, thick and thorny with no hint of an entrance. As we spread out, working our separate paths to the edges, we found there were two ways down to the campsite. One at either end of the thicket, kind of like a prairie dog hole. You start diggin' at one end, he goes out the other.

On a signal from Gabe, I started tiptoeing down the narrow track. Out in the river, bright-white egrets picked among the shallows and sandbars. A squadron of brown pelicans floated overhead. And then I could hear him—ahead of me in the undergrowth, low and musical, as if he were humming a childlike tune to himself.

As I neared the river, I saw that the bushes ran all the way into the water. If I was going to step around the corner into the campsite, I was going to have to take at least one wet step.

I was standing there, trying to decide which foot I was willing to get wet, when I noticed the thick branch with the missing bark. I reached out and touched it. Smooth but bony and dry. Bark peeled off a long time ago. And then I knew how he got around the corner. I took three steps up the bank, reached out and grabbed the barkless branch, lifted my feet, and swung myself around the corner like an orangutan.

I landed right in front of him. About three feet away from where he was sitting in one of those low beach chairs, eating Dinty Moore stew out of the can. Before I could react, he powered off the canvas chair like a bottle rocket, the can of stew pinwheeling in the air as he headed for the opposite end of the campsite on a dead run.

My mouth opened to shout a warning, but the words caught in my throat when I heard the collision of flesh. Sounded like somebody'd dropped a heifer from the roof of an apartment building.

"Goddamn," I heard Gabe grunt, right before it all got swallowed by the sounds of somebody thrashing the underbrush. I crossed the short section of riverbank and started up the opposite path. Gabe was sitting on the ground, using two fingers to wipe at a bloody nose. I could hear Boy Bar Code forcing his way through the thick cover to my right. He was still humming.

I reached out with both hands and pulled Gabe into a standing position and then started chugging up the bank, trying to beat our quarry to the top of the berm. My right knee hated the strain, but I kept pushing until I popped out onto the bike path, hands on knees, bent over, breathing like a steam locomotive.

The kid was twenty yards away by the time I looked up, pumping across the park like a long-distance runner. Gabe stumbled to my side, red in the face, still trickling blood from one nostril.

The precise reasons why we started to chase after him I suspect had more to do with psychiatry than common sense. Took both of us about fifty yards of sprinting to devolve from running like the wind to running like the winded. Only reason we made it that far was because neither of us wanted to be the first one to give up.

We stood there on the grass, hunched over, barking at invisible ants as the kid hotfooted it off into the ozone on the far side of Robb Field.

"Few years back we'da caught him," Gabe eventually huffed.

I stifled a snicker. "Whatever you say."

Gabe threw an arm around my hunched and heaving shoulders.

"We know where he lives. Let's give him a couple of days to settle back in. We'll get him next time."

• • •

Lamar slid back from the counter and wiped his mouth with a paper napkin. When he straightened his back, the big Browning semiautomatic ground into him like a knuckle. He reached behind himself, checked the crowd, and made sure the Browning stayed under his shirt. They'd been forced to find a joint with counters to eat at 'cause the only booth Chub was fittin' in was a tollbooth and maybe not then neither.

Chub ate like every bite might turn out to be his last. He was on his sixth steak-and-shrimp taco, savoring every great white bite he took, which was about two per taco.

"Well . . . we showed that picture to about every damn person in this town. I'm thinkin' it might be time to update our plane reservations and report back to the brass."

Chub finished chewing, downed half a beer, and set the taco back in the little checkered container. "Told you, man . . . you wanna go . . . go."

"What else is there to do?" Lamar wheedled. "We already done everything."

"We still ain't done the south end of town," Chub said as he manhandled the second half of the taco into his mouth. "So . . . go."

"I can't do that, man. A major part of my job is to get both of us back up north safe and sound." Which had seemed to Lamar way better than telling the big guy that what the Brotherhood really wanted was for Lamar to blow his fucking head off. "I leave you here and come back without you, those Brotherhood fucks are gonna be all over me like ugly on an ape. Nope, man . . . where you go, I go."

"We'll sleep in the truck," Chub said around a belch.

It was at that moment when, for the first time, Lamar began to seriously consider the possibility that he might, before this was over, have to maneuver Chub someplace where they could be alone and then turn out his lights. The idea scared the living shit out of him.

. . .

Took us about twenty knee-knocking minutes to walk back to Newport Avenue, where a couple of mahi-mahi tacos and double margaritas at the South Beach Bar & Grille eased our pain considerably. An hour or so later, we were spent but still saucy, and the streetlights had just hissed to life as we turned onto Del Monte Avenue and started hoofing it up the block to the building.

If we'd had any wind left in our sails, it surely would have luffed out at the sight of Sergeant Saunders standing on the sidewalk in front of our building, trying not to look like a cop.

"Wonder what she wants," Gabe whispered sideways. We were both thinking the same thing. Maybe she had some news about my tests. *Hold your breath* time.

I gave her a small wave. "Sergeant," I called.

She was wearing blue pants, but without the badge on the belt. No jacket. Just a plain white blouse. She was standing in the entranceway, with a red file folder clamped under her arm, wedged between the wooden fence and the little hedge. I surveyed the area, looking for her partner. Nowhere in sight.

"I need to have a word with you two."

She saw Gabe and me pass a look. "This is something new," she said.

Gabe's flattened lips meant *what the hell*, so I gestured with my hand, and the three of us tromped up the stairs and into the apartment.

Five minutes later, everybody had something to drink and a place to sit.

"So?" I said.

"So . . . ," she began. "Before we got the cause of that boy's death from the ME, I did what I always do: I sent samples to the lab for analysis. Standard procedure in a case like that. When it came back that he'd died of the flu . . . well then, that made further analysis kind of a moot point." She wagged a hand. "But . . . you know . . . at least we'd have a DNA profile in the system in case anybody ever came looking for him."

"And?" I prodded.

She looked embarrassed. "It bothered me. You know. A kid like that. It just pissed me off to see something like that happen."

"Bothered me some too," I admitted.

She took a deep breath. "This is where it gets dicey for me," she said. "Like I said, I was bothered . . . so . . . when I didn't get a match from the system, I also sent the DNA profile to an open-source registry."

"Like they did for the Golden State Killer," Gabe said. "They traced him through his family tree."

Saunders nodded. "Definitely outside of protocol, but you know, it was in the news and on my mind, and like I said . . ." She looked from one of us to the other. "I could get fired for this," she said. "Swear to God, I was just gonna let it go at that. Get it behind me and get on with my job. You know . . . onward and upward."

"But?"

"I got a familial match."

"No shit," I said.

"All those people giving each other DNA test kits for Christmas . . . you know, 23andMe, AncestryDNA, Living DNA, all those kinds of things. All the samples are given voluntarily, which means people like you and me don't need a warrant to annex the database, so I did."

"So what's the rub?" Gabe asked.

"The match is a twenty-three-year-old Mexican national."

I shrugged. "Close as you guys are to each other, there must already be some sort of procedure in place to deal with that sort of thing."

Saunders was shaking her head. "First of all, it's not my case any-more, which in the SDPD is either a suspension or a firing offense, depending on who it is you piss off. Secondly, we got a president claim-ing he's gonna build a wall and make them pay for it. We got the State of California suing the city of Tijuana over polluting the Pacific with its sewage runoff. Was a time I could have made a couple of calls and gone down there myself and followed up on this thing, had a nice lunch, and come back. These days, cooperation is a thing of the past. They're strip-searching American grandparents."

When neither of us said anything, she went on. "Even on our end, open-source information is not welcome in court. Things like crime scene integrity, contamination, chain of custody, transportation, and storage of the DNA samples have yet to go through the U.S. court system. You spit in a container, which may or may not already be con-taminated, then send it off to be handled by multiple people, who then mail it off to God knows where, to be processed by God knows whom. All that crap still needs to be worked out for open-source information to be legally viable."

Gabe frowned and leaned forward. "So you're telling us this why?"

I watched as she began to color. "I was thinking . . . hoping, really . . . that I could talk you two into going down there and follow-ing up on this thing." She waved a breezy hand. "You know, like a little Mexican vacation."

"Where in Mexico?" Gabe pressed.

"Tijuana."

"A true garden spot."

"Real close, though," Saunders said. For the first time since I'd met her, she made a joke. "Besides . . . when am I ever gonna have a pair of pistoleros like you two at my disposal again?"

"Nobody's called me a *pistolero* for years," Gabe said with a laugh.

"Surely an egregious oversight," Saunders threw in.

"But there's no way we can show up at the border with guns," Gabe pointed out.

"No way," Saunders parroted.

"We'll be *fistaleros*, then," I said.

"Not sure I like the sound of that." Gabe swallowed the smile.

"What have you got for a match?" I asked her. "How close a relative?"

"Half brother—they've got the same mother."

"And how are we supposed to find this guy?" Gabe asked.

"I know where he lives, where he works, and where he likes to drink." She looked over at Gabe. "Your sheet says you speak Spanish."

"I worked for a Hispanic gentleman for a number of years," Gabe allowed. "You pick it up."

Saunders lifted the file folder from the coffee table. Pulled out a sheet of paper. "Here's all the information on Henrique Asevedo," she said. "I made a few calls and am assured he's still alive and kicking around the neighborhood. He's married and got two kids."

Gabe and I were still reading when she reached into the folder again and came out with a photograph. The dead kid, but with eyes this time.

"I photoshopped eyes back into his face," she said. "I don't know how accurate they are, but I couldn't see how anybody could show it around . . . you know . . . with the eyes pecked out like that."

Nobody disagreed.

I looked over at Gabe. "Whatta ya think?" I asked.

"I'm thinkin' she's got us by the short hairs," Gabe said. "That this is one of those *one hand washes the other* moments . . . You know, like how she's holding on to our little secret and hoping like hell we'll feel like we have an obligation to return the favor."

"Whatta ya say?" I asked.

Gabe gave me the *what the hell?* face. "I think she may have a point."

"I'd sure like to find out what happened to that boy," I said.

Gabe was nodding. "Me too."

Chapter 6

Borders are lines in the sand. Bloody lines. Lines that people fought and died for. Perhaps that explains the otherworldly flow they have about them, like walking in the front door of a strange house and then out the back, without ever bothering to look around. Always feels as if my identity has been canceled and I've been reduced to merely a number in transit, neither a piece of the continent nor a part of the main.

Gabe and I crossed the border at San Ysidro at a little after seven A.M. and followed the trickle into Tijuana on foot, past the historical markers and the roundabouts and all the fierce, rearing statues of the nation's heroes.

You know how people like to pretend they're more familiar with places than they really are, so that they can be the one who knows the way? That was us. We were looking for a little restaurant named Las Morelianas, where we'd eaten several times before, but neither of us wanted to admit we didn't quite remember the way, so as we'd also done before, we'd hooked a wrong turn somewhere among the maze of streets and had wandered about the adjoining neighborhood for half an hour before realizing our mistake and sheepishly asking a truck driver for directions.

Thus frustrated and overly exercised Gabe ordered an Omelette de Chicharron y Lengua big enough to feed a Malay village. As for me, I wasn't much in the mood for breakfast, so the staff graciously kept the eye rolling to a minimum and whipped me up Chilaquiles Marevca, even though it wasn't what sane adults ate first thing in the morning.

The best news was that they weren't playing the usual earsplitting mariachi music this early. Some days are better than others.

It was five past nine by the time we stepped back into Elkalla Street, suitably fueled and ready for action. Gabe let go with a belch that rattled the windows of nearby shops. "That was some good shit," Gabe said with a shake of the head.

"We keep eating like that and we're gonna need to order the Metamucil Mole for lunch," I said.

Gabe smiled. "Where you wanna start?"

I shrugged. "It's after nine on a weekday. I'm betting he's at work," I said.

Gabe got directions from a traffic cop, and we took off walking the streets. Remnants of the onshore flow drifted among the buildings like airborne gauze. The weather was at the *hot in the sun, cool in the shade* stage of things.

When you're at large on foot in the Third World, the first thing you notice is that things are much more in flux than they generally are in America. Everywhere you look, buildings are going up, buildings are going down, and it's almost impossible to tell the difference. In this part of Mexico, change was the permanent order of the day. If that makes any sense at all.

Twenty minutes later, we were standing next to a square city block of pollution, plastic, and aluminum scaffolding running up about five stories. We stopped at the battered trailer they were using as an office and asked the guy behind the desk for Henrique Asevedo. He spoke into a handheld radio and then told us that Henrique would be right down.

We saw his boots first, as he climbed down from the scaffolding. Work boots, jeans, then white tank top, yellow helmet. Henrique Asevedo was a young-looking twenty-three. Didn't even look like he shaved yet. Hard to imagine he had two kids of his own.

"You asking for me?" he asked in perfect English.

We introduced ourselves. He didn't offer a hand. Just stood there with his hands on his hips, shifting his eyes back and forth between Gabe and me. So I reached into my pocket and pulled out the photoshopped image of the boy, unfolded it, and held it up in front of his face.

"You recognize this young man?" I asked.

He slid his eyes over the image and then quickly looked away.

"Nope," he said. "Who's that?"

But he did. I could tell by the way the blood began to rise to his face, by the pulsing blood vessel in his neck and the sudden problem he was having keeping his feet still. "You get one of those genetic tests done lately?" Gabe asked.

He folded his muscular arms across his chest and jutted his chin way out.

"What about it?"

"Genetic science says you and this young fellow have the same mother," I added.

He tried to slough it off. "Must be some kind of mistake," he said with a violent shake of his head. "Computer must have fucked up."

"Probably not," Gabe said.

Henrique Asevedo swatted at the dusty air. "Hey . . . you two got no cause to be comin' down here to where I work, talking about my family. I got a job to do here. And like I told you, I never seen that kid before."

He did an abrupt about-face and stalked off, sweeping aside a black plastic tarp and pushing his way into the darkness beyond.

Gabe looked at me. "He knows."

I pushed the black plastic aside and started after Henrique. The tarp was intended to shield one side of the massive project from the other. As I stepped inside, I could see Henrique double-timing it away from me in what was now a plastic tunnel beneath what seemed like the spiderweb of scaffolding overhead. Here and there along the plastic corridor, shafts of brilliant sunlight streaked diagonally across the space, illuminating the floating dust motes like tiny stars. I picked up my pace, stretching my legs now, gaining ground. I could feel Gabe close behind me. A sudden blast of sunlight told me that Henrique had punched his way out the other side. I held up a hand to ward off the glare and started to jog.

We burst out into what turned out to be the alley behind the construction project. Narrow. Filthy. Bent-up burglar bars covering the back doors of whatever was on the next block. Overflowing dumpsters. Mangled wooden pallets. Loose trash. Coupla mangy dogs and maybe half a dozen feral cats lurking here and there amid the putrid squalor.

The air swarmed with airborne construction debris, the roar of machinery, and the smell of rotting organic matter. Rodeo Drive it wasn't. And that was the good news.

The bad news was that Henrique had found four burly members of the construction crew, and it didn't look much like he was extolling our virtues. As I stepped out into the filthy air, Henrique was gesturing in my direction with both hands. I could feel everyone go tense.

Gabe leaned in and whispered in my ear. "When this starts here—and it's gonna—pick somebody and knock him out. The odds will be a lot better that way."

I nodded. I was in the process of deciding who got the honors when Henrique and his pals made up my mind for me. The big guy on the far right started sidling his way around us. The guy on the left slid a claw hammer from his tool belt just about the time all five of them started to inch forward. Apparently, further discussion of Henrique's family tree was not on this morning's agenda.

So I made a hard right turn and bull-rushed the guy who was trying to flank us. I swallowed the eight feet that separated us in two quick steps. He saw me coming but wasn't quick enough to do anything about it. I feinted a left hook at his head; he brought up a thick hand with a cross tattooed on the back. I bowed my neck and head butted him right in the middle of his Emiliano Zapata mustache. I felt his front teeth fold inward and heard the cartilage in his nose crinkle flat. His anguished howl pinballed off the buildings. As he brought both hands up to his flattened face, I stepped back and aimed a straight right at his solar plexus. I started the punch from my toes up, pushing off my right foot and following through like a pitcher delivering a fastball to home plate.

My fist landed just above the spot where his bulbous gut began. Felt like it sunk all the way to his backbone. From the expression on his face, it felt that way to him too. One second he was sucking air, next he was bug-eyed, slack-jawed, clutching his chest like he'd just had the big one. A red-handled drywall knife dropped to the ground in front of him. He collapsed to his knees as if to pay homage and then bent at the waist, put both hands on the ground, and puked all over it.

I turned back toward Gabe just in time to see the guy with the hammer learning to fly. Gabe's left foot landed solidly in the middle of his chest as he leaped forward; it caught him in midair, with the hammer raised above his head, growling like a hound from hell.

The kick not only stopped his forward momentum but actually propelled him back in the opposite direction, sending the claw hammer pinwheeling off into space. And then for a second or two after the hammer clattered to silence, the only sounds filling the air were those of two guys gagging bile while desperately trying to force air into their deflated lungs. The alley's feral menagerie was suddenly nowhere to be found.

Counting Henrique, there were three of them left standing upright in the alley, but I could tell right away these guys were fresh out of fight. Apparently loyalty to a coworker was one thing, but getting your ass kicked by a couple of professional thugs was something else entirely. All three of them took off running up the alley. The two new guys went right. Henrique veered left.

"Aw Jesus . . . another fucking track meet," I heard Gabe mutter in the seconds before we took off after Henrique.

Twenty yards up the alley, we burst out onto a street—a big-time under-construction street. Looked like they were expanding the side-walks and putting in new sewer lines as well. Three wide ditches ran down the middle of the street. Henrique was tight-roping across a one-board bridge spanning the nearest ditch. That's what saved us. This wasn't a running track; this was an obstacle course.

The bouncy board bridges were strictly one person at a time, espe-cially for a couple of gorillas like Gabe and me. Worse yet, the bottoms of the ditches were filled with several feet of lumpy green liquid, the toxicity level of which I imagined had to be somewhere north of radio-active isotopes. Falling in was not an option.

I was tiptoeing between the second and third bridges when Henrique made it to the far side of the trench. I pulled my eyes up from my feet just in time to see him dart into a narrow alley on the left.

I held out my arms for balance, like a high-wire walker, hurried across the final ditch, and sprinted left. It was that low, hollow whistle that saved my ass. Turned out Henrique was waiting in the gloom. He'd found himself a six-foot section of aluminum fence pipe for the purpose of putting a permanent dent in my head. As the hollow pipe moved through the air it emitted a low whistling sound, a noise something in me immediately recognized as danger.

I dove for his ankles. I felt the breeze, heard the pipe plow into the wall, bounce off, and clatter to the ground. I grabbed his ankles and jerked them out from under him. He landed flat on his ass right in front of me. And then Gabe was all over him like a cheap suit, and the struggle was more or less over. Took us about five minutes of holding him down before he finally stopped flopping around like a beached trout.

Gabe looked over at me. "You okay?"

"Stop it," I said.

Gabe chuckled out loud.

Henrique's struggles had left him winded and mouth breathing. Gabe and I got off him and stood up. We both offered him a hand. He thought about it for a moment and then took us up on the offer.

"Listen, man, we didn't come here to make any trouble for you," I said as he dusted himself off.

"But we gotta know about the kid in the picture," Gabe added.

"I told you I—"

I raised a cautionary hand. He flinched.

"Don't fucking tell me you don't know who he is . . . 'cause you do. People been lying to me for the better part of twenty-five years. I know bullshit when I hear it."

Henrique opened his mouth. Then changed his mind and stared down at his shoes.

"He probably don't have a name. Mostly she don't give 'em names, 'cause she knows they ain't gonna be around for long and she don't want to get too attached to them."

"Who?"

"Her."

"Your mother?" Gabe pressed.

Henrique averted his eyes. "I guess . . . if you say so," he whispered.

"Where do we find her?" I asked.

"Where she belongs," Henrique spat and turned his face away again.

"Where's that?"

"At the fucking dump."

For some reason, Gabe was appalled. "Hey, man . . . you only get one mother."

"She ain't nothing but a whore and a baby machine," Henrique said. He looked from one of us to the other and back. He could tell we were dubious. "She sells her babies, man. That's what she does. That's how she lives."

"Are you trying to tell me . . . ," Gabe began.

Henrique pounded his chest. "I oughta know, man. She sold *me*," he blurted. "When I was eight. I ended up with some rich old lady on Coronado . . . some old navy guy's wife. I spent almost three years cleaning her toilets and sweeping her fancy floors." He slashed the air with his hand again. "She wouldn't let me wear no clothes in the house neither . . . not the whole time I lived there. Only time I seen clothes was if we had to go out someplace." His eyes got hard as gravel. "She liked to touch me. Said that was how God intended it to be. You know . . . like in the Garden of Eden."

His long-smoldering shame radiated from him like heat waves, thickening the air. He looked away. I didn't much want to hear any more either.

"And then what?" I pressed.

"And then my father . . ." He hesitated. Made a face. "Or at least who we *think* is my father . . . he found me and took me back home."

"Can we talk to him?" Gabe inquired.

Henrique shrugged. "He died a couple of years back. He was a good man."

Gabe kept poking at it. "Howsabout the Coronado lady?"

For the first time, his dark eyes lit up. "She died," Henrique said. "Fell off that chair lift thing she had on the stairs. Busted her fucking neck."

He grinned, and I didn't blame him.

"How do we get to the dump?" I asked.

■ ■ ■

"See . . . this is the end of the commercial shit right here." Lamar pointed at the rash of mansions despoiling the mountainside in front of them. "This here's what they call Sunset Cliffs. This ain't even Ocean Beach no more. These ain't the same brand of stoners as back in town.

These here are the swells who can afford to buy themselves a genuine ocean view."

When Chub didn't say anything, Lamar kept talking. "We start knockin' on doors up there and Mr. and Mrs. Rich Bitch are sure as hell gonna call the cops on us."

Chub turned in a half circle and gazed back the way they'd come.

They'd driven down from Dog Beach, where they'd spent a spine-crushing night sleeping in the car and then parked and walked south from Point Loma Boulevard, down the part where it was all cliffs and there was no way to get down to the ocean. No houses on the ocean side of the street at all, just a brown dirt path that wove along the serpentine face of the cliffs. On the east side, it was like strictly McMansionville.

This was Sunset Cliffs Nature Park or something like that. A thousand signs telling you what you could and couldn't do. No smoking. No drinking. No this. No that. Stay back from the unstable cliff edge, all that kind of pushy government shit. Signs had always pissed Lamar off. Something about being told what to do invariably gave him an almost uncontrollable urge to do the opposite. The shrinks said he had a problem with authority. That pissed him off too.

"Yeah," Chub said finally. "Ain't nothin' we can do down here. Let's go back and do that neighborhood where we parked the car." Without further discussion, they turned around and started north, back toward the last of the businesses on Point Loma Avenue.

Half a dozen surfers now rode the swells; the parking lots were full. A pair of middle-aged married types jogged by in identical jogging suits, red-faced, huffing and puffing as they passed. Lamar turned his head, watched them wobble off, and snickered to himself.

He first saw the woman when he turned his attention forward again. She was standing on the ocean side of a little fence designed to keep gawkers back from the edge of the cliff. Standing all stiff and straight, like a ballet dancer or something. Great ass on her too. Whooooie! Some firm-lookin' cheeks there!

HEAVY ON THE DEAD

He looked up at Chub and was about to make comment regarding her unusually symmetrical posterior when suddenly Chub dribbled to a stop.

"Where'd she go?" Chub asked nobody in particular.

"Who?"

He pointed. "The lady that was standing there."

Lamar looked back to the spot where he recalled seeing her. Nothing there.

He checked the path in both directions. She wasn't there either. Either she'd learned to fly or . . .

"Holy shit," Lamar whispered.

■ ■ ■

I sat on an empty wooden spool and watched Gabe work the dump for nearly an hour, moving from shack to shack, from tent to tent, from one haggard garbage picker to another, making conversation at every stop along the way, as an endless armada of garbage trucks washed through the gate like beached whales, disgorging their rancid entrails upon the ancient mountains of waste.

Above my head, a swirling maelstrom of seabirds wheeled and screeched with the sound of tearing metal. On the festering piles of refuse, an army of stray dogs and piebald pigs sniffed and snuffled its way from pile to pile in search of sustenance.

Gabe was coming my way now. Crossing one mountain of refuse and then disappearing down into a trash trough before reappearing again atop the next.

I scooted over on the cable spool. Gabe plopped down beside me.

"So?" I said.

"Anytime you get to thinking people like us had it rough, all ya gotta do is spend some time talking to these folks," Gabe said. "These folks will cure your ass of feeling sorry for yourself . . . fucking forever, man."

"The mother here?"

Gabe nodded. "Way over on the far side. Lives in an ancient camper. Been there for as long as any of them can remember. Couple of them told me she was born here."

"We gonna . . . ," I began.

Gabe started to talk. "From what they tell me there's about two hundred people who live here full-time. Most of 'em recycle things for a living—glass bottles, metal, cardboard, wood—anything made in the U.S." Gabe swung an expansive arm. "And it's all real territorial . . . folks have died defending their territory. Other people been killed for poaching. Everybody has their own little area they pick. They sell whatever they find to middlemen who sell it to recyclers—you know, except for the food they find. That they either eat themselves or feed to the pigs."

I watched another garbage truck regurgitate its load. "How the fuck do you eat anything from this place?"

"Don't think about it," Gabe advised.

"Anybody hear anything about her selling babies?"

"Just all of 'em," Gabe said with a sigh. "And she ain't the only one doing it neither. Around here selling kids seems to be a major part of makin' ends meet."

A red wave of anger washed over me. "How the fuck can anybody rationalize selling their own kids, for Christ's sake?"

"They think they're doing them a favor. One lady I talked to said she figured they'd end up with a better life no matter where they ended up than they would if they stayed around here."

I'm not often at a loss for words. Gabe sensed it and pointed west. "Over there, by the ocean, there's a big graveyard. Costs fifteen bucks to bury your dead. To these people . . . far as they're concerned, that's the alternative over there."

We sat in silence for a while beneath the swirling, keening birds, interrupted at intervals by the rattling knock of diesel engines and the whine of hydraulics.

"We should talk to her," I said finally.

"About what?" Gabe asked disgustedly. "About how she should be a nice lady and stop selling her kids?" Gabe's jaw clamped down hard, jaw muscles quivering like cables under strain.

I thought about it some. "We should ask her about how she lets them know she's got another one ready." I shrugged. "Some way or another, she has to have a way of getting in touch with whoever it is she sells them to."

There was no arguing with that, so we didn't bother. Rather than marching hill and dale over the garbage Alps, we fanned way out to the east side of the dump and walked along the fence line to the very back of the landfill.

Her abode was a scabrous old cab-over camper mounted on cinder blocks instead of a pickup truck. A peeling red logo on the cab-over part announced it was a Caveman camper. Grants Pass, Oregon. The slider window on the near side was broken out and had been replaced with a jagged piece of plywood.

She was sitting on a bent patio chair stirring a pot of something on an old Coleman stove. There were three children sitting on five-gallon paint buckets in an arc around the stove. Ages two to six or so. Genders uncertain, as none of them looked like they'd ever had a haircut.

Her age was anybody's guess. People who spend their golden years hanging around the pool in Palm Springs tend to age a mite slower than people who scavenge the Tijuana dump for a living. She was somewhere between forty and sixty. Long graying hair and an overall layer of grime that looked like it had been on her for years.

First thing she did at the sight of us was hustle the kids into the camper and close the door. She stood like a sentry, peering out at us with a puffy red eye through a slit in her cascade of falling hair.

I put a hand on Gabe's arm. We both stopped walking. I reached into my back pocket, pulled up the folded photograph and handed it over.

"Let's not scare her any more than we have to," I whispered.

Gabe got the message. I hung back as Gabe slowly approached the woman.

When Gabe unfolded the photo and held it up in front of her face, she shook her head violently and tried to escape into the camper. Gabe threw an arm around her waist and hauled her back to the ground. She punched Gabe in the face with the side of her fist. Gabe ignored it. She started pounding Gabe's chest. Gabe just stood there and looked at her as she pounded away. Eventually, she ran out of gas. Her limp arm dropped to her side and stayed there.

The wind brought me several snippets of Spanish as the two of them went back and forth, shouting above the din. Finally they walked over to the camper door together. The second she opened the door, Gabe slid into the doorjamb. Couple of minutes passed before she reappeared holding a filthy scrap of paper in her hand.

Gabe turned my way. "Lemme have that pad and pencil you always carry."

I moved slowly. The woman eyed me like I was a pack of circling wolves.

Gabe stuck out a hand. I put my little spiral-bound private eye notebook and green golf pencil in Gabe's hand and then backpedaled to where I'd previously been standing.

Took another two or three minutes before Gabe started walking back my way. The second Gabe turned to leave, the woman rushed for the camper and disappeared inside. I heard the snick of the lock. Gabe heard it too.

Gabe gave me a bob of the head that said, *Let's get the hell out of here.* I followed along in Gabe's wake, back along the fence, taking the long way around, until we were back by the gate, sharing the same wooden cable spool we'd shared earlier.

"So?" I said again.

Gabe pulled out my notebook and pencil and handed them to me. "She's got something she wants to sell, she calls that number," Gabe said.

I flipped through the pages. "San Diego number," I said. I've always had a keen perception of the obvious.

"She says two guys always show up for the pickup. Both Americans. One she describes as the fancy guy. Says he wears fancy shoes. He's the one who hands out the money. The other one she refers to as a mechanic. Big man, she says. Says he always wears some shirt with a name on the front."

"I still can't wrap my head around anybody selling a kid," I muttered.

"I said the same thing to her," Gabe mused. "You know what she asked me?"

"What?"

"She told me how she's already lost two children to malnutrition, and then . . . then she asked me if I was sure what *I'd* do to keep them from starving to death?"

I floated it through my circuits for a while. It wasn't a comfortable ride.

"So . . . we found one end of this daisy chain . . . What are we gonna do about it?"

"Go back to O.B., see if we can unwind the other end."

I nodded. I felt weary—lead heavy and out of sorts, kinda like my imaginary dog had died or something. "Yeah . . . for sure," I said. "I don't see how making that poor woman's life any more miserable . . ." I threw a futile hand into the air. "I just can't see how it's gonna make the world a better place."

"Wouldn't work anyway," Gabe said disgustedly. "I mean . . . who we gonna call? The Federales? Like they're gonna do anything about it."

"Ghostbusters," I suggested.

Gabe stifled a bitter laugh. "Maybe Saunders can trace the phone number," Gabe added, trying to find something positive amid the refuse of the morning.

"Let's round up the sheep and get the flock out of here," I said.

Took us a sweaty hour to walk back to the border and then another forty-five minutes to ride the trolley back to San Diego. I don't think we shared ten words the whole time.

Chapter 7

Lamar skidded to a stop six feet from the edge of the cliff, flopped down onto his belly, and began to crawl forward like an inchworm on meth.

"You better stay back, man," he yelled over his shoulder at Chub. "You're too heavy."

He kept inching along until he was able to peer down at the beach. The missing girl was there, all twisted up on the black rocks. Lamar winced. Above the roar of the surf he could hear her low moan. He winced again and then crawled backward on his hands and knees. As he pushed himself to his feet, he said to Chub, "She's still alive, man, but there ain't no way down there."

Chub pointed toward the surfers. "They got down there."

The big guy had a point. Lamar didn't know squat about surfing, but by his estimation, the surfers were way too far from the beach for anybody to have paddled a board down here, so there pretty much had to be another way down to the water.

Chub jerked a thumb back over his shoulder. "I'll go this way. You go that way," he said and took off south, moving right up to the edge of the cliff so's he could see over the top.

Lamar started north at a lope. About seventy yards north of where she'd gone over, he noticed a worn trail of bare footprints that crossed the main trail. He inched over to the edge and looked down.

Looked like a rocky mountain trail. More like a series of footholds worn into the side of the crumbling cliff face.

Lamar brought two fingers to his lips and let go with his best whistle. A quarter mile south, Chub stopped in his tracks and looked back.

Lamar gave him a double *get your ass here in a big hurry* wave. Chub began lumbering in Lamar's direction.

Took a minute or two. Speed wasn't necessarily Chub's strong point. As he approached, Lamar pointed wildly at the spot.

"They go down here," he shouted.

Lamar had sort of assumed they'd work their way down to the rocks together, but Chub ran by him like he wasn't there, stepped down onto the first cutout, and disappeared over the side.

Lamar hurried over to the edge. The big guy displayed the nimble dexterity of a mountain goat as he descended the cliff face in a series of precise hops and lunges.

With a prayer on his lips, Lamar poked a toe over the edge, made sure it was in the groove, and stepped off into space. And then another step and another. He was doing fine until he was only about ten feet above the beach, at which point he missed a step, lost traction, then plopped down onto his ass and slid the rest of the way, coming to a stop when his shoes banged against a Subaru-size rock. Lamar pushed himself upright, leaned back against the nearest boulder, and looked around. Sometime in the past, this section of coast had been filled with large black boulders in an attempt to prevent further erosion of the cliff face.

Chub was twenty yards away, taking off his jacket. Lamar started picking his way over, moving carefully so he wouldn't bust an ankle on the slimy rocks. When he looked up again, Chub was winding the jacket around the woman's left leg.

Lamar didn't have to wonder if her leg was broken because her shin bone was sticking out through her skin. Looked like her left arm might be broken too, and a thin trickle of blood rolled down her chin. She groaned piteously. Lamar swallowed hard.

"Shoulda picked something a bit higher, honey," he mumbled to himself as he picked his way around a final glistening boulder to Chub's side.

Chub looked over. "Don't think we ought to move her," he said, slowly turning a piece of driftwood to tighten the makeshift tourniquet he'd put together. "We need a real medic here."

Out in the ocean, the surfers had picked up on what was going on and were paddling like hell for the beach. "Go back up," Chub said. "Get somebody up there to call 911."

Lamar looked around. "Maybe we shouldn't get involved with the heat," he said. "Those surfers can probably handle it," he said.

"We don't get her help, she's gonna bleed out," Chub growled.

Lamar hurried back the way he'd come, moving faster now, taking more chances on his footing as he scrambled up the cliff face.

Two minutes later he was at the top of the cliff. He pulled the burner phone from his pocket and dialed 911. Almost instantly, sirens began to wail from the north end of town. Lamar reached around to the small of his back, nervously fingering the Browning wedged against his spine, making damn sure his shirt was all the way down.

• • •

We called Sergeant Saunders from the downtown parking lot where we'd left the car this morning. She wasn't in, but after a bit of wheedling from me, they patched me through.

"It's your private pistolero patrol," I said when she picked up. "We've got something."

Short silence. Somebody else said something I couldn't make out. Another silence before a car door opened and closed.

"How long will it take you to get to the west precinct?" she whispered.

"Maybe twenty minutes," I said.

"Make it half an hour and I'll meet you out front," she said and broke the connection.

"Half an hour," I said to Gabe. "I think maybe she needs to ditch the partner."

Gabe nodded and buckled up. "Take the 5 to the 8 . . . then over the bridge into Mission Bay."

"Ooooh . . . don't we sound like Californians now," I joked.

"When in Poway," Gabe said.

I headed downhill toward the freeway, found the 5 North ramp, goosed it up to eighty so's I could at least keep up with the geriatric traffic, and followed the **BEACHES** signs onto the 8 West. From there it was just a few miles till the freeway up and ended in Ocean Beach, except we didn't go quite that far. Instead, I took the bridge over the river into Mission Bay, running along Sea World Drive, through the water wonderland that was Mission Bay Park, past hotels and marinas over to Gaines Street and the SDPD west precinct.

I found a place to park on the west side of Napa Street, turned up the AC, and waited. Gabe was playing some sort of game on the phone. I just sat there and stared out the window, wondering if the dump woman had been right. Wondering whether anyone, if pushed hard enough, would do whatever it took to survive. Supposedly, survival is the first instinct of human nature, but something deep inside me didn't like the sound of that at all. At least not as it applied to me. No matter how many times I went through it, a voice in my head could not be silenced. *But not me,* it shouted inside my skull. *Yeah, maybe for other, weaker people, but it couldn't possibly be true about me. No friggin' way. Not with all* this *moral fiber. No sir.*

Saunders was ten minutes late. It was nearly noon before she pulled the unmarked car into the SDPD parking lot and got out. I popped open the door and put one foot in the street. She caught the movement, made eye contact, and started walking our way.

By the time she caught a break in the traffic, Gabe and I were waiting for her on the sidewalk. We walked up Gaines Street a ways, found a bench in the shade, and sat down. First I handed over the phone number. Then I gave her the *Reader's Digest* version of how our Mexican morning had gone.

"I'll make a few calls to the Mexican police," she said.

Gabe leaned forward on the bench. "No."

Saunders seemed startled. "Whatta you mean no? The woman's selling her babies. I'm going to notify the human trafficking division about this."

"No . . . don't," Gabe said.

Saunders frowned.

"She's got all she can handle," I said. "Let's see if we can't unravel it from this end."

"What? We're all of a sudden having a pity party for a human trafficker?"

"I know it sounds weird, but yeah, something like that," I said.

An uneasy silence settled on us like coastal fog. A slow minute passed. Another.

Saunders got to her feet. "Okay," she said. "You two aren't exactly the little sisters of the poor. You think her plate's already full, I'll take your word for it."

"Thanks," I said.

"So let's go see who this number belongs to."

• • •

The fire department guys had done this kind of rescue before . . . lots of times. Lamar could tell. In no time at all, they'd hooked the jumper up to an IV, stabilized her compound fracture with a blow-up bandage thing, and patched up a bunch of scrapes, before they strapped her to an orange plastic sled and hauled her ass back up on top of the cliff. By that time whatever pain juice they'd given her had come on strong. Her eyes were shut, and, as far as Lamar could see, she was all the way out in dreamland.

That's when the cops showed up. Two of them. One a short little guy. Wiry hair. Olive skin. Looked like he might be Italian. The thick tuft of hair sticking out from his shirt collar suggested he might be haired all over like a gibbon.

The other one looked more like a romance novel cover model. Slicked-back surfer boy hair and that air of confident superiority Lamar always had the urge to stab a few times.

"You the guys called it in?" the smaller cop asked.

"Yeah," Lamar said.

"We'll need you to come down to the station and give us a statement," the big kahuna said.

"We didn't see her jump, man. One minute she was standing there. Next minute she wasn't. That's all we seen," Lamar said. "Ain't nothin' other than that to make no statement about."

"We'll still need you to give us a statement," the short guy said.

Lamar's voice rose. "Okay . . . we didn't see nothin'. There's your statement."

He swiveled and began to stalk off. The big cop blocked his way. When Lamar looked over, Chub was slowly shaking his head.

"You guys have a car?" the cop asked.

Chub nodded.

"I'll drive you back to your car and then you can follow me over to the west precinct. That way you won't have to wait around until I find somebody to drive you back after you give us a statement. Save you a lot of time that way."

• • •

Sergeant Saunders waved a well-manicured hand at the screen and then pushed back from the desk. "It's a restricted number," she said through clenched teeth.

"What's that mean?" I asked.

"The mayor's got a restricted number. The DA's got one. Anybody who needs to keep their private lives private no matter what, people in public positions—they have restricted numbers."

"But you can find out who it belongs to . . . right?" Gabe added.

She made a disgusted face. "If it was still my case and I had a warrant and about six months to take the cell provider to court . . . 'cause that's what it takes these days. Lately everybody's so paranoid about security that cell providers take you to court if you want records. Strictly legal CYA as far as they're concerned." She leaned in and lowered her voice. "At which point you two would probably have to tell your story to a judge."

"Ain't gonna happen," Gabe said quickly.

Saunders help up a *take it easy* hand. "Not to worry. Like I been telling you guys, this is not my case anymore, and all the phone number adds to the equation is that whoever we're looking for is probably somebody with a whole lot of powerful friends. Which, if anything, makes things even worse."

Voices from the uniform squad room filtered in. Out in the parking lot somebody's car alarm started chirping like an urban cricket.

"I'll make a few calls," she said finally. "See if maybe I can't call in a couple favors." Her face said she wasn't holding out a hell of a lot of hope.

Gabe stood up.

"Come on," Saunders said, "I'll walk you out."

Saunders pushed open the station house door. Flicked her eyes up at the CC cameras mounted in the doorway and another on the wall outside.

"Thanks for your help," she said for the benefit of closed circuit posterity.

■ ■ ■

"I'm tellin' ya . . . That's them. That tall fella right there. He's the one. He's Waterman."

"Come on, man. You said it yourself. It's a lousy picture."

"No. The other one."

"What other one?"

Chub lifted one cheek off the seat and pulled the folded photo out of his back pocket. He snapped the CC photo from the bank open in front of Lamar's face and pointed to the person in line behind the guy in question.

"Same one who's with Waterman here right now."

Lamar would have put up more of an argument, but at that moment, the west precinct front door swung open and the two of them stepped out onto the sidewalk. He snapped his eyes back and forth between the picture and the two bruisers walking up the sidewalk.

Lamar watched as they crossed the street, panicked for a second when the pair kept walking directly at them, and then relaxed as they veered to the right and climbed into a rice burner SUV three or four cars in front of them.

Chub grinned and started the engine.

Chapter 8

Traffic on the bridge back to Ocean Beach was lousy. Mostly Gabe and I made it a point not to drive around during the rush hour, so the ride home served as a vivid reminder of why. Around here, other than a couple of hours in the early morning and a couple more at the other end of the day, everything was twenty minutes away by freeway. Odd-numbered highways ran north and south, even numbers east and west. Easy as pie and a far cry from the constant paraplegic gridlock of my old Pacific Northwest stomping grounds.

"Long as we're up at this end of town, what say we see if old Creamed Spinach ain't home," Gabe said as I eased the car around a soft right turn onto Sunset Cliffs Boulevard and began to roll along the east side of Robb Field.

I turned right on Voltaire, drove down to Bacon, got lucky and found a parking spot in front of Te Mana, from whence we walked around the corner to the car entrance to the Robb Field complex. Some sort of kite-flying confab was going on up at the far end. The sky was filled with a flock of shapes and colors, whirling and diving, some long tailed and languid, nearly still in the sky, others veering around like angry hornets.

As we walked up the drive working our way over to the river, Gabe got all philosophical. "Funny, ain't it . . . how much everything depends."

"Whatcha mean?"

"Well, you know . . . the other day when we went through this place asking around about ol' Bar Code . . . I had a big case of *there but for fortune* . . . you know, like I was feeling like I ought to give thanks for my life and wondering how an affluent society like ours . . . how they can allow our fellow citizens to live outdoors like animals. It was like feeling real sad and real fortunate at the same time."

I knew where this story was going because I'd felt the same way myself. "But after our visit to the Tijuana dump . . ."

"No shit," Gabe said. "This place is like the friggin' Ritz compared to that."

"But people don't want to hear that shit either," I said. "It's like the lady in the dump said. How bad would it have to get before you sold a child? It's like that with subjective and objective too. Educated people recognize—you know, on an intellectual level anyway—they know the world is subjective, that everybody sees something different from every-body else, but somewhere deep inside they've got a voice whispering *except for me, of course. I'm the exception to the rule. I see it like it really is.*"

"That's what keeps us going, ain't it?" Gabe asked. "The idea that we can forge order out of chaos."

"Some people think so," I admitted.

We labored up to the top of the berm. Bar Code's campsite was down the bike path maybe four hundred yards east of where we stood. To the left, Dog Beach was packed with pooches dashing after balls, running in circles, bowling one another over in insane spurts of doggy joy.

The river looked as if somebody'd pounded white stakes into the sandy shallows at random intervals . . . until suddenly a stake moved, and then another, and I realized I was looking at a stick-legged squadron of snowy egrets picking among the reeds and shallows, one staccato step at a time.

Out at the end of the sandbar, some bald drunk was wading in the water. From here it was hard to tell whether he was just trying to cool down or maybe he thought he was fishing. The fact that he was wearing nothing but a full-length tweed topcoat gave me an inkling he may have started the self-merriment a tad early today.

"Shall we?" I said.

"Long as you don't ask me how I'm feeling."

"Okay."

Behind us the sun burned low on the horizon, and the shadows were getting long. Maybe another hour or so of daylight, I figured.

"I'll go down the near side and run him out in your direction," I said as we hiked up the bike path. Another fifty yards and we started to hear it. The guitar. And the singing. He was singing.

"What's that he's warbling?" Gabe asked as we got closer.

"The Guess Who—'American Woman,'" I said.

"But . . ."

"Yeah," I said. "I hear it."

We stopped at the near end of the thicket. I started down the well-worn path.

"Bump stock woman, honey let me be. Bump stock woman, baby set me free. Don't come knocking round my door. Don't want to see you anymore. I say woman . . ." I eased down the path toward the river. The guitar was way out of tune, but apparently that minor sonic imperfection didn't much matter to him. He was lettin' it all hang out, wailing on the thing. *"Now woman, I said stay away. Bump stock woman, listen what I say, bump stock woman, listen what I say. Bump stock woman, mama let me be . . ."*

I grabbed the handhold, swung around the corner, and damn near ended up in his lap. The kid was quick, I'll say that. I guess speed's an asset when you're living in the streets. He pulled the same stunt as the last time, scooting out the other end like a prairie dog, only this time Gabe was ready, blocking the other exit like a boulder.

The kid started to back up. "Hey . . . hey . . . ," he was yelling as he backed out into the river, balls deep, holding the guitar high over his head to keep it dry. Gabe walked to my side. The kid pointed with his free hand.

"You fuckers was here the other day."

"Careful with that guitar," I said. "Those things don't like getting wet."

"That bar code on your forehead there," Gabe pointed. "That thing really read out as creamed spinach?"

"Who tole you that?" he demanded.

"A little birdie," Gabe said.

"You a man or a woman?" Bar Code asked Gabe.

"Does it matter?" Gabe countered.

"Probably not," the kid said.

"What's the bar code for?" Gabe pressed.

"Succotash," the kid said.

"Come on in, man," I said to him. "We need to talk with you about something. We're not here to bust your balls or roust you out or nothing like that. I just need you to help me with something."

"Like what?"

"You remember the other day when the cops chased you up the Santa Cruz stairs?"

He frowned, wrinkling the bar code. "What about it?"

"You bit me, man." I pointed at the dental decoration on my neck. "Right here."

He started waving his free hand in my direction. Like he was wiping off a blackboard. "No . . . no . . . no, man . . . I didn't mean to . . . things was . . . fuckin' cops . . . that fat bastard up on the cliff . . . always . . ."

I cut him off. "Look, man . . . here's how it is . . . either I've got to wait for the rest of my life to find out whether or not I've contracted some kind of infectious disease from you, or you've got to go get a blood test so's I can know for sure one way or the other—you know, and then maybe get on with my life."

"Huh?"

"Come on, man. I can't have this shit hanging over my head forever. Help me out with this. I'll make it worth your while."

He was indignant. "I got no damn diseases. Who said I got diseases?"

"I gotta make sure."

The kid's feet slipped on the muddy bottom. He wobbled, waving the guitar above his head like a torch. Gabe stepped up to the water's edge and offered him a helping hand. He hesitated, swaying in the current like a reed, and then took it. Gabe hauled him ashore like he was lighter than air.

First thing he did was walk the guitar over to the case and tuck it inside.

"So . . . how you gonna make it worth my while?" he asked as he straightened up.

"Tell you what . . . You go with me over to the Scripps Clinic in Mission Valley, get a blood test and maybe let 'em run a big Q-tip around your mouth, and I'll buy you dinner when we get back. Also I'll be eternally grateful—"

"Hodad's," he interrupted.

"Okay, Hodad's . . . and . . ." I paused for effect. "And . . . I'll give you a nice crisp hundred-dollar bill when I bring you back here."

"Twenties," he said immediately. "Ain't nobody around here gonna cash a hundred for me."

"Done."

I stuck out a hand. He looked at my outstretched palm like I was trying to hand him a dog turd.

"When?" he asked.

"Right fucking now," surged from my throat like a cheetah. Even surprised me. That's when I realized I was having one of those moments when the sound of my voice had pushed something to the fore—something I'd been keeping at arm's length.

I was shit scared. Probably as scared as I'd ever been in my life. Over my twenty some years in the private eye business, I'd pondered and pictured and personally experienced all manner of violence and mayhem and had gone through many moments where I'd figured the jig was finally up for me. The way I saw things in those days, it just came with the territory . . . But this . . . dying from some slow wasting-away disease, in some shitty hospital room with strangers standing around me like I was some kind of exhibit. That was too horrible for me to contemplate even from a distance.

I looked over at Gabe and shrugged an apology.

Gabe grinned. "I'll walk home and take the bus to my karate class."

• • •

Lamar pointed through the dirty windshield. "There's the other one," he said.

They watched as the other one exited the park and started walking south on Bacon Street. Ten seconds later, the car they'd come in rolled out the park entrance. Leo Waterman and somebody new turned left onto Voltaire.

"He's got somebody with him," Lamar said as the car went by.

"We'll follow the one on foot," Chub announced.

Took less than fifteen minutes. The freak walked down to an apartment building near the middle of the block, turned into the narrow walkway, and disappeared.

Lamar and Chub were still deciding what to do next when the freak came back out, walked down to Cable Street, got on the number 35 bus, and dieseled out of sight.

Chapter 9

Marshall took his time cleaning his glasses. He was lost in thought when his phone began to blink. He put it on speaker.

"Lamar Pope on line one," the young man's voice said.

Click. "You motherfuckers hear me, you want Greenway dead you better drag your white Aryan Brotherhood asses down here and do it yourself, 'cause I'm telling you right now I'm not good for it. You know what they say: if you can't do the time, don't do the crime, and motherfuckers, I'm not doing hard time for nobody. And that big ol' boy ain't about to give up anytime soon neither, so if . . . y'all got any . . ."

Marshall settled his glasses onto his face and broke the connection. He leaned back and laced his fingers together. "Well," he whispered into the silence. "That settles that, doesn't it."

Greenway and Pope had officially gone from being a dubious asset to being a definite liability. Quite simply put, for the good of the cause . . . they simply had to go. No doubt about it. The way he saw things, it was wise to assume that every time Pope had called, including this one, the cops had been listening. The cause couldn't take any more heat at this point and neither could he. No . . . those two had to be removed . . . posthaste and permanently.

The problem was that the white separatist movement, at least this particular end of it, was just about flat broke. He sat there leaning back with his eyes closed for the better part of twenty minutes, going over his options in his head. The phone buzzed again.

"Fresno on line four."

Marshall wasn't surprised. Of the various West Coast chapters of the Aryan Brotherhood, Fresno was the most hardline and the most difficult to manage. Their founder, Paulie Kopecnick, known among the members as Paulie K., was the most militant and outspoken of all the chapter leaders. Nobody would say it out loud, but Paulie was the chief instigator of blaming Marshall for the Conway disaster.

Truth was Paulie had always wanted Marshall's job. Thought he should have had it from the beginning; despite being virtually illiterate and about as inarticulate as humanly possible, he had always thought himself a great leader of men. Marshall heaved a sigh and picked up the phone.

"Paulie," he said.

"You get that Waterman guy yet?"

"We're working on it."

"Something needs to happen, man. The guys are coming apart. I've heard from other chapter presidents. They need somebody to pay the price for what happened up in Washington. Way I see it, it's either this Waterman guy or it's you."

"Paulie—" Marshall began.

"They're done with your bullshit, Marshall. No more hiding out while the scum of the earth take this country away from us. No more lying low, driving around in PTA vans, leaving our bikes in the fucking garage. That shit's done. My boys have had it with that. They need something to happen. They need somebody to pay the price for what happened up there. Right fucking now!"

"I couldn't agree more, but it has to happen surreptitiously."

"What the fuck does that mean?" Paulie growled.

"We can't take any more heat," Marshall said.

"Get it done, Marshall. If you have to, do it yourself."

Marshall started to speak, but Paulie cut him off. "And don't start that executive delegation shit of yours with me neither. I knew you *when*, you little motherfucker. I remember the time you put one in

Shorty's ear. And that shit hole greaser from Victorville too. You got quite a history of sneaking up behind people and putting out their lights. If you can't get it done by someone else, then do it yourself."

Marshall was working up his chain-of-command speech when the connection broke. He again sat back in his chair and pondered what to do next. He'd heard through the grapevine that Paulie K. had showed up at the Portland chapter earlier in the week, so he'd been expecting him to sooner or later show up here. As Marshall saw things, the only way to maintain his position and come out of this smelling like a rose was if he did the job himself, so in that sense Paulie was right. Which meant that he needed to get Pope and Greenway out of the picture once and for all.

After a considerable interval he slowly stood up and pulled a small silver ring of keys from his pants pocket. He sorted out a small brass key and used it to unlock the bottom drawer of the desk.

He removed two items, set them on the desk in front of him, and slid the drawer closed with the keys still in the lock.

He pushed the "Power" button on the disposable phone and watched it blink to life, then opened the leather-bound journal. Three pages from the back and then back to the inside of the front cover for the code sequence. Took him several minutes to work out the random algorithmic sequencers. He dialed the ten-digit number he'd block printed on the page. Somebody picked up but said nothing. "I'd like to speak with Mr. Garrett," the little man said.

"Your name?"

"Marshall."

"Does Mr. Garrett have your number?"

"Yes."

Click.

He dialed another number. Waited.

"*Hola*. BanRegio Bank."

"Mr. Romero, *por favor*."

He waited through three rings before somebody picked up.

"Romero," the voice snapped.

"Mr. Romero . . . earlier this week you provided us with some information . . ."

"What? I don't know . . ."

He let Romero sputter and deny for a while, then said, "I imagine the BanRegio bank would not look kindly on one of their IT employees selling confidential client information. I think it most likely that they would relieve you of your responsibilities were they to find out."

Long silence, then, "What do you want?"

Marshall told him. "No money actually involved. It simply appears and then disappears, and nobody's the wiser."

Romero started to sputter again. Marshall cut him off. "And better yet, you'll never hear from us again."

"When?"

He told him.

. . .

I heard the squeak of her shoes on the floor and perked up. An official-looking hospital brunette, athletic looking, wide in the shoulders, long of limb in that healthy California-girl manner. Coming my way. Smiling.

"Tomorrow afternoon," she said. "One . . . two o'clock."

"Huh?"

"That's what everybody asks first," she said, clipping her pen into her lab coat pocket. "We'll call you with the test results."

She checked her paperwork and then recited my phone number, making sure she had it right. She did.

"Where's he?" I asked.

"Mr. Succotash?"

I laughed for the first time today.

"Mr. Succotash had the worst case of head and body lice any of us have ever seen, and we've got some grizzled vets around here. We cleaned him up in the shower and then more or less sheared him like a sheep. Head to toe. Stem to stern. We're treating him for the parasites right now."

"He agreed to that?" I asked.

She arched an eyebrow. "He signed the waiver . . . remember?"

"Aaaah." I made a mental note to have the car sandblasted when this was over.

Twenty minutes later Bar Code eased out the swinging door, cleaner than I'd ever seen him, dressed in a pair of bright-blue scrubs and the neat little color-coordinated booties. I wolf whistled.

"They burned my clothes, man . . . cut every damn hair off my body. Gonna sue these motherfuckers . . . gonna come back here with—"

"You signed the release," I interrupted. "You gave them permission."

"They got no . . . no goddamn . . ."

I stood up. "Come on, man, we'll go get you a fresh set of duds."

He mumbled and grumbled and bitched all the way back to Sports Arena Boulevard. I wasn't really listening, but I could pretty much swear he mentioned the Supreme Court several times as we fought the traffic snarl down past Midway to the mall.

We parked in the lot and moseyed into DICK'S Sporting Goods, where we fitted him out with a whole new set of clothes. For reasons of his own, he insisted on camouflage everything, including both the sneakers and the sunglasses. When he pulled the camo stocking cap down over the bar code, I started pretending I couldn't see him, but I don't think he got the joke.

By the time we made it back to the car, he'd decided that The Habit burger joint on the far side of the mall parking lot was plenty good enough for this evening's repast and that we could forget about Hodad's. I sipped at a lemonade while he worked on two Santa Barbara burgers and a large order of onion rings.

Between burgers, I asked him, "What's your name?"

"What's yours?"

"Leo Waterman."

He swallowed. Took another bite and then started to answer.

"Really," I said before he could dream something up. "No frozen vegetables."

"Brandon," he said after another bite of burger.

"Brandon what?" I pressed.

"Pitts," he said before swallowing and then washing it down with Dr Pepper.

"So how'd you end up on the streets?"

"Why? You writing a book?" he asked without looking up from the plate.

"Just curious."

He finished the second Charburger. Ignoring me.

"Where you from?" I tried.

"Redding," he said around a mouthful.

"How long you been homeless?"

He wiped his mouth with a paper napkin. "Since I was fourteen. Damn near ten years now." He knew where I was heading. He set the mangled burger on the plate, used a couple more napkins to clean himself up, and let out a sigh.

"Okay, man . . . ," he started. "Look . . . it's not even exciting, bro. My dad died when I was little. The doctors told me he died of tuberculosis, but you ask his men friends and they say he was a little too fond of drinkin' and carrying on to last very long at all . . . so anyway, after that things were hard for a while. We moved around a lot. Redding, Crescent City, Central Point, Roseburg, Canyonville . . . places like that. Mostly my mom cleaned motel rooms for a living. I was about eight when the boyfriends started coming round . . ." He waved an angry hand. Shook his head sadly. "From then on it was mostly just a question of which one of us they'd rather fuck." He picked the burger back up. "About a month before I turned fourteen I just picked up and left. Seemed like just about any other place was better than where I was."

He grinned through a mouthful of burger. "Got me waterfront property now."

"You still talk to your mom?"

"We're done. She made her choices, and I made mine."

I had a feeling that I'd heard all I wanted to, so I changed the subject.

"And . . . and . . . if you don't mind me asking . . ."

He cut me off. Almost smiled. "Why the bar code?"

"Yeah."

"Seemed like a good idea at the time. Felt like I was nothin', so I made myself into somethin'. Simple as that." He tapped the bar code with his index finger. "I'm whatever this thing says I am, man." He snapped his fingers.

Silence settled over the table like a shroud.

"What were the cops chasing you for that day on the cliffs?" I asked.

His neck began to redden. "That fat fuck . . . motherfucker calls the cops every fucking time he sees me . . . And you know . . . that's not even the weird part. Weird part is the cops show up every time he calls . . . like he's got 'em on a string or something. So . . . you know . . . I figured if that fat bastard was working for the guy on the cliff, he couldn't be down at the big building at the same time, so I was running that way figurin' I could lose the pigs on the stairs."

He went back to the burger. Stayed at it until the last morsel disappeared down his throat. "You got my money?" he asked.

I counted five twenties out onto the table. Brandon Pitts snatched them up like he was catching a fly. "Howsabout you drive me back to the river, man," he said. "Don't want nobody messing with my shit."

I leaned forward. "I live on Del Monte, Brandon. The building with the bright-yellow window frames. You know where I'm talking about?" I asked.

"Yep. Just about in the middle of the block."

"You ever decide you want to have that tattoo removed . . . you come and find me, and I'll make sure it happens."

He seemed puzzled. "Why would I want to do that?"

"Maybe you're already somebody. Maybe you don't need a label on you anymore."

• • •

Garrett didn't look the part at all, which was at least partly why he'd lasted so long in the business. If you saw him in the street, suburban lawns would come immediately to mind. And cul-de-sacs and backyard barbecues and Little League games . . . those sorts of things. Last guy on earth who killed people for a living. No way. Not ol' Harve. *Insurance, I think,* someone would say. But Marshall had used him before when they'd required professional help, and with excellent results.

They'd agreed to meet at a local discount mall south of Portland. Over by the north parking lot, by the Nike store. They were seated side by side on a blue steel Metro bench; Marshall had filled him in on the details thus far. Garrett hadn't uttered a syllable since Marshall stopped talking. Marshall had given up trying to read his expressionless granite eyes. Talk about a sphinx.

At this point the only thing Marshall was sure of was that the guy gave him the willies in a manner few other people ever had. Something about the way he sat there, not saying a word, staring holes in you with those flat gray eyes. That pouchy face and double chin with all his features crammed into the middle like they were having a meeting, the shiny, bald head and scuffed-up boat shoes. Joe Everybody.

They'd been sitting there listening to the ebb and flow of traffic for what seemed like half an hour, when Garrett finally spoke again. "So . . . you sent these two guys down to Mexico to get some data on a guy you were hunting for. Right?"

"Yes."

"They were supposed to report right back to you, but one of them had other ideas and decided to off the original guy for himself."

"Yes."

"And you told his partner he'd have to take care of him, even scrounged him a piece for the job, but he either can't or won't do the do. Is that right?"

"Yes."

"And now you want me to off them both for you. Like right now. Before they can fuck things up even worse for your people, who, I don't have to tell you, are hotter than the freakin' surface of the sun right now."

Marshall nodded his grudging agreement.

Garrett smiled. "You do realize this has a certain irony to it, don't you?"

"Most things do," Marshall said as he handed a manila folder to Garrett. "He's using the name Leon Marks and lives on the coast in San Diego. Your fee will be posted to an account in the Tijuana Rio branch of the BanRegio bank. First thing tomorrow morning." He handed Garrett the envelope. "All the necessary information to transfer it wherever you please is there for you."

The man known in the trade as Garrett got to his feet. "I'll handle your two guys," he said. "The Waterman guy is strictly your problem. He's involved in your disaster up north. That whole Conway thing is way too hot for me, and I hear your membership is blaming the Conway thing on you. I don't want any part of it. I'll check the account for the money first thing in the morning. As long as the money's not mythical, I'll be in San Diego by afternoon. This is the only time we'll meet."

Marshall sat and watched the man waddle across the access road, amble beneath the covered walkway, and disappear into an Eddie Bauer store.

. . .

Soon as I got back to the apartment, took a half-hour shower, and ate
a peanut butter sandwich, I called Tim Eagen in Seattle. Went right to
voicemail. Ten minutes later, he buzzed me back. Eagen wasn't big on
preambles.

"You been to your computer?" he asked.

"Not in the past few hours," I said.

"I got a make from immigration on the two guys the Brotherhood
sent down to Mexico to trace your bank accounts. I sent it to your
computer. Coupla small-time losers. Not the sorta assholes you'd expect
the Brotherhood to send after anybody."

"What . . . no swastika tattoos?"

I heard him flipping pages. "No tattoos period, either one of them.
No felony convictions either, or the Mexicans wouldn't have let their
sorry asses into the country."

I didn't say anything.

"They rented a different car for their return to the States than the
one they drove down in. The info's in the file. They been charging things
to eat and drink in Ocean Beach, so it's a good bet they're still around
someplace."

"What about lodging?"

I sat there and listened to pages turning.

"Nothing for lodging. Just gas and food."

"Thanks," I said.

"How you feeling?" he asked.

I told him about catching up with Brandon Pitts and taking him
in for a blood test.

"At least you'll know," he said. "I was you, I'd take a little time to
see if you can't confirm the information. It's task force info . . . you
know . . . it's a cooperative multiagency thing. Politics sometimes wins
out over getting it right."

I was still processing the question of whether or not I actually *wanted* to know, when Eagen said, "I got a charity dinner. Gotta go." Click.

He wasn't big on goodbyes either.

I made another peanut butter sandwich on my way through the kitchen and took it with me into my bedroom where my desk was. The sounds of my chomping were accompanied by the soft bong of the iMac turning on. Every Wednesday night, year-round, O.B. has a farmers market. One of the regular merchants specializes in homemade coconut peanut butter. I was so bonkers for it, I always kept a spare in case I needed a "go-to jar." As far as I was concerned, if that stuff wasn't a controlled substance, it damn well ought to be.

I scrolled through my email until I came to one without a hint of who the sender was, and there was Eagen's file. Lamar Pope and Chub Greenway. A couple of marginal white supremacist types with no criminal records. I clicked on pictures. Stopped chewing and sat there openmouthed and gaping squished peanut butter and white bread. One was a weaselly-looking fucker with greasy hair and a rodential grin. The other was the largest SOB I'd seen since . . . goddamn . . . since earlier today.

"No shit," I said to nobody in particular.

. . .

They'd been at the Little Lion Cafe for over an hour, waiting for dark. Lamar was sipping his latte and checking the street. Chub was across the street in the mini-mart. He'd taken one look at the menu and lost his damn mind.

"What kinda stuff is that?" He dropped the menu on the table, then just as quickly snatched it up again, reading out loud, "Belgian Lion Potatoes." He waved the menu like an orchestra conductor. "What in holy hell is that?" He snapped the menu with his finger. "What? It speaks French or something. Something called a Buddha Bowl. Only damn thing on here I recognize is the Apple Crisp."

"It's just a menu, man," Lamar offered, sipping at his latte.

"No it's not," Chub insisted. "It's all those snooty types out there on the Facebook . . . postin' pictures of hundred-dollar lunches, when my folks are out there buyin' Wonder Bread and Top Ramen. And worse yet, they're rubbin' our damn noses in it every freakin' day. Braggin' how they eat better, and dress better, and own better houses and cars . . . and have better kids, who end up livin' better lives than our kids." He dropped the menu again and folded his arms across his chest.

Lamar started to say something, but Chub cut him off.

"It's all that, man. All the crap we got going on in this country right now is 'cause of the same thing. Whole buncha regular people in this country would as soon elect a baboon president or jump into a hand-basket headed for hell just so they could shut those snooty Facebook types the hell up. Like they're sayin' that if they're gonna be down there in the mud, everybody else might just as well be down there in the muck with us."

He grated the chair backward and got to his feet. "I'm goin' across the street and get me some real food for later," he announced.

Fifty feet up, the palm trees swayed like hula dancers. Buncha people using the Laundromat. Pretty good crowd at the Mexican joint up by Ebers. A few random skateboarders. That was about it. Except for the chickies. Whatever this joint was lacking, it sure as hell wasn't good-looking chiquitas. They were everywhere. Armies of blue-haired, leg-tattooed woman flesh crawled along the sidewalks like a motorcade.

Lamar hadda admit it. This place had its charms.

He was leaving in the morning. Gettin' the hell out. He'd already decided that. No way he wanted to be around when Chub killed the Waterman guy, so he was getting out of Dodge first thing in the A.M.

He watched Chub come out of the mini-mart with a bale of snacks and head up Point Loma Avenue to dump them in the car. Lamar dug into his pants pocket and grabbed the burner phone, thumbed in the number, and waited. *The number you are trying to reach is no longer in service. Please leave a message at the tone.* He tried again. Same result. Goddamn thing was on autodial, so he hadn't misdialed. Third time he left a message.

"We found your boy Waterman," he said. He found the paper he'd written the address on. "Forty-eight ninety-six Del Monte Avenue. We ain't sure what apartment yet. And I'm tellin' you, man, Greenway's gonna cancel his ass tomorrow. I ain't got no doubt about it." His voice rose. "I also ain't got nothin' to do with this shit. I done everything I could to talk some sense into the guy. This shit's all on Greenway. Not me. All of it."

Almost in slow motion, Lamar hung up, set his cup on the little round table, and sat back in the seat. *They've cut me loose,* his brain told him. Why the hell would they do that? Unless . . . you know, unless for some reason, they didn't give a shit about Waterman anymore, which was real unlikely as far as Lamar was concerned. If anybody needed a scapegoat, it was the Brotherhood brass. With half the membership blaming them for the disaster up in Conway and over a hundred other guys either dead, hiding out, or in jail, they really needed to make an example out of somebody, and this Waterman guy was it. No changing horses neither. Not this late in the game. Waterman was it.

Then there was the question of whether or not to tell Chub what he was thinking. The guy had a right to know if the Brotherhood was still looking to kill his big ass, but on the other hand Lamar couldn't tell him about it without letting on that he'd been ratting them out the whole time they'd been in California. The big gorilla wasn't going to like that at all, so that sure as hell wasn't gonna work neither.

Lamar went back to watching the palm trees and sipping at his latte. The painted ladies at the other table got up, threw some money on the table, and headed up Sunset Cliffs Boulevard. The wobble of their resplendent asses held Lamar's attention like flypaper. Wasn't till Chub sat down across from him that Lamar looked that way.

"I'm going back in the morning," Lamar said. Which was of course a bald-faced lie. Showing up at the supposed meeting place after Chub killed Waterman was not one of life's possibilities as far as Lamar was concerned. Might as well take the Browning and blow his own brains out. No sir. Lamar was headed for the unknown parts of parts unknown.

As was his nature, Lamar gave it one last try. The old *up close and personal* approach. "I'm tellin' you, man, these Aryan assholes ain't the forgive-and-forget types neither. No sir. Those fuckers eat hate for breakfast, man. They're gonna be lookin' for you forever if you go through with this . . . and if you don't mind me saying, Chub, your dimensions make the prospect of hidin' out a whole lot more difficult than it would be for, how shall I say, us more diminutive folks. Those fuckers are gonna be all over you like fleas on a cockapoo."

"Tomorrow's the day I make my folks proud," Chub said.

• • •

"Who ate all the damn peanut butter?" were the words that yanked me from my stupor.

My eyes snapped open; I ran a hand over my face. I'd crapped out sitting at my desk. I had a major case of Igor neck. When my vision reorganized itself, I was looking at Gabe's head peering at me around the doorjamb. "Where's the stash?" Gabe asked.

"The little cabinet over the stove. Behind the flour."

Took me a couple of minutes to recalibrate my faculties. "After you chow down," I yelled out to the kitchen, "come in here. I've got something to show you."

Gabe strolled into the room, coconut peanut butter sandwich in one hand and big glass of milk in the other. "You get Bar Code down for his tests?"

"Yeah," I said, "and his name's Brandon."

"So . . . when do you . . ."

"Tomorrow afternoon."

I hit the iMac's space bar to wake it up. "Eagen called. Here's the two guys the Aryan Brotherhood sent after us."

The images on the screen stopped Gabe midchomp. The big forehead wrinkled.

Gabe pointed with the milk. "Isn't that . . . those guys . . . those two . . . didn't we see them earlier today at the cop shop?"

"Yep."

Gabe made the peanut butter sandwich disappear, then chugalugged it down with the rest of the milk. "You got any idea what in hell's going on here?"

"None," I said.

"Or why they were at the cop station today?"

"Nope."

"They can't be hitters," Gabe pronounced after a minute of staring at the screen. "Neither of them's the type. That greasy little runt can't weigh over a buck fifty, and I mean . . . for Christ's sake, who's gonna hire a nine-hundred-pound hit man?" Gabe pointed at the screen. "You gotta be able to blend in. That ol' boy can be seen from space."

"Good point," I conceded. "What then?"

"What's in the computer file?"

"The skinny one, Lamar Pope, is a small-time grifter and con man. Short cons. Identity theft . . . credit cards, that sort of crap. He was living in Arkansas and about to take a lot of local heat for credit card fraud, probably looking at his first felony conviction, when he got the offer from the Brotherhood to take a trip to Mexico. The cops think he got affiliated with the Brotherhood during one of his county jail stints. One of those lockups where you got no choice but to pick a side and get on it. He's not a true believer at all. More like a hanger-on. They think he only accepted because he needed to get out of town for a while. And like you said, he's definitely not muscle, either by trade or inclination."

"And the big guy?"

"Chub Greenway. He's a little easier to figure out. His older brother Randy was killed up in Conway. Randy was a true believer. Hated everybody. Vaporized, as I understand it. So the task force is thinking that for Greenway, this is probably personal—you know, revenge for his older brother. Defending the family honor and stuff like that. Pope and Greenway were supposed to collect some information in Mexico and then hustle back to the nest and tell all. Nothing but that. But . . . seems somewhere along the way, Mr. Greenway decided to hunt us down on his own. Pope called it in, even though he wasn't supposed to break radio silence. Told the Aryan Brotherhood how Greenway had gone rogue and he didn't know what the fuck to do. They go back and forth until they finally tell Pope he's gonna have to stop Greenway on his own. Put out the big guy's lights singlehandedly for the good of the cause. Pope about shits his pants. This isn't his kind of thing at all. Meanwhile they arrange for Pope to get a gun, hoping to either embolden or shame him into doing the deed, but Pope calls back the next day and tells 'em gun or no gun, he isn't killing anybody, not now, not ever. They get pissed and tell him if he doesn't pop Greenway, he better stay awake for the rest of his days 'cause they're surely coming for his scrawny ass. Pope tells 'em to stuff that too—says he still isn't gonna do it." I let my hands flop into my lap. "That's where we are," I said. "The number they were tapping is no longer in service, and recent credit card purchases say that, as of this morning, Pope and Greenway are right here in O.B., still looking for us."

"Sounds to me like maybe we ought to find them before they find us."

. . .

Garrett had been assured the gun was cold. The supplier assured him the piece had never been registered anywhere. That it was a World War II souvenir. Spent the past fifty years in a trunk in somebody's attic. The source said he'd picked it up at an estate sale, cleaned it up, tried it out, and pronounced it a great little pocket gun. A .765-caliber Beretta. Fired 32 autos. They'd agreed on both a price and a delivery system.

Garrett sat in the rental car half a block south of the little neighborhood lending library. From his distance it looked like an oversize birdhouse or maybe an overdecorated mailbox. Definitely handmade. He watched an older Hispanic woman rummage through the donated books, select one, and close the little glass doors.

Right on schedule, the blue Toyota he'd been told to expect looped around him and pulled up next to the lending library. He watched as the driver unbuckled himself, got out, and checked the immediate area. The driver waited until the Hispanic woman turned right on Voltaire and disappeared, then walked over and added what looked like a book to the donated collection and drove off.

Garrett started easing the rental car forward even before the Toyota was back in motion. He jammed the car into "Park," got out, and pulled open the glass doors. He reached over the top of the shelf of books, found the package's smooth cardboard finish, and eased it back over the reading material. He slipped the package under his arm, closed the doors, and hustled back to the rental car. The package was about the size of a book but way too heavy. He smiled and eased the rental out onto Muir Street and drove off.

• • •

Gabe and I had decided to keep it low-key, like we were going downtown for breakfast and taking a nice walk on the beach before wandering back home. We did that several times a week, and we thought it would be better than staging a full-scale search for Pope and Greenway, which would surely set off the local underemployed tongue-wagging grapevine. Instead, we'd simply be a couple of locals out for a stroll, talkin' with our neighbors as we communed with nature.

A dozen surfers were riding the swells alongside the pier. The tourists hadn't arrived yet. Those left here had no place else to go.

Later in the day, when the beach scene was in full swing, the sea wall would have morphed into a steamy mix of locals availing themselves of beach culture, and hordes of tourists snapping ocean selfies while chewing on take-out tacos, all this going on while the dazed and confused stumbled among them like gypsies in the palace, panhandling, selling trinkets and peace and love and art and handmade this and that, all to the melodic strains of four or five wretched self-taught guitar players wailing away, hoping to separate a few coins from the passing parade of tourists.

Gabe caught up to me while I was crossing the parking lot by the big lifeguard station at the bottom of Santa Monica. We slipped between cars, out onto the grass, and kept heading north until we ran out of green.

Up here, between lifeguard stations 3 and 4, the beach was deserted, so we kicked off our flip-flops, walked out onto the sand, and headed back the other way. Gabe hiked up the Nike shorts and waded out into the water . . . knee-high.

"Still cold," was the pronouncement.

First person we ran into was an older Asian woman wearing a straw Chinese coolie hat, carrying a picker and an orange plastic bucket. The old woman was a regular. She scrounged from the beach garbage cans three or four times each day. Fast as the tourists filled them up with cans and bottles, she came along and cleaned them out. Over the months I'd said hello to her half a dozen times as I walked the beach in the morning but had never received so much as a syllable in response, so we gave her a polite nod and kept walking.

The second guy was so stoned on something, he'd morphed into a restaurant critic. I made the mistake of asking him how it was going.

He responded with, "Whatever you do, don't order the octopus tacos."

Gabe grinned and asked, "Why not?"

"Tough, man . . . like chewing bungee cords."

We let it go at that and kept moving south. He, for some reason, decided to tag along with us as we moved down the beach. Babbling as we walked along the sand. I recall something about the illuminati secretly running San Diego and the notion that while love may be eternal, the blow jobs tend to taper off. The rest of it I just tuned out.

Somewhere south of lifeguard station 2 he vaporized back into the atmosphere.

Wasn't until we ran into the bubble guy that we picked up some of the gossip we were looking for. I didn't know the guy's name, but I'd bandied words with him quite a few times. He was a multitasker. His life's work seemed to consist of flying kites, throwing a boomerang, and blowing huge bubbles that floated over the beach, mesmerizing the jumping children as the giant silvery orbs floated across Abbott Street and spent themselves on the front of the Ocean Beach Hotel. He was unpacking his stuff for the day.

"What's up, man?" I asked.

"Same ol', same ol'," he said. "Another day in paradise."

I unfolded a copy of Pope's and Greenway's passport photographs that I'd printed before we'd left the apartment. "You seen these guys?" I asked him.

He stopped what he was doing and walked over to peer at the pictures.

"Oh yeah," he said. "They been around for a few days, showing some picture around, asking if anybody knows where to find the guy in the photo."

"You recognize the guy in the picture?" Gabe asked.

Mr. Bubbles shook his head and began to dump water into the bucket. "Real bad picture," he said as he mixed the concoction. "Coulda been anybody from Tina Turner to Karl Malden as far as I was concerned."

We thanked him and kept walking south along the sand. The beach was thick with kelp; swarms of sand flies buzzed and settled before the next high tide rolled in and the ocean reclaimed it.

A Heermann's gull skittered across the sand in front of us before launching himself into the breeze and flapping indignantly away. By the time we'd walked back to where Abbott makes the big turn and becomes Newport, we'd been told more or less the same thing by at least five different people, none of whom had recognized the guy in the photo Greenway and Pope had shown them. The most common descriptive phrase about the two men was "biggest SOB I ever saw," or something to that effect.

"So Eagen's info was spot on," Gabe said as we dodged an Odwalla truck crossing Bacon Street on our way back home.

"There haven't been any lodging charges on their credit card," I said.

"So they're either sleeping rough or sacking out in the rental."

"We've got the plate number on their rental."

"I'm betting Dog Beach," Gabe said. "That or someplace along the river."

"Good bet."

Wasn't till we got up to Cable that the final piece fell into place. Otherwise, we'd gotten what we came for. We'd confirmed Eagen's information and were strolling back home to decide what in hell to do about it when Tran, the guy who made keys out of a little kiosk in a furniture store parking lot, started waving his arms to attract our attention.

"Leon," he shouted through the thick morning air. I waved back, and Gabe and I veered in that direction.

Tran was a beloved town character. A former marine, he was in his mideighties and had lived in O.B. since the ice had receded from North America. Seventy years back, as a teenager, fresh from Texas, he'd helped plant Newport Avenue's famously photogenic palm trees. As usual, he was wearing a Padres hat and a portable oxygen unit. As always, the jazz channel was blaring from his boom box. Sounded like Hank Mobley workin' the sax to me.

The three of us exchanged pleasantries. "Folks saying you looking for them guys showing a picture around town."

We admitted it was true. "Funny thing about that," Tran said. "Picture wasn't worth a shit . . . coulda been just about anybody . . . 'cept . . ." He gave it a dramatic pause.

"'Cept what?" I prodded.

"'Cept the T-shirt, man."

"What about it?" Gabe pressed.

"Whoever was in the picture was wearing that same Blue Rush Fishing Charters shirt you wear sometimes. The light-blue one. The one from Puerto Rico with the fish on the back. Got no idea who was in the picture, but it was the same damn shirt. Swear to God." He held up two fingers, like scout's honor.

We made a little more small talk, had the obligatory conversation about the weather, thanked Tran for the info, and started toward home.

Soon as we were out of earshot, Gabe asked, "You remember the last time you wore that shirt?"

I ran it through my circuits for half a block. "Maybe a month ago. Tijuana. It was a hot day. Remember? You went with me. The bank was an oven. I sweat it up pretty good. It's been in my laundry basket ever since."

"So that answers the question of how they got on to us to begin with."

"Yeah. Somebody in the bank's flapping his lips."

"Dog Beach," Gabe said. "Let's find those fuckers."

"What then?" I asked. "Not like we can call Saunders. Pope and Greenway haven't committed any crime that we know of, and if we get the cops involved there's a real good chance our identity cat is going to get let out of the bag."

"We could off them ourselves, I suppose."

"Maybe they can be persuaded," I suggested.

Gabe said, "Giants aren't in my job description."

"Yeah, but like you said, either we find them, or they find us."

• • •

I prefer optimists to pessimists. What's gonna happen is gonna happen. No sense getting all worked up over it beforehand. That way you suffer twice. Or at least that's what I regularly told myself when things went to shit.

The woman at the hospital had been a bit of an optimist. The supposed afternoon email didn't hit my phone until nearly seven in the evening. The muted bong said I had a message. Scripps Clinic in Mission Valley. Confidential.

Took a few minutes to answer all the security questions and then find the report. I turned my eyes away and didn't look. Gabe was sitting on the other side of the glass table. The *Beacon*, a local advertising rag, was spread out over that end of the table. Gabe was cleaning the automatic on it. Or had been anyway. Right then Gabe was staring at me like I'd grown an extra head.

"Well?"

"You know what I was thinking about?"

"Do tell."

"Remember those old brainteasers where people were asked whether they'd like to know their futures—assuming, of course, that such a thing were possible—and I remembered how I'd always answer no, that I'd prefer to live it out and see what happens?"

"Whenever you get through talking . . . what does it say?"

I winced as I jabbed at the phone. You know . . . you'd think that with something like this, something in the same area code as life and death, they'd just come right out and say it. Bold print. Above the fold, so to speak. *You're going to die in three weeks. You're fresh as a spring lamb.*

But no, you had to read through the damn thing and the damn readings and numbers that you had no idea what they measured, till finally way down at the bottom of the second page was the verdict.

"Your lips were moving as you read," Gabe commented.

"And apparently they're going to keep moving into the foreseeable future—no HIV, no hepatitis, no nothing," I said. "The only things the kid . . ." I corrected myself. "The only things Brandon had were head lice and crotch pheasants."

"You feelin' itchy?"

"No."

Gabe stuck out a hand. "Congratulations." I took it and shook it.

Gabe went back to oiling and reassembling the gun, while I cc'd the message to two different police departments. Eagen in Seattle. Saunders in San Diego. I thought about calling the media, but that seemed a bit excessive.

. . .

Garrett knew from experience that you had to be in just the right size city to have this work. Like you could never do it in New York or L.A. Too many people, too many pizza joints. But a place like this, most of which seemed to be homegrown noncorporate businesses, maybe. Just maybe. Took him six calls. Out of habit he'd started with the big chains. Dominos, Round Table, Little Caesars, that kind of thing. Second time he got told they don't deliver to that part of town, he figured it out and started calling the local pizza joints. Surf Rider, it was called.

"Hey . . . this is Leon Marks. How's about shooting me over a big sausage pie."

"You still at 4896 Del Monte number 4?" the girl asked.

"Yep," he said.

"Thirty-five minutes," she said and hung up.

He knew the address was close enough to walk but decided to drive down, trying to keep his street presence to a minimum. He rolled down Sunset Cliffs Boulevard and turned right onto Del Monte.

Nice palm-lined street maybe six hundred feet from the Pacific Ocean. A few private houses but mostly small to midsize apartment buildings from the forties and fifties. Nothing over three stories tall, 'cause that's all the California Coastal Commission would allow. But you could add as many rental units as you could fit onto the property's footprint, because what used to be family beach cottages were now worth millions and required a bunch of rentals just to pay the taxes.

He drove slowly, braking once in the middle of the block as a trio of young people on electric scooters zipped across the street in front of his rental car. Forty-eight ninety-six looked to be pretty much par for the course. Ten, twelve units. Two stories. Concrete steps up to the upper floor. Wedged into the lot sideways so's they could fit an extra unit or two. Had he been going any faster he might well have missed the SUV along the south side of the street, way down at the end. With that eerie ocean light behind the vehicle, nothing was visible but the silhouettes of the occupants, one of whom was the size of a Hereford heifer. He broke out into a grin. You needed to find a guy who was looking for some other guy, all you had to do was find the guy he was looking for.

He turned his head as if he were studying something on the other side of the street as he drove by, stopped at the stop sign, memorized the SUV's license plate, and turned onto Cable Street.

• • •

Ten minutes later we were sliding between the hedge and the board fence, heading for the inner courtyard of our apartment complex. As Gabe and I popped out into the courtyard, we skidded to a sudden halt. People were milling around. Our neighbors. Several of them. Adam from upstairs. Cat from the other end of the building. The older couple from down below. All seemed to be huddled around Kevin, the young guy whose ground-floor unit ran along the back alley.

"What's up, Kev," I hollered.

"Somebody stole my truck, man," he yelled back.

"Right out of the parking lot?" Gabe asked.

"No shit," Kevin growled.

"You call the cops?"

He choked out a short, bitter laugh. "They told me to fill out an online form and if they found it, they'd get back to me." He waved an angry hand. "I mean . . . man, it's not like I expected a SWAT team or anything . . . but you'd think . . . Jesus . . ."

I didn't hear whatever Kevin said next because that's when it clicked for me. One of those millennial moments when the extinct crater of my mind finds a long-forgotten ember and begins to glow red. Kinda like when, all of a sudden, your car's engine light comes on. Sorta.

Detective myth has it that Sherlock Holmes could logically work his way from one thing to another, deducting his way to the truth. Not me, though. I didn't work that way. Sure, I can generally follow the obvious to the more obvious, but with me there was always a bit of pure intuition involved. Something that came to me out of the blue, rather than something I'd rationally stalked. All twenty years working as a PI had accomplished was to make me way better at noticing the light.

"What?" Gabe said, nudging me toward the stairs.

"I've got an idea," I whispered over my shoulder.

"Remind me to update my will," Gabe groused, closing the apartment door behind us.

. . .

I made it down to the river at about ten A.M., just as the marine layer was turning to lace in the sky. I slid down the path and called his name.

"Brandon," I hailed. "It's Leo. You here?" I waited for the Southwest airliner to pass overhead and then called again.

His head slid out of the thicket. "Hey, man," he said.

"I need to talk to you."

"Come on down," he said and disappeared.

I swung around the corner and took a seat on an orange plastic bucket.

"How you doing?" I asked.

"Good, man. Real good. Tell ya the truth, feels real good not to be itchy." He offered me a half-gone bottle of Gatorade. I shook my head but thanked him for the offer.

"Lots of shit down in the park last night," he said.

"What are you hearing?"

"Cops found a couple of tourists murdered. One of 'em stuffed down inside one of the shitters." He shook his shaved head. "Bad stuff, man . . . I'm tellin' ya. They rousted everybody. Tested everybody to see if they'd fired a gun. Checked everybody's ID and shit. Busted a couple of people with old warrants. Bad bunch of shit like that. Lotta people real upset about it. Saying they're gonna get the hell out of here."

"Anybody actually see what happened?"

He pointed west. "Old Vera—lives in that beater van down the end—Vera says the only person she saw other than the local yokels was some tourist in a bucket hat and some loud-ass shorts."

"No shortage of those types," I said.

He nodded and took a big swig of the Gatorade.

"So what can I do for you, man?" he asked.

"The other day . . . you told me that the same guy on the cliff calls the cops on you every time he lays eyes on you."

"Son of a bitch," Brandon said. "Motherfucker's such an asshole."

"And you said the cops show up every time this guy calls. Right away."

"Like he keeps 'em in the garage. What about it?"

"Well . . . you know, man, whenever you hear people talk about crime in O.B., the big bitch is that the cops won't come down here for anything short of armed robbery or mass murder. People have their apartments broken into. They have their cars and surfboards and stuff stolen, but the cops never show up. They just have the victims fill out a report online and let it go at that."

"Yep."

"So how come they come every time this guy on the cliff calls?"

He thought about it for a bit. "Well, man . . . that little area there . . . you know, like it's like a snooty district . . . kinda like an island of high-rent types hiding out by the ocean . . . you know . . . and I mean the joint's got security like fucking Fort Knox . . . so he's obviously got some kind of serious-ass clout."

"Show me," I said.

"Huh?"

"Show me the house you're talking about."

"You mean . . . like now?"

"I always mean like now," I said.

He grinned. "Yeah, you do. Okay, let's go."

He was damn near as fast a walker as he was a runner. Took everything I had to keep up with him as we headed south on Bacon.

"So . . . ," I asked him as we walked along. "You done any thinking about my offer?"

"You mean the tattoo?"

"Yeah."

"A little."

"So?"

"I think I'd feel like I was joining something."

"Joining what?" I asked.

He shrugged. "Maybe the human race."

"You got a belly button?"

"Shit yeah . . . why?"

"Then you've already joined."

We hooked a right on Saratoga and walked down to Abbott and turned left, walking along about as close to the beach as you could get. I could feel he was uncomfortable with the subject of the tattoo, so I buttoned my lip.

"What's your favorite rock-and-roll song?" he segued out of the blue.

"'Gimme Shelter,'" I answered right away.

"Rolling Stones. Real retro, man."

"Feels urgent to me. Always has."

"I can dig it. The Betty can really sing."

We followed Abbott down to where we had to walk out into the sand to get to where the town beaches ended and the cliffs began. Twenty minutes later, we climbed up the stairs to Niagara Avenue, from whence one had three choices. You could turn right and walk out on California's longest concrete pier. Gabe and I had done it once, which, as it turned out, was sufficient. Or you could turn left and walk into the adjacent end of the Niagara neighborhood. Or finally, you could, in a severe fit of pique, throw yourself over the rail and dash yourself on the jagged black rocks below.

Brandon wisely chose the Niagara route. But not for long. We'd barely gotten across the ramp connecting the pier to terra firma when Brandon scuttled over to the small cottage on our right and pushed his back against the wall, arms spread like angel's wings.

He gestured with his head. "Around the corner, man. I step out into that alley, that big gorilla comes out and starts busting my balls, and then the cops'll be here in under five minutes. Sure as shit."

I shrugged, stepped around him, and walked out into the alley. Took me a minute to get my bearings. This side of Niagara looked out over the town beaches toward Mission Bay in the distance. On the other side of Niagara, the jagged cliff face jutted out farther into the ocean than the rest of the shoreline. As it wasn't possible to put a fire lane in front of the rocky node, they'd carved a fire alley out behind the buildings, thus creating several oceanfront properties, slightly isolated from the rest of the neighborhood.

I ran a hand over my face, took a deep breath, and stepped around the corner. On my right a newer ten-unit condo development faced the Pacific. Nothing showing along the alley side except everyone's bathroom windows. The rest of the block it was hard to tell. The green house in the middle was definitely a dwelling. The buildings on either end showed only faceless garage doors to the alley and could have been just about anything.

I got about five more strides before the guy stepped out from between buildings. Mexican, I thought. Sunglasses. Thick black hair brushed straight back from his forehead. Maybe six feet tall. Black Ralph Lauren polo shirt and jeans. Standing there with his hands clasped behind his back pretending he had a serious alley fetish and wasn't watching me.

I pulled out my camera and began filming my approach. Out in front of me, the alley abruptly ended at a set of white metal garage doors that appeared to belong to a three-storied building that fronted Narragansett Avenue. Nothing showing on this side of the building except another collection of bathroom windows.

I swung myself and the camera around in a circle and then kept walking. When I got abreast of the guy, he stepped forward.

"This is private property, sir," he said.

"No it's not," I said. "If it was a private road, it would say so on the street sign." I pointed back in that direction. "It doesn't, so it's public property."

I wasn't sure that was true, but it sounded good. I kept walking all the way to the dead end, where I made a U-turn and filmed my way back.

None of the buildings in question had house numbers on the rear sides except the condos on the corner, which claimed to own *numeros* 5010–5020.

He didn't say anything when I came abreast of him for the second time. The only thing that had changed was that he'd brought his hands out from behind his back and was now holding himself up by the balls. Other than that, it was all pretty much status quo.

I ducked around the corner and started waving my arms at Brandon, who was still painted onto the cottage wall like graffiti. "This way," I hissed as I jogged past the entrance to the pier, down the angled ramp that passed between the South Beach Bar & Grille and the public parking lot that fronted the beach.

By the time I got down to Newport, I was moving at the speed of lava, and Brandon was hard on my ass. We swung right, moving against the beachward flow on the crowded sidewalks, skittering across Newport and diving into Mike's Taco Club, where we found a couple of outside cube seats where we could watch our wake.

A minute passed. And then another. First person to roll down the ramp was a blonde girl on a skateboard, followed by a couple of tourists on motorized scooters. Then an SUV full of people. I kept watching until a blue garbage truck lumbered around the corner, made the turn, and groaned up the ramp like a ruptured rhinoceros. No one who seemed to be following.

I was panting like a terrier, so I pretended to be loosening up my neck while I tried to correct my oxygen debt. Brandon immediately got hip to me and smiled.

"Told ya," he said. "Place is like a bank."

"Mexican guy came out and tried to tell me it was private property."

"Yeah . . . they got a bunch of them guys too. Mr. Muscles must be workin' down at the other building."

"What other building?"

"You know . . . top of the stairs at Santa Cruz. Right where, you know . . . you and I . . . all the blood tests and shit."

I held up a *stop the music* hand.

"So . . . you're telling me the muscle-bound janitor from the building on Santa Cruz works here too?"

"Nasty asshole. Real jerk. Likes to throw his weight around."

"Guy named Russell?"

"Who knows, man. Got him a million of these mechanic-like shirts with names in circles on the front. All different names . . . like he bought a bunch of them on sale at the swap meet or something."

I reached into my pocket and pulled out some cash. Brandon waved me off.

"I don't need no money from you. I'm good."

"You sure?"

"Preserving my integrity."

"Howsabout a taco?"

"I never turn down a taco."

Half an hour later, I was walking off a couple of spicy shrimp tacos on my way back home. I was strolling along Bacon Street when a flash of color caught my eye. Up at the end of Narragansett. A rental banner draped across the front of the three-story building. Without wishing it so, I veered in that direction.

Turned out to be the building at the end of the alley I'd filmed earlier. The one with all the bathroom windows looking down on the alley behind the house Brandon had taken me to.

I had a sudden spasm of lucidity. A flash of an idea sufficiently audacious to bring a smile to my lips. I took out my phone and told Mrs. Google to put the rental agency phone number on my shopping list. She did.

• • •

It was one of those rare occasions when I managed to get modern technology to work for me on the first try. I emailed my video recording of the alley to myself and then opened up a bigger, better version on my iMac. Voilà! Gaze upon my work, ye Spielberg, and despair.

"What's that?" Gabe asked.

"Little film I shot today."

I started to fill Gabe in on my day but only got as far as "you remember that guy threw us out of the parking garage?" when Gabe's face clouded over.

"That son of a bitch. I haven't wanted to kick someone's ass that bad in years."

I finished my tale.

"We know that asshole's name?"

"No. But I'm betting we can find out."

Gabe moved close behind my seat at the desk.

"Play the thing."

I did. A minute in, Gabe grabbed my shoulder. "Stop. Back up."

I did.

"Stop."

Gabe tapped the screen. "Bullets. A shitload of them."

"Huh?"

"The cameras. That whole end of the street is covered by bullet cameras . . . you know, like the kind they use on liquor stores and jewelry marts and that kind of shit. Eight of them that we can see. Probably more of them on the ocean side. Big-time overkill on a private residence. Big-time."

Gabe pointed again. "Stop."

"Look," Gabe said. "Same brand of cameras on all three buildings. Look at the logos on them. They're all ZOSIs."

"Making it real, real likely the buildings are owned by the same person."

"You betcha."

"Let's see if we can't find out Mr. Muscles's name and who owns that property."

"Okay."

"And . . . I've got another idea. Something I noticed on the way home."

. . .

Gabe and I met Sergeant Saunders at Café 21 in the Gaslamp Quarter. She looked wrinkled and tired. She turned down a drink but downed a couple of tumblers of ice water before we got started.

"The janitor's name is Ronald Reeves. Known to his friends as Heavy Ronnie. Years ago he won a couple of local powerlifting titles and has been trading on it ever since. Nothing on his record but a couple of misdemeanor drug busts and a couple of assault beefs that were mysteriously dismissed. He's worked at the building for six and a half years. His driver's license says he lives out in Lemon Grove." She read the address out loud. Gabe wrote it down.

"And the property owner?" I pushed.

"That you're going to have to get from the plat maps. They're online, but you have to sign in in order to annex them, so it would be better if you two did it instead of me, since it's not my case." She held up a stiff finger and waggled it in our faces.

"You know that call I made about the restricted phone number?" she said.

"At the station the other day?" Gabe said.

She nodded. "Today I get a call from the deputy chief's personal assistant wanting to know why I wanted to know who owned that number."

"Is that standard procedure?" I asked.

"Couldn't be further from standard," she said. "I've worked for the department for eleven years, and nobody from the chief's office has ever called me before."

"What did you tell them?" Gabe wanted to know.

"I told them I'd typed the wrong number, and then . . . you know what he said?"

"What?"

"He said I better dial more carefully in the future. That careful dialing could possibly save me a great deal of trouble." She waved a hand. "A very low-key, passive-aggressive threat, as far as I was concerned."

Gabe stood up. "Gonna powder my nose."

I poured myself another glass of water and watched as Gabe squeezed between tables and disappeared inside the café.

"You know," Saunders began, "me personally, I couldn't care less . . . But just out of curiosity, is Gabe . . . I mean, what does Gabe consider . . ."

I helped her out. "Gabe considers gender to be a highly personal matter."

"Ah," was all she said.

"I, on the other hand, am strictly a *vive la différence* guy myself."

She shot me a look. "I've noticed."

"You ever get a day off?" I spread my arms wide. "Leading medical experts have declared me fresh as a spring breeze. I thought maybe we could do lunch or something."

She hid behind her water tumbler. All I could see were her blue eyes above the rim. "I've read your file, you know," she said. "Ne'er-do-well son of a wealthy and very corrupt Seattle politician. Spent twenty some years working the streets as a PI. Supposed to be a pretty tough guy. A pain-in-the-ass smart guy but supposedly somebody who can be counted on to do the right thing." She took another sip of water. "Came into the family fortune a few years back and quit the biz."

"So . . . what do you say?"

"Maybe," she said after a moment. "I like the rich part."

Chapter 10

It's not every city that's got a three-thousand-pound lemon sitting on the corner of Main and Broadway. No sir. The citrus groves for which Lemon Grove was named had long since been squeezed out by suburban sprawl, but the world's largest concrete lemon had defied the juicer for the better part of a century now.

We drove to the end of Cardiff Street and found Skyline Hills, the neighborhood we were looking for. We pulled to the curb and checked the houses for numbers. Most of the neighborhoods we'd driven through to get there were best described as where the sidewalk ends. The sort of places where netless garage hoops had been bent straight down and where people parked beater cars on their browned-out lawns.

But this end of the hill was a different matter. It looked out over Spring Valley and the looming mountains beyond. Quite a view by anyone's standards. If Lemon Grove had a high-rent district, this surely was it.

"Gotta be another block downhill," Gabe announced.

Santa Rosa Street snaked down the side of the hill in a series of tight loops. Gabe recited the progression of numbers as we slid by the houses, finally pointing to the house at the very bottom of the street.

"That one with all the bougainvillea," Gabe announced.

I eased my foot from the brake and began to circle the cul-de-sac. Gabe reached over and squeezed my shoulder.

"Let's stash the car and see what we can see," Gabe suggested.

"Isn't that usually my line?" I asked as I pulled over to the side of the road and set the emergency brake.

"Just trying to spread the blame around for whenever things go to shit like they always do."

We parked on a little dirt lane and walked over to Santa Rosa Street. In the near corner of the property, behind the six-foot adobe wall, a huge ficus tree spread across the sky like a giant mushroom cloud. The rest of the wall in both directions was covered with a blanket of red, lending a colorful, festive quality to an otherwise somewhat forbidding landscape.

We stayed close to the wall. All the way up to the gate. I got down on one knee and peeked through the steel slats. Classic California mission style. One story. Red tile roof. Nothing very ornate, not like the humongous Tudor I'd left smoldering back in Seattle, but in this real estate market, it looked like several million bucks' worth of terra firma.

We skittered past the gated opening and walked all the way down to the next corner. Same deal. Bougainvillea all the way down to the back corner, except for a little patch down near the center of the south wall where the bougainvillea was absent.

I started walking that way. Fifty yards down I stopped. A black metal gate. Lots of tire tracks. Big tires. Sets of two in tandem. Big rigs.

"Must be how they got the farm equipment into the grove," Gabe offered.

"Hasn't been a working grove for years now," I said.

"Somebody's sure as hell still using this one," Gabe commented.

"Wonder what for?"

We wandered back up to Santa Rosa Street. We were on our way back to the gate when Gabe slid to a halt and turned around to face me.

"See it?" Gabe whispered.

"What?"

"The light. The blue light. We're on CCTV."

I swiveled my head but didn't see anything.

"Up in that eucalyptus tree."

Took me a while but I finally managed to see the light. Just a dot among the maze of branches. Bright blue. Gabe began to walk. The camera swiveled and began to track Gabe's movement. "Motion activated," Gabe whispered, then pointed toward the huge ficus tree at the far end of the yard. "One up there too. Probably a bunch more we can't see."

Gabe hustled up to the corner and looked up into the tree. Pointed.

"Bullet cameras. ZOSIs. Same brand as the cameras on the cliff house."

We hurried back to the car; I did a K-turn and headed back up the hill.

Halfway up, a U-Haul truck was parked at the curb facing in the wrong direction with the back door wide open and a ramp hanging down like a metal tongue. I looped around the truck and pulled the car to the curb.

By the time I got out and walked around the front of the car, Gabe was standing on the AstroTurf that separated the sidewalk from the street.

"Those cameras," I said. "They see all the way up here?"

"Set up right, by a pro, they can count your nose hairs from this distance," Gabe assured me.

One house uphill, two Mexican guys were dollying a clothes dryer out of the garage. One house downhill, an older woman in a huge straw sun hat was picking litter from the manicured succulent garden that was her front yard.

From this vantage point, I could make out a series of terraces spilling down the hillside behind the house. Blotches of brown and green. Far as I could tell, the property went east and west as far as the hill would allow. Not your basic suburban house lot by anyone's standards.

A combination of curiosity and gravity seemed to urge us back down the hill. Next thing we knew we were abreast of the woman gardener. One of the Mexican movers walked past us. *"Senora,"* he called. The woman turned his way.

He handed her the key to the house. "Dat's it," he said. "We got it all."

She reached out and took the key in a gloved hand. "I'll give it to the Realtor next time I see her," she said.

"Gracias," he told her.

We watched as the mover walked back up the hill, got in the moving truck, and rumbled up the hill and out of sight. We were standing on the sidewalk watching the truck crest the hill and disappear from view when the gardener spoke to us.

"It was the last lemon grove in Lemon Grove," she said.

"The house at the bottom?" Gabe asked.

"Yes," she said. "But the new tenant, he don't like trees. Didn't want to pay for the water, they say." She shook her head sadly and removed one green glove. "The Martini family must be turning over in their graves. They spent five or six generations creating and tending that grove. And then they get behind on their taxes, the city steps in and throws them out."

"Who lives there now?" I asked.

"A big muscle-bound moron, name of Reeves. *More money than brains* type." She pulled a paper towel from her pants pocket and wiped her brow. "Couple years now. Mr. Martini was in the later stages of Alzheimer's. The family needed the money for his care. They were behind in their taxes. Wasn't the first time either, but this time the city came down on 'em like a landslide. Broke the ninety-nine-year lease and returned the property to the investment company that owned it. That's when that Reeves fella moved in."

"He friends with anybody? You know, like tight with any of his neighbors?"

She shook her hat. "Nope," she said. "Not sociable at all. Just had that security system and an electric gate installed and moved in.

Doesn't, to my knowledge, ever say a word to anybody. Leaves early in the morning. Comes back after dark. I hear a big truck coming and going sometimes in the middle of the night." She leaned back onto her heels and stretched her back out. "Whole neighborhood used to smell like lemons. Not anymore."

She put the glove back on and went back to picking cigarette butts and bits of plastic from her cacti. Gabe and I headed back toward the car.

"What do you suppose that place cost?" Gabe asked as we chugged up the hill.

"Multiple six figures," I guessed.

"On a janitor's salary?"

"Not even close," I said.

"So where's all the cash coming from?"

"I'm thinkin' maybe we ought to find out."

"Didn't we pass city hall right after we got off the 94?"

"Yes. I believe we did."

"Let's find out what he paid for it."

"Sounds like an idea," I said.

• • •

At the time of the tax seizure, the Lemon Grove city auditor had valued the property at $659,000, and then, almost overnight, without any of the usual bureaucratic delays or paperwork snafus, they'd deducted the thirty or so grand the Martini family owed the city in taxes, voided the family's long-term lease, and returned the property to the owner.

All I could think of was that the Martini family didn't have a lot of wiggle room. The wolf was at the door. The city wanted its damn tax money. Their dad was wasting away in a six-grand-a-month elder care facility down in Spring Valley.

The joint turned out to be owned by a private trust called Allied Investments of San Diego. That's where all the actual folding money had come from. Also interestingly, there was no record of Heavy Ronnie paying rent. If public records were any indication, Ronald Reeves was living on twenty-two acres of god-awful-expensive San Diego County real estate for free. Nice work if you could get it, but no matter how you looked at it, it didn't make a hell of a lot of fiscal sense.

The other interesting aspect popped up when we decided to check the tax-related evictions for 2013, the year the property had changed hands. Lemon Grove had nearly sixteen hundred residents who were, at that time, seriously behind on their taxes. Some of them more than a decade in arrears. Some owing considerably more than what the Martinis had owed. But, in all that time, only three properties had been forcibly seized for tax liabilities. Two commercial properties back at the other end of the city by the freeway, which, I was guessing, were probably gas stations by now. And this one. Definitely looked like somebody had tilted the playing field in favor of Allied Investments. Especially since the records showed Allied was the only bidder, a fact which both Gabe and I found nearly inconceivable. Something was rotten here.

It was a little after noon when Gabe squeezed us back onto the 94 and started zooming back toward Ocean Beach. We chewed over what we'd found out and came to the conclusion that there were only two real possibilities. Either Allied had something very good to protect, or they had something very bad to hide. Nothing else made any sense. The way we figured it, the key to the puzzle was finding out who or what Allied Investments was. Simple as that.

The wind was up. We were tooling down Sea World Drive, dodging fallen palm fronds and about to cross the San Diego River, when I pulled out my phone and called Saunders. They patched me through.

"Saunders," she said.

"It's Leo. Returned from the wilds of Lemon Grove."

"Hang on," she said.

She came back on a minute later. "Have any luck?" she asked.

I told her about what we'd discovered.

"Lemme see what I can find out about Allied Investments," she said. "Gotta go. On my way to a home invasion in Mission Beach."

Click.

. . .

"We have a problem, I think, Mr. Pemberton."

The man who billed himself as Samuel Rice Pemberton III looked up from his *Architectural Digest*. "How so, Hector?" he inquired.

Hector gestured toward the room across from the library. "If I might," he said.

Pemberton rose gracefully from the brocade couch and followed Hector out into the richly carpeted hall. He had a manner of walking that made him look like he was on wheels, as if someone were pushing him along on a cart like they did for the Pope.

They walked to the second doorway on the right, where Hector stepped aside and allowed Pemberton to enter first. In earlier manifestations of the house, this room had been an enormous walk-in closet. These days they referred to it as the media room.

The uppermost bank of eight TV monitors were direct feeds from the eight cameras surrounding the house and the pair of flanking buildings, which they still referred to as "the sheds" in deference to their original use as storage facilities for the floats, nets, and other commercial fishing paraphernalia belonging to the property's original owner, Mr. Mark C. Haller, way back in the early forties.

Hector seated himself in his office chair, massaged the keyboard a bit, and an image appeared on the lower bank of monitors.

"This gentleman appeared on yesterday's report."

They watched as the man in the fishing charter T-shirt entered the alley behind the house, filming with his phone as he walked along. They watched as one of the security men said something to him. Whatever words were exchanged, they certainly had no effect whatsoever on the guy. He kept right on going, all the way to the end of the alley, then turned around and went back the way he had come, still filming.

"And this is significant why?" Pembroke asked.

Hector massaged the wireless keyboard again. Another video appeared on the adjacent lower-row screen. "Mr. Reeves's domicile, this morning," Hector said.

At that point two people wandered onto the screen, walking along in front of an adobe wall covered with masses of red bougainvillea. Hector stopped the action.

"Same guy," Hector said, pointing at the taller of the two.

Pemberton leaned closer. Looked from one screen to the other. "Yes, indeed it is."

He tapped the other person. "Is that a man or a woman?" he asked.

"Not sure, sir," Hector replied.

They spent the next five minutes watching in silence as the pair on the screen went about what could only be described as casing the joint.

Pemberton straightened up. "Have Mr. Reeves come here at his earliest convenience. Tell him it's an important matter and won't wait."

"Yes sir."

"And tell your Ms. Cisneros it might be better if she were present too."

• • •

Gabe was taking an art class, and I was zoning on the couch, binge-watching the last season of *Game of Thrones*, when somebody started banging on the security door. I paused *G of T*, pushed myself up, and wandered over to the door. Saunders was standing on the landing, walking in tight little circles, looking seriously pissed off. I pulled open the door and motioned her inside.

"Thought you had a home invasion gala to attend," I said.

"So did I," she said as she squeezed by me in the doorway, the friction of which ranked right up there on my *best things to happen to me* list.

Before I could frame another question, she started in talking.

"So we're waiting outside the home invasion house, waiting for forensics to finish up inside, and while I'm standing around, I decide to call in a request for information on Allied Investments of San Diego. Ten minutes later I get a call from my immediate superior. Says I'm off the home invasion case as of right now and need to get my butt down to headquarters posthaste . . . like immediately."

"Sounds ominous."

"So I fight the traffic all the way from Mission Beach to downtown, trying to figure out what in heck's going on. When I get there, there's a couple of Internal Affairs assholes waiting for me. They want to know why I made the request about Allied Investments." She spread her hands in resignation. "We go round and round, and then who do you suppose shows up?"

"Same guy who told you to mind your business the other day," I guessed.

She nodded. "The deputy chief's personal assistant. Only this time he's got my precinct supervisor with him. When I can't come up with a good reason for making the inquiry . . ." She stopped and caught her breath. "My supervisor suggests I take a little time off—use up some of my comp time. Stops just short of telling me I'll be out of a job if I don't. Tells me it might be a good time to reorganize my priorities."

"Which means what in cop speak?"

"It means I better mind my own business or face the consequences."

"Just for asking for information?"

"Apparently."

"Guess what?"

"What?"

"I looked up the plat maps for that house on the cliffs."

"And?"

"Same thing. It's owned by Allied Investments of San Diego."

"I get it, Leo. There's some kind of shit going on." She put her hands on her hips and took a deep breath. "But . . . they made it clear. If I push this any further, I'm gonna end up as a school crossing guard."

"I know somebody who can probably find out on the sly for us."

"Same person who created those fake identities for you and Gabe?"

My turn to nod.

"The way Gabe and I see it, seems like somebody with a whole lot of money and clout is trying real hard to keep something out of sight. Somebody with enough heft to influence government offices in Lemon Grove and now apparently in Ocean Beach too. We're in heavy company here."

Her upper lip curled. "Someone a lot like your father."

I must have looked surprised.

"I told you. I read your file," she said with a grin.

"Yeah . . . I guess so," I admitted. "But you know . . . those were different times . . . things were . . . people were . . ."

"Money still talks," she said. "And everything else still walks."

Hard to argue with that, so I didn't bother.

"So you're on vacation now."

Her face clouded over. "A week," she said.

"Breakfast?"

She thought it over. "Where?"

"Fiddler's Green?" I said, naming a joint on Shelter Island.

"What time?"

"Nine?"

"Let's make it ten. It's not very often I get to sleep in."

I walked her down to the car. Soon as I was back in the apartment I called Carl Cradduck in Seattle. Carl Cradduck had once been one of America's most prominent battlefield photographers. His work had appeared in every big-time magazine I could think of. Came through the jungles of Vietnam without so much as a hangnail and was sitting on top of the world when a random piece of Bosnian shrapnel severed his spine in September of 1993.

Twenty-five years later, he'd morphed into what he liked to call security consulting, which actually meant that if there was a piece of IT information you needed—for your personal security, of course—Carl could get it for you, with the help of several highly talented computer monkeys with whom he was professionally acquainted. These were the same people who had created total new identities for Gabe and me, back when disappearing suddenly became a major priority for us.

Charity answered on the second ring.

"Cradduck Data Retrieval," he said in that lilting Jamaican voice of his.

"Hey, man," I said.

Pause. "We good on your end?" he asked.

"It's a burner," I said.

"Leo, my mon. Good as hell to hear your voice."

"Same here," I said. "Carl around?"

"In Chicago, visiting his brother. Got the big C. Bladder."

We exchanged sympathies, traded compliments, and shot the breeze for a couple of minutes before I told him what I wanted.

"Allied Investments of San Diego," he repeated. "So what you want, mon?"

"Everything you can get, particularly where the money comes from."

"Easy meat," he said. "You gotta wade through all de dummy holding companies, de offshore corporations, de blind trusts and all dat crapola, but mostly it ain't very hard. I got a cousin . . ."

I laughed out loud. "You always do, Charity. You always do."

"We'll send it along when it get done. Same email?"

I said it was.

"Got somebody on de other line," he said.

"Later, my old friend."

• • •

"Nice of you to join us, Mr. Reeves."

Reeves looked around the room. Other than the two of them, it was empty.

"Us? What us? You got a tapeworm or something?"

"I was referring to a metaphorical plurality."

"I'da been here sooner except I had to clear two toilets and a garbage disposal before anything else. You know how people get when they're stopped up."

Ronald Reeves spread his feet, as if to better stand his ground. Normally he liked to keep his distance from Pemberton. Being in the same room with the guy always made Reeves feel disheveled. The guy never had a pleat or a wrinkle in his thousand-dollar trousers. He gave the impression that he slept standing up, like a horse in a stall, and stepped out each morning just as polished and perfect as he'd been the day before.

"Like I told you before, Pemberton, I'm getting real sick of this shit. I don't need to be cleaning other folks' toilets anymore. I got enough stashed to—"

Pemberton cut him off. "And as I've told *you* on several occasions, Mr. Reeves, we have a very busy season coming up. This is our final push before closing things down. Any changes in the players or the program makes things exponentially more dangerous than they need to be. So we're going to keep everything just as it is until we get past this juncture. After that . . ."

Pemberton trailed off. He looked away and began to pinch the pleats in the front of his pants. "It would have been better if you had not brought that boy here."

"Where the hell was I supposed to take him? He was sick as a dog, and that quack doctor of yours wanted to bring him here. So I did. I didn't know the little shit was going to die. I'd known that, I'da buried his ass out in the old grove someplace. What in hell was I supposed to do?"

Pemberton opened his mouth to respond. Somebody knocked on the door.

"Yes," Pemberton said.

The door opened. Hector ushered Corinna Cisneros into the room. She was on the far side of fifty, built like a fireplug, but, as was her custom, showing mile-deep cleavage to the universe. She'd inherited Western Security from her late husband, Daniel, and to everyone's surprise turned out to be a far more able administrator than her predecessor. In the course of five years, Western Security had morphed from primarily providing low-rent security guards for warehouses in the south end to operating as a high-tech, single-client security firm, while quadrupling the company's profits in the process.

Hector pulled out one of the upholstered chairs for her and poured a glass of ice water. She thanked him with a nod and took a hit of the water. Trying to hide his anger, Reeves found himself a seat in the far corner of the room. Hector then pulled out the office chair and sat down behind the console.

Pemberton wiped the corners of his mouth with his fingers and then began.

"As Hector has so ably pointed out, we seem to have a bit of a problem," he began. He nodded at Hector, who tapped the keyboard in front of him on the desk.

"This was a day or two ago," Pemberton recited. "This gentleman wandered onto the street and filmed our little corner of the world. The usual admonitions as to this being private property seemed to have had no effect on him whatsoever."

Reeves rose from his chair and walked closer.

Hector worked the keyboard again. Reeves's house jumped onto another screen.

"Your residence, Mr. Reeves. Yesterday morning. Same man and a companion of indeterminate gender."

Reeves leaned over Hector's shoulder.

"Yeah . . . I know those two," he said. "From the Santa Cruz building. Pair of smart-asses. I threw them out of the parking garage a few days back. They were on foot."

"Which probably means they're from someplace here in Ocean Beach," Hector threw in. Nobody disagreed.

"This isn't good," Cisneros said.

"I'll need you to find out who they are and where we can find them if necessary."

"Consider it done," she said.

"Also, we're going to require an increased security presence for the foreseeable future. We cannot allow anything untoward to interfere with our present schedule."

"I only have six men left," she said. "Everyone else has been let go."

"Half a dozen will have to do, then," Pemberton replied. "We have parcels arriving tonight and another eight coming in five days." He raised a finger. "Also . . . I've added Dr. Trager to the procedure. I'm going to have him do a health check on all of them before we deliver—as I'm sure you understand, we can't be having a repeat of what happened last time."

"Trager's a quack," Reeves said.

Pemberton waved him off. "Dr. Trager's already on board. As the estate's executor, I'm required to provide quarterly health reports. Trager, for all his warts, serves a useful purpose. Mrs. Cisneros, we need to find these people as quickly as possible. Anything that might help us identify and locate them. We need to be quite proactive here."

• • •

One bedroom. One bath. Maybe five hundred square feet. On a month-to-month basis, eighteen fifty a month. I was out the better part of five grand by the time I put up the security deposit and first month's rent and paid for a credit check of myself, a modern rental custom that never fails to piss me off. Sure . . . I understand why a landlord would want to check a prospective renter's credit. Just makes sense. But the logic behind why the renter should be forced to pay the check has always escaped me.

Mercifully, the camera and recording equipment were cheap. Gabe and I tooled it over to the Best Buy in Mission Valley and picked up a motion-activated Spy Tech camera and a camcorder for under a hundred bucks. 'Tis a paranoid world we live in.

On the way back home we stopped at Home Depot and bought a roll of duct tape and a couple of fairly comfortable deck chairs so we could at least sit down if we had to be there for any length of time.

I picked up the apartment keys from the property management company later in the afternoon and met Gabe over at the new joint. Faced with a level of technology above our general area of competence, we did the most unlikely thing imaginable—we read the directions. It was awful, but when we'd finished and had kicked it around between us a bit, it took us under twenty minutes to get the whole shebang up and running.

We set the camera up in the lower left-hand corner of the bathroom window, a placement that gave the camera a cinemascopic view of all three buildings and the street below. We set the camcorder to keep track of it all and then programmed the digital controller. Worked perfectly on the first try. Both of us were amazed. There was something about filming the former filmers that appealed to my sense of the absurd. I even considered the possibility that somebody else might be filming us filming them . . . you know, etc., etc.

We kicked around the question of whether the camera was going to take decent pictures at night, decided the answer was no but couldn't come up with a viable solution. Lights of any kind were out of the question. Might as well put up a neon sign that read "We're filming you!"

So we'd walked back home, resigned to being strictly daytime spies.

· · ·

By the time ten o'clock the next morning rolled around, I'd shaved, showered, and managed to find a shirt with a collar. I'd been taking in the scenery and sipping at a cup of coffee for about five minutes or so when she arrived at the top of the stairs, in a boat-necked tropical floral-print dress that fit her like feathers.

I'd never seen her in a dress before, which was a damn shame, 'cause despite Gabe's notion that gender was a personal matter, it sure didn't seem to be a problem for Sergeant Carolyn Saunders, and it sure as hell wasn't a problem for me neither.

We were seated outdoors, on Fiddler's Green's upstairs balcony, looking out over Shelter Island and the jagged skyline of downtown San Diego in the hazy distance.

We'd ordered breakfast and were waiting for the food when she asked:

"How come you've never been married?"

I thought it over. "I've asked myself that for years," I said. "And I never come up with an answer. It just turned out that way, I guess."

I wagged an accusatory finger in her direction. "You know, it's not fair that you've read my file and know everything about me, and yet I don't know a damn thing about you. Where's your file?"

"I was married once. Long time ago. Less than a year. A real cup of coffee romantic relationship."

"Never had the urge again?"

She shrugged. "I guess I figured . . . you know . . . my judgment was so bad the first time around, maybe I just ought to give it a rest." She took a hit of coffee. "After that, I buried myself in my career. I more or less became what I did. I passed the sergeant's test, and . . . like they say, life goes on. Next thing you know you're fortysomething and so entrenched in your ways it'd be a miracle if you found anybody else who could fit in the box with you. And worse yet, all that time you've been doing a job and seeing things that are pretty much guaranteed to erase any romantic ideals you might still be carrying around in your pocket."

I knew what she meant. Twenty some-odd years working as a private investigator had made quite a dent in my romantic idealism too. Shattered dreams and severed limbs have a way of doing that. "I used to tell myself I just wasn't needy enough for permanent relationships," I said, "but you know . . . long-term . . . that's got a real self-serving quality about it, so these days I just content myself with I don't know."

"You and the medical examiner . . ." She let it trail off.

"Believe it or not, the subject of marriage never came up."

"Weird. In all that time?"

"I think we both knew—right from the beginning, back when we were kids—I think we both knew that on some level, our life dreams were so far apart that sooner or later our relationship wasn't going to work out. But . . ." I stifled a shrug. "We enjoyed each other's company, most of the time anyway, and we're both real good rationalizers . . ." I stopped picking at it and left it at that.

The waitress saved the day by arriving with the food and coffee refills. For the next ten minutes, we traded inane pleasantries regarding the weather and local politics.

I watched as she forked in a bite of omelet. Some women pick at their food. I'd never been altogether sure whether they were on a perpetual diet or if they merely wanted to appear refined. With Saunders here, it'd be a good idea to keep your hand out of the eating zone—assuming, of course, you wanted it back. This was a woman of strong appetites.

"You know what I was thinking?" she asked.

"I'll bite."

"If whoever's behind that little boy's death has something to do with that house—if that's true—and if, like you guys think, it's part of the same organization as that house in Lemon Grove that Reeves lives in, then they've got you and Gabe on CC tape. More than once. They're probably already looking in your direction."

I swallowed a bite of toast. "Could well be," I allowed. "We've been made for sure. No doubt about it. They know by now that we've been poking our noses into their affairs." I waved my piece of sourdough toast like a semaphore flag. "Gabe and I are working on it."

"Working how?"

I told her about renting the apartment and about Gabe and I setting up the camera to keep track of what went down at the cliff house next door. I put a set of keys to the new surveillance apartment on the table in front of her. "You know," I said. "Just in case." She left them on the table for a long minute before shoveling them discreetly into her clutch purse and snapping it shut.

Then I told her about my call to Carl regarding Allied Investments. About how the minute Charity and his "cousins" started hacking their asses to pieces, Allied was gonna know somebody was asking impertinent digital questions and how, from that point on, we were figuring things had the potential to get serious in a hurry. "Either that, or these people have nothing to hide, or nothing much will happen."

"You guys need to be careful," she said.

I nodded my agreement and went back to the bacon and eggs.

"Is that what finally drove her off?" she asked.

"What?"

"That you seem to have an almost casual disregard for either the law or for your own safety."

"To a great degree . . . I guess . . . yeah, that was probably a big part of it."

By the time we'd both finished eating and the staff had cleared the rubble, she leaned her elbows on the table, leveled those blue eyes at me, and asked, "Why should I get involved with you?"

"I'm rich."

She laughed. "Besides that."

"Well . . . ," I hedged. "You know . . . Other than such tawdry considerations as material wealth . . . I am still able to form complete sentences. I believe I have retained most of my sense of humor and some of my good looks. And you don't have to worry that I'm not the person I claim to be. You know, like in digital dating. Like you said earlier, you've read my file."

"Are you good in bed?"

"Doesn't everybody think they are?"

"Probably."

"Tell you the truth, it's been so long I don't remember."

She sat back, folded her arms over her chest, and was silent.

I filled the void. "And don't forget I've been declared positively virginal by prominent medical authorities."

"I know," she said. "I read your medical history too."

I must have looked aghast.

She shrugged. "Just checking," she said.

We shared a laugh. She insisted on splitting the check.

. . .

I'd tried my best to talk her into spending the day with me, but she'd already set up an afternoon meeting with her union rep and had to beg off. She said she'd stop by the apartment when the meeting was done.

I ran a half a dozen errands in Point Loma, grabbed a prime rib sandwich at Liberty Station, then took Cañon back over the hill to O.B., and as I was tooling up Sunset Cliffs, almost as an afterthought,

I stopped by the new apartment to make sure everything was working according to plan.

Not only was it working but the blue light was blinking, which, according to the directions, meant the setup had recorded something going on downstairs.

Took me a couple of tries, but I eventually coaxed the pictures out of the camcorder. Two things became immediately clear. Security had increased significantly. There was somebody in front of the house trying to look busy all of the time now, not just when the cameras told them someone was in the street, which led directly to the realization that watching all of this stuff was going to take a whole lot more of my time than I'd figured.

I quickly learned to fast-forward, racing through what must have been three hours of Hispanic security types mucking about the front of the house, until 11:13 in the A.M., when a UPS truck arrived with half a dozen packages, followed almost immediately by three women in matching yellow T-shirts.

They were still inside the house three hours later when an older gentleman arrived at the door wearing what was in all probability the only twilly tweed sport coat in Ocean Beach and carrying a battered gladstone bag.

I couldn't see who let him in the door either, but Tweedy stayed for a little over an hour. I was about to give up binge-watching when the yellow T-shirt women reappeared on the front stairs. Whoever let them out was wearing a wristwatch the size of a Chevy hubcap and a shirt with French cuffs. When one of the women turned toward the camera to let one of her companions pass her on the stairs, I could see that the shirts had a logo on them. I stopped the action. Backed up a little. Zoomed in. And then in again. A half circle with the image of somebody swinging a mop and the words BUSY BEE CLEANING SERVICES.

The rest of it didn't amount to a hill of beans. Not until the very end of the show anyway. Just before it got too dark for the camera, I got my first look at the guy with the French cuffs. He came out onto the front porch and had a few words with a security guy who was pretending to garden the flower boxes.

Maybe six-two. Hundred eighty pounds. Great shock of styled white hair. Fiftysomething. Dressed to the nines. Whatever he said to the inconstant gardener sent the guy scuttling around the side of the house and into the alley between the house and the nearest shed. A minute later, a different guy came out of the alley and took his place. Mr. Smooth said something to the new guy, surveyed the street for a long moment, then disappeared back inside the doorway. Another five minutes of fast-forwarding and it got too dark for the camera to function properly, so I closed up shop and headed back home.

Gabe had the yoga mat spread out on the living room floor and was in some pose that looked like it hurt. Knowing that Gabe preferred to be alone during yoga sessions, I fetched a San Pellegrino from the fridge and then cleaned up my bedroom before deciding to take a gander at my email.

I'd gone through a bundle of the usual spam and sales pitches before I came to the one with no address. Charity and his "cousins" had been hard at it. Allied Investments of San Diego was an umbrella of private trusts and shadow corporations designed to obscure the fact that Allied was the family trust of the Haller family, specifically the widow of the late Hiram Haller, whose father, Peter, had accumulated the family pile through a highly successful commercial fishing company back in the forties. Florence Haller, now eighty-one years young, was listed as the executor of the estate but appeared to be taking less of a personal hand in the operation in recent years and divorcing herself from the day-to-day operations.

More to follow, the email said. And a little personal note from Charity to the effect that the rest of the information should be easy to get, as Allied's cybersecurity left a great deal to be desired, by current standards anyway. Said he'd get back at me tomorrow.

I was still chewing on the information when Gabe knocked on the door.

"Yeah," I said. Gabe poked that big head in the room.

"You see the tape from yesterday?" Gabe asked.

"Maids always hate the people they work for," I said.

"Wouldn't you?"

"Absolutely."

"Any idea about the guy with the valise?"

"None except maybe he looked out of place."

"What about the guy in the Valentinos?"

I must have looked dumbfounded.

"The guy with the French cuffs," Gabe said.

"What about him?"

"Those were Valentino trousers he was wearing." Before I could ask, Gabe brushed me off and went on. "That's what Joey used to wear all the time. I used to take them to his tailor up on Broadway to be altered." Gabe smiled. "He always claimed they were making them smaller every year. Refused to buy the next size up. They're sixteen hundred bucks off the hanger. By the time he paid that Chinese broad a few hundred to let 'em out a bit, he had the better part of two grand in a pair of pants."

Joey Ortega and I had grown up together. His father, Frankie, had been my father's chief bagman and leg breaker. A guy whose claim to lasting fame was that he'd once cut off a guy's ears in defense of my father.

Joey and I had spent our formative years playing together in my old man's backyard, while they plotted away inside my old man's office. When Frankie died, Joey had taken over the ship and turned his father's ill-gotten gains into a virtual empire of card rooms, strip joints, and massage parlors that specialized in what they liked to call "a rub and a tug."

Gabe had been Joey's personal bodyguard for nearly fifteen years. We'd known each other for over a decade before we'd blundered into something we weren't prepared for and had paid the price in blood—our own.

"Interesting," I said and then mentioned what I'd gotten from Charity.

"What say we find the maids," Gabe said when I'd finished.

. . .

I felt the warm glow of familiarity rise in my cheeks. It was like old times again. I was on the phone lying like a motherfucker to somebody. A licensed PI spends quite a bit of time lying to people. People only hire private eyes out of desperation, after they've already tried everything that made sense, and desperation is real hard on the truth. Back people into a corner and they'll lie their asses off. Every time. I hadn't had occasion to outright bullshit anybody in quite a while, and to tell the truth, I found I'd sort of missed the thrill of it.

I told the woman who answered the phone I was a neighbor of Mrs. Haller's and gave them the address of the apartment building on the corner. I said I had heard simply fabulous things about her cleaning crew and wondered if perhaps we couldn't schedule them to do my place after they got through with Mrs. Haller's house one of these days. We had a brief chat as to the impossibility of getting good help anymore. And yes, of course I understood they were both licensed and bonded, but, equally of course, I'd need to vet them personally beforehand.

Took a little cajoling and a bit of the *mordida*, but we eventually put something together. They got off at four. She'd call them back to the office in Chula Vista, and we could chat there at about four thirty. She'd be gone by then of course. Slip the envelope to the young man who'd be manning the desk.

. . .

Ten miles south of downtown, Chula Vista was another of those citrus grove towns gone suburban. So many World War II vets decided to stay in the San Diego area after the war that places like Chula Vista had changed from rural to suburban seemingly overnight.

Busy Bee had an office halfway down G Street from Third Avenue. One of those neighborhoods where crass commercial and ratty residential had been mixed together to create its own brand of urban squalor. The building used to be a gas station. They'd painted the outside in bold black-and-yellow bee stripes. Used the overhead gas sign for the bug eyes. The left side was a big rolling overhead door that at one time led into the service bay, which was now stocked floor to ceiling with cleaning supplies and such accouterments. The right side was still the office area. Out front you could see where the gas tanks had been wrenched from the ground and then patched over. An alley full of fifty-five-gallon drums separated the building from the Expert Hands Body Shop next door.

We pulled up to the garage door about six minutes early and were surprised to find that the maid crew was already on hand. We handed the guy the agreed-upon envelope and traded pleasantries for ten seconds with Mr. Anonymous before he opened the door to an adjoining room and quickly walked away.

Gabe and I had talked it over on the way down and decided to be straight with them. They introduced themselves as Felicia Gomez, Maria Hueso, Gloria Del Rio.

Gabe walked around behind them and put a crisp new hundred-dollar bill in front of each of them. "We want to know about what goes on in the Haller house," I said. "We're not criminals. Nobody's gonna get hurt. We just want to know what goes on inside the house."

"You the cops?"

We said we weren't.

"Immigration?"

No to that too.

"Nothing said in this room goes anywhere else," Gabe said.

The women exchanged *I've heard this shit before* looks.

"The money's yours either way. No hard feelings." Gabe then translated it into Spanish in case anybody didn't *habla*. What followed was a forty-five-second Maalox moment, lots of darting eyes and low-key squirming, at which point the woman on the right began to babble in Spanish.

"She's scared," Gabe said. "Wants to leave."

"Tell her she can go. The money's hers. All we ask is that she doesn't tell anybody about this." Gabe translated and then put a finger across both lips.

The woman snatched up the bill and fled, banging the door behind her.

"She got no papers," Felicia Gomez explained. "She scareda ICE."

I told her it was okay. That we weren't here about that.

"Those people . . . ," Maria Hueso said. "They got a lot of secrets. Crazy private. We only clean part of the house. The rest of it they don't never let us in."

"They keep some of it locked all the time," Felicia Gomez added.

"Got all kind of security guys all over the place. Tellin' you where you can and can't go today."

"What's Mrs. Haller like?" Gabe asked.

They both shrugged. "Never seen her," they said in unison.

"How long have you been cleaning the house?" I inquired.

They looked from one to another as if communicating on some psychic level.

"Little under two years," Felicia Gomez said. "Me and Maria anyway. Gloria . . . she's new . . . maybe five months now."

"And, in all that time, none of you has ever met her?"

They shook their heads.

Gabe took out an iPhone, cued up last night's footage, found the guy with the gladstone valise, and set the phone on the table in front of them. "Who's that?"

"The doctor . . . namea Trager," Felicia Gomez said.

"We call him *tembloroso*," Maria said with a hint of a grin.

"Shaky," Gabe translated.

Felicia held her hands in front of her and vibrated them like she was using a jackhammer.

Gabe lifted the phone from the table, fast-forwarded to French Cuffs and the fabled two-grand trousers. "And this guy. Who's he?"

"El jefe," Maria said. "Mr. Pemberton."

"He's the major dodo." They both laughed out loud.

"Yeah," said Felicia, smiling now. "He runs the place."

"Not a very nice man," her partner added. "Got a mean spirit. Got all this money and don't never give a tip. Not once. Not even at Christmas."

"Better than that Reeves *pendejo*," Felicia snapped.

"They got this big maintenance guy comes in sometimes. Always trying to catch us alone. Likes to feel us up whenever we get within reach. You give that fool a chance, he'll stick his hand up your dress."

We stayed at it for another five minutes, didn't come up with anything but household gossip, and sent them back home with a little extra pocket change. The question of whether they'd keep their mouths shut about our visit was very much up in the air, but the way we saw it, we'd already been made a couple of times, so the fact we were checking on them wasn't going to come as much of a surprise to anybody.

Gabe drove. I called Charity. Got the company machine and recited the names Pemberton and Trager and what precious little we knew about them. The machine thanked me. Traffic was passable until we got about a mile from home. Once we turned south onto Ebers, we got passed twice by a woman with a walker.

■ ■ ■

I was standing behind Gabe's office chair peering at the computer when Saunders knocked on the security door. I tore myself away from the screen and let her in. Gabe gave her a wave and kept reading Charity's latest email aloud.

"Trager, William D. for Donald. Medical degree from Farley University in Iowa. Bottom third of his class. Started out in private practice in Oklahoma forty-eight years ago. After settling a couple of malpractice suits, he couldn't get insurance anymore, so he moved on to something called the Hartwell Clinic up in Oceanside. Stayed there for more than twenty years, until the State of California jerked his license about five years back. Doesn't say what for. Whatever it was, he sued to have the records sealed and won the court case. Charity says he's still working on that end of it but is pretty sure he can swing it. For the past three years Trager's worked as the private medical consultant for Florence Haller. She's his only patient and, as far as the boys can tell, his sole source of income."

"What did he make last year?" I asked.

Gabe clicked through a number of on-screen pages. "He reported income of just under two hundred grand in 2018."

"From one old lady?"

"Must be a miracle worker," Gabe said.

"Especially for a guy with no medical license," Carolyn Saunders added. "What about the other one. The Pemberton guy?"

"That's where things really get interesting," Gabe said, tapping the keyboard.

"Samuel Rice Pemberton the Third. Hired on with Mrs. Haller about five years ago. Before that there's no record of him, at least not under that name. They're working on that too. Get this: he was originally hired as her driver. If you read between the lines, seems like he just sort of took over things as he went along. One function at a time. These days he's the executor of the estate and has her power of attorney. Signs all the checks for Allied Investments and calls himself the majordomo."

"Pretty upwardly mobile for a chauffeur."

"With a bullet," Saunders threw in.

"She have any kids?" I asked.

"Two," Gabe said. "Mary Jean, who'd be fifty-eight if she hadn't died of ovarian cancer a few years back, and Jack, who has been suing Allied for one thing or another for the past few years." I started to ask another question, but Gabe cut me off. "Eighteen months ago, Allied Investments and Florence Haller took out a restraining order against him. He can't be closer than a hundred yards to anything owned by the company."

"The only son expelled from the garden?"

"Bit of family conflict there, I suspect," Gabe said.

"More than a bit," I said.

"Let's see if I can get an address for him," Gabe said and started tapping away.

I looked over at Saunders. "The whole thing sounds real sketchy to me," I said. "Something just ain't right here."

Saunders looked grim. "Me too," she admitted, "but sketchy isn't going to be enough if this has anything to do with Florence Haller. We're gonna need a smoking gun, Leo. Florence Haller is about as *Social Register* as you can get. One of the biggest philanthropists in the San Diego area for the last fifty years or so. Her mother-in-law was a grand dame named Ruth Rader. Florence Haller built Rader Children's Hospital out of her own pocket and named it after her. Major contributor to the library. That kind of stuff. Sits on every board of directors in the county. If you've got anything criminal on her, it better include HD pictures."

"White pages says a Jack Haller lives on Mission Boulevard," Gabe announced.

I walked over and checked the street address over Gabe's shoulder.

"Twenty-nine fifty-eight," I read. "Just south of the roller coaster."

Gabe shut down the computer and stood up.

"Let's go."

Gabe and I started for the door. I stopped and turned to Saunders, who hadn't moved. "You coming?" I asked.

"I can't," she began. "If I—"

"You're on vacation."

She thought it over. "Yeah, you're right," she said. "I'm on my own time."

Chapter 11

Something about post-middle-aged men with ponytails always rubs me the wrong way. Seems like they've stayed too long at the fair. Like maybe it's way past due for something new to happen. Something a little more grown-up maybe.

We were on one of those short-term vacation rental streets that run at right angles to the ocean. Almost Disney-like in its pastel cuteness, the sole concession to livability was a single condo building about half a block from the water. That way the city planners could pretend it was still a neighborhood where regular people lived.

Haller's place was on the third floor, which was as high up as things were allowed to get this close to the Pacific. We climbed the stairs and knocked on his door.

Jack Haller was using a Ferragamo necktie as a headband when he pulled open the door. Midfifties. Thin and in shape. The wheatgrass-enema type. Wearing biking shorts with enough ass padding to give the impression he'd baked a load of brownies in his drawers. His head was bald in front with a long white shock of hair hanging down his back. Haller the Hun.

I could see all the way through the condo, past the sliding patio doors, out onto the Mission Beach boardwalk and the hordes of tourists biking, scootering, or merely strolling along, backed by battalions of beach umbrellas, and beyond the blaze of color, the rippling muscles of the Pacific Ocean.

"Whatcha need?" he asked.

"We wanted to have a few words with you about Allied Investments," I said.

He made a rude noise with his lips and slammed the door.

"That went well," Gabe commented.

I knocked again. Nothing happened, so I really put the knuckles to it.

He jerked the door open and stepped out onto the landing. His face was twisted into an angry knot. "Do I need to call the cops?" he demanded.

"How come Allied got a restraining order against you?" Gabe asked.

A super loud Harley came roaring by out on Mission Boulevard, setting off a couple of car alarms as it passed. The bleatings of urban crickets suddenly filled the air. Nobody said anything until they finally stopped chirping.

"I had the gall to want to see my mother," Haller said bitterly. He looked us over. "Who the hell are you anyway? That asshole Pemberton send you?"

"Nope," I said and left it at that.

"We're looking into something," Carolyn said, "something that may have to do with your family trust."

"It's not my family anymore. They cut me loose. Might as well have set me adrift on an ice floe." He wiped the corners of his mouth with his thumb and forefinger. "At least Pemberton did. Couple years back, I got pissed and insisted on talking to my mother directly. Said I wasn't going to leave until I saw her. Next thing I knew, they hurled me out the front door and then hauled me into court and handed me that restraining order."

"When was the last time you spoke to your mother face-to-face?" Carolyn asked.

Haller thought it over. "Damn near two years now. Even before that, she was always either sleeping or indisposed in some manner every time I showed up at the house. Eventually, when I kept insisting,

Pemberton had his pet gorilla throw me out into the street and then slapped that restraining order on me."

"I mean . . . ," I started. "Did something happen between you and your mother—you know, some kind of argument—something that would have . . ."

"It wasn't her," he scoffed. "No . . . no . . . she'd never do that. It was that Pemberton asshole. He just sort of took over her life." He stopped talking and seemed to go elsewhere for a moment. Gabe was all over it.

"What?"

"A while back . . ." He sighed and looked around. Unsure he wanted to spill it. "Back when he first started taking over for her . . . I don't know . . . I know how weird this sounds, but . . . I know this sounds crazy, but . . . I think he might have been sleeping with her." Haller shook his head and held up a restraining hand. "I know . . . I know . . . she's thirty years his senior and all . . . but it was just a feeling I got the last time I saw them together. Just something about the way they moved with each other . . . something about how they handled the space . . . you know, between them . . ." He let it peter out.

This didn't seem to be the occasion for a jaunty quip, so everybody shut up.

Haller began to talk again. "From then on, one step at a time she signed things over to him. I got a call from my mother's former business manager. He told me the Allied Investment property is being offered for sale. The cliff house, the Lemon Grove property—all of it. They're looking for a private buyer for the whole thing."

"Could Pemberton do that? You know, just on his own without your mother?"

"Oh yeah," Haller said. "He's like some kind of fucking parasite. Nowadays he's in charge of everything. He's the executor of the estate. He signs all the checks. You want to deal with Allied Investments and you gotta go through him. That's all there is to it anymore. He fired all her doctors and lawyers and accountants. Nobody sees Mother except him and that quack doctor he hired."

He studied our faces for a long second looking for signs of disbelief and then went on talking. "It's not just me, man. Check with her friends. Check all those corporate and city boards she sits on. Nobody's seen her in public in forever. It's everybody. Pemberton's walled her off from the world."

"Why would he do that?" Gabe asked.

"He's sold everything. The boats, the equipment. Every piece of land the trust owned. Only reason he hasn't sold off Mother's house and the property in Lemon Grove is that I've got them tied up in court. Those properties are mentioned in my trust fund, so they need my signature, otherwise they'd be gone too. My attorneys have put a restraining order on them. All their accounts are frozen until the courts rule on my suits."

He grabbed the door again, pulled it open. The reddish hue of his face told me he was embarrassed and wished he hadn't shared with us. "Now if you'll excuse me, I've got things to do."

We were about halfway back to the car when Carolyn said, "This is the definition of frustration. We keep pumping. We keep picking up more and more information, and none of it does us a bit of good."

Up in the eucalyptus trees a mourning dove was cooing his broken love song. Somewhere in the distance an approaching siren began to sing sad harmony.

■ ■ ■

Hector knocked on the study door. Waited and then pulled it open.

"Did we have a visitor?" Pemberton asked.

"Yes. One of the young women who clean the house."

Pemberton frowned. "They were just here, weren't they?"

"Yes sir."

"What did she want?"

"She had a tale to tell. I thought you would be interested."

"Pray tell."

"She said that those two people we have on tape, the ones who've been poking their noses into our affairs . . . they set up a meeting with our house cleaners earlier this evening. At the company office in Chula Vista. She said they wanted to know all about us. About the house and the residents. About Mrs. H. and what goes on here."

"And what did they tell them?"

"She didn't know. Says she left before the interview really got started." Hector kept talking. "She also said that one of her crew called her later, after they all got home—making sure she was all right and such. The men told her they had CC images of us as well. You and Dr. Trager in particular."

"Really?"

"What now, sir?"

"Inform the cleaning company that we will no longer require their services. Pay them off for whatever we've contracted for. We don't need minor annoyances gumming up the works right now."

"Yes sir."

"And get me Mrs. Cisneros on the secure line."

"Yes."

Pemberton paced the room until the light on the desk phone began to blink.

She wasted no time. "I found them," she said by way of a greeting. "They go by the names Leon Marks and Gene DeGrazia. They live on Del Monte. And guess what?"

Pemberton said nothing.

"Two days ago, Marks rented an apartment on Narragansett, in the building at the end of your alley. Number eight in the back."

"Well, that answers that question, doesn't it?" Pemberton murmured.

"Huh?"

"We're going to have to do something about them."

"Something like what?"

"Like Mr. Pickett."

Long silence. "You think they're getting that close?" she asked finally.

"I think they're closer than anybody's gotten before. And most of all, I think we've milked the situation here for nearly everything it's worth. We can't keep up this charade forever. The arrangements for departure have already been started. It's time for all of us to sit back and let the dust settle."

She didn't say anything for a while.

"When?"

"As soon as possible. Certainly in the next few days."

He told her how and where he thought it should be done. She agreed.

"I'll see to it," she said and hung up.

• • •

We blew the rest of the day trying to find a surviving member of the Martini family—anybody who knew the full story of how the Martinis got separated from the family homestead—but we came up dry. From what we could find online, the youngest daughter, Serena, used to live out east in Santee. We found our way to Santee and eventually found the last known address of Serena Martini. The babysitter wasn't even sure what town it was, she just knew how to get there, but the little girl in the fairy costume playing out in the yard said her family had lived there for as long as she'd been around, which was, judging from the princess herself, about five years or so. As we started to leave, the purple princess said she hoped Serena Martini had gone to Jesus. We said we hoped so too.

Traffic back to O.B. was shitty, but we drew Schadenfreudian solace from the fact that most of the bumper-to-bumper traffic was crawling in the other direction and the mean-spirited notion that we'd probably beat most of those poor suckers home.

"This is like riding an escalator backwards," Saunders said as we cut down onto Sea World Drive. "No matter how fast we walk, the thing just keeps us moving in the other direction. We don't have one damn thing we can use. Nothing."

I was going to agree, but Gabe looked up from the phone.

"Charity."

Carolyn unbuckled her seat belt, leaned forward, and pushed her head between Gabe and me.

Gabe began to read from the screen. "Trager got caught with his hand in the cookie jar. More than once. Charity says the clinic doesn't say it in so many words due to the legal ramifications, but he thinks Trager is a full-scale junkie. They sent him to rehab twice before they fired him. He says the clinic Trager was working at when he lost his license is what amounts to a private sanatorium, and that they've been investigated and fined for the overmedication of patients on four occasions. Sued more times than that. Won some. Lost some. Says they were headed for bankruptcy when the opioid epidemic gave them new life."

"Pill pushers," Carolyn muttered.

"So how does a guy with no license still get to practice medicine?" I asked.

Gabe looked up. Made a face. "It's not like he's got an office someplace. He's only got one client. I'm betting that as long as nobody complains, he's pretty much invisible to the medical authorities."

Gabe tapped the screen. "But somebody did complain," Gabe said.

"Who?" Carolyn asked.

"Guy named Pickett. Simon Pickett. An old guy who'd known Mrs. Haller since they were kids. About five months ago, he lodged a complaint regarding elder abuse with social services."

"What happened?"

"The report says he failed to follow up on his complaint. Seems this Pickett guy just up and disappeared. His family reported him missing two days later. Nobody's seen or heard of the guy since. The case was referred to missing persons and is still unsolved."

"What else?" I pushed.

"He says Allied Investments has been selling off its inventory for the past couple of years."

"What inventory is that?"

"Various parcels of land in San Diego County. Old fishing boats. The original Haller fleet. Thirty-four of them. Auctioned off one at a time over the past two years, mostly in Mexico. Took in nearly nine million bucks, not counting the nets and equipment, which were shipped back to San Diego for later disposal." Gabe went on. "Nine million of which never appeared anywhere in the Haller trust accounts. Nine million whose whereabouts are presently unknown."

"Why not sell the equipment with the boats?" Carolyn asked.

"Good question."

Both Gabe's and my phones bonged at the same time.

"More Charity," Gabe said and began reading the screen.

"You know," Carolyn said from the back seat. "The elder abuse angle might be a slick way into this thing."

"Why's that?" I asked.

"Because it's trending these days. SDPD's run a couple of mandatory staff workshops on elder abuse lately. They say we've got a generation coming up that's not going to have it nearly as good as their baby boomer parents did and that some of them are in a real big hurry to come into the family money. There's a special hotline to report it on. It's presently cause du jour in the anti–domestic violence campaign."

"Maybe we should lodge an anonymous complaint," I said.

Carolyn nodded. "I've got a friend on the task force. Let me make a call and find out the best way to go about it, but yeah—that might be a real good idea."

"You wanna hear the scoop on Samuel Rice Pemberton the Third?" Gabe asked.

We waited for the rim shot.

"He's dead," Gabe said. "Died of complications following pneumonia at Brushy Mountain State Penitentiary in Petros, Tennessee, in 2013. Survived by nobody."

"Then who's the guy running the Haller show?"

"Pemberton was in Brushy Mountain for the last fourteen years of his life," Gabe read. "Ran a red light drunk and got T-boned by a cement truck. His wife and six-year-old son were declared dead at the scene. He decided to act as his own attorney, which got him fifteen to life for negligent homicide. Like half the known world, he supposedly found Jesus while he was on the inside." Gabe swiped at the phone. "He had nine different cellmates over that period. Charity's cousin says he thinks the most likely candidate is named Walter G. Hall. Did four and a half for bank fraud and money laundering. Did the last three of it in a cell with Pemberton. Was released two weeks before Pemberton passed away. Looks like Hall saw the handwriting on the wall and used Pemberton's name to sign up with something called Heavenly Forgiveness, a Torrance, California, charity whose mission is to get recently released inmates started on the path to redemption. They run an interstate prison ministry, half a dozen halfway houses around the West Coast, and a job counseling service. They're the ones got Pemberton hired as a driver for Mrs. Haller, who was inclined to support second chances for guys like Pemberton. Supposedly, after her husband passed away, she gave jobs to dozens of them on the fishing boat fleet. Also there's no paper trail of any kind for Walter G. Hall. Not one thing since the day he was released. Not a traffic ticket, not a library card. Never reported to his parole officer. Disappeared into the ozone."

"All of which gets us exactly nowhere," Saunders groused. "We can't even tell anyone how we came by this information, and as long as what's-his-name has Mrs. Haller's power of attorney, it's gonna take a smoking gun to get anybody official to knock on that door." She sat back hard into the seat. "None of which leads us any closer to what happened to that little boy, and all of which is very likely to mess up your personal witness protection program if we keep pressing."

"So what—lemme get this straight—the best we can do is to file an anonymous elder abuse complaint and hope they get off their collective social service asses and do something about it?" Gabe muttered.

"That's our only option," Saunders said. I checked her face in the mirror, hoping to find at least a trace of irony in her expression, but came up empty. She believed in the system, which was way more than anybody could say about either Gabe or me.

"So what you're saying is that the best a couple of old pistoleros like me and Leo can do is to call social services on these jokers."

"They'll demand to see Mrs. Haller. I know that from the workshops. They'll notify whoever answers the phone that there's been a complaint filed and then show up with a warrant. That's the protocol."

"Sounds pretty limp dick to me," Gabe muttered.

"You might want to rephrase that," I suggested.

Gabe shot me an angry glare. "How the mighty have fallen."

"There's got to be something we can do," escaped my lips.

"What if we . . ."

"Don't start," came from the back seat.

As we rolled up to the curb, half a block behind her car, I said, "Maybe we could . . ."

Carolyn clapped her hands over her ears. "I don't want to hear this. I'm an officer of the court." She popped the rear door and stepped out onto Niagara Avenue. She walked up and tapped on my window. I rolled it down.

"We're gonna check the camera later. Why don't you stick around?" I tried.

She was tempted, but the cop in her won the struggle.

"I'm thinking that medical examiner girlfriend of yours back in Seattle might just have been right about you," she said and then stalked off.

I looked over at Gabe. "She'll be back," I predicted.

Wishful thinking, as it turned out. We mostly wasted time until right after nine, when we decided to hop down to the OB Noodle House for a bite to eat.

• • •

Lamar had planned to skip town. He really had. They'd stayed outside Waterman's in the SUV all night, rather than driving over to sleep at the dog beach, because Chub, having located Waterman, didn't want to let him out of his sight. Lamar had made one last attempt to convince him to stand down, and before he could leave, Waterman had done something shifty—and intriguing.

They'd followed him uptown to the dog beach, then watched as he and some homeless kid had trekked over to a set of houses and condos on a cliff, where Waterman had later returned to rent a condo. Why did he need a place when he already had one? Waterman was clearly up to something. Suddenly, Lamar had an idea: If he could keep Chub from killing Waterman long enough to find out what the guy was involved in, maybe he could pass that info on to the Brotherhood and it would be enough to convince them to give him a pass for not killing Chub. Maybe he wouldn't have to go on the run for the rest of his life.

They'd followed Waterman around for two days. All the way up to Lemon Grove, to breakfast with his girlfriend, etc. All public places, and even Chub wasn't stupid enough to go after Waterman then. They'd been spooked too by a Taurus that had been parked outside Waterman's building, a guy just sitting inside. Looked like a tourist, but Lamar had managed to convince Chub that it might be an undercover cop waiting to move on them, or someone Marshall had sent. Chub seemed to buy that. Lamar had even started to relax a bit, thinking maybe he'd get out of this mess after all.

But then Waterman had returned to this alleyway, and now it was all going to hell.

Chub pointed out the front window and then popped his seat belt.

"There they are," he said, sliding out of the seat.

"Maybe we oughta . . . ," Lamar began, but Chub was already gone, double-timing it down Del Monte Avenue about half a block behind Waterman and the freak.

"Fuck," he muttered at the inside of the truck and then climbed down into the street and hurried to catch Chub, which was harder than it sounded, 'cause the big guy was really stretching them out. Lamar checked the Browning stuck in the back of his belt. Pushed it deeper and then broke into a dog trot.

■ ■ ■

Garrett blinked twice, as if not believing his eyes. Looked like *Zoo Parade*. Waterman and his keeper leading the way down the opposite sidewalk. Greenway and Pope bringing up the rear, staying in the shadows of the swaying palm trees as they trailed them down the street. He lay down on the seat until they were well past, then sat up, got out, and followed along on the opposite side of the street.

He'd cased the neighborhood hard earlier and was trying to recall any place secluded enough to do his work. Problem was, they were so close to the beach that space was precious. Everybody was jammed up tight to their neighbors. He just couldn't bring to mind a place secluded enough for wet work.

Wasn't till they turned the corner onto Bacon Street that he finally understood. Greenway didn't give a shit. He was out of patience. He was gonna do this wherever and whenever he could. The big guy was no more than twenty feet behind when they seemed to sense someone behind them. The freak turned first. Greenway kept coming. Like a boulder rolling down a hill.

Garrett crossed the street, ducking behind parked cars as he moved in.

"Hey," the freak shouted at the sight of Greenway. Waterman turned quickly.

Greenway swept the freak aside with an elbow to the head. The freak went down hard. Greenway grabbed Waterman in a bear hug and lifted him from the ground. Waterman butted him in the face. Greenway held on, pressing his huge red face into Waterman's. "You killed my brother," he screamed.

Waterman pistoned up a knee . . . and then another. Garrett saw Greenway's shoulders slump. Waterman slid out of his grasp and began crawling out of reach.

Greenway's partner arrived in the frame. Waving a gun around. Pointing it at the freak, who was rising from the sidewalk.

"Don't you move, motherfucker," the little turd was yelling.

Garrett moved two cars closer. Waterman threw a straight right. Connected with Greenway's face with a wet thud, actually drove him back a pace. All it seemed to do was piss the big guy off.

"I'll kill you, motherfucker," the big guy screamed.

Greenway had Waterman in a choke hold now. Waterman's face looked like it was about to explode.

The little guy stepped forward and put the barrel on the freak's temple. "You stay there. You hear me . . . stay there."

Looked to Garrett like the smaller guy was trying to work up the courage to kill. Garrett slid past the final car, stepped up onto the sidewalk, and shot the guy in the side of the head. The big black automatic clattered to the sidewalk. Porch lights were coming on all over the neighborhood.

Waterman's eyes were closed. His arms and legs gone limp. Greenway had just about choked him out when Garrett slid the barrel along the side of Waterman's head, rested it on top of his left ear, and shot Greenway in the face. Chub went down in a heap. Garrett walked over and put another round in his ear. He could hear shouting and the roaring of engines.

When he turned back, Waterman was on his knees. Coughing, choking, spitting all over himself. The freak was struggling to get upright. Garrett checked the street.

The freak looked up at him.

"You guys oughta be more careful," Garrett said as he picked up the black automatic, pocketed his own gun, crossed Bacon Street, and disappeared from view.

• • •

The cops showed up about two minutes later. En masse. Gabe and I were waiting. We'd talked about maybe getting lost before the cops showed up but decided that was probably a bad idea. Since we were neighborhood regulars and neither of us were armed, we'd just claim we'd been attacked by the two guys lying dead in the street, and then somebody had stepped out of the shadows and shot them. We had no idea who the guy was. Some local concerned citizen perhaps. Maybe somebody else had seen him better than we did. "I don't know" is hard to take issue with.

We spent most of the following day getting tested for gunshot residue, lying to the authorities on a variety of subjects, and standing behind the one-way glass looking at all the suspects they'd rounded up the night before. Mercifully, the shooter wasn't among them.

We'd already talked it over. What do we do if the shooter is in the lineup? Gabe had asked. I thought it over.

"He could have offed us too," I said.

Gabe had nodded. "Easy."

So even if he had been among those they'd rounded up, we wouldn't have ratted him out.

Back home several hours later, we put a makeshift dinner together from leftovers, spiffed up the apartment, and were still pretending to be upright, law-abiding citizens when eight o'clock rolled around.

"Let's go see if there's anything new on the tape," Gabe suggested.

I'll admit it. At some level of consciousness I knew it was a bad idea. Something in me understood that it might be better if we gave it a break and took it up again after we'd cooled down a bit and weren't feeling quite so frustrated and flaccid. But God help me, I didn't.

Five minutes later we were walking up Del Monte Avenue under a full moon before hooking a quick right onto Cable and heading north. The wind had risen. The onshore flow had the palm trees swaying like ghostly dancers in the wet tropical breeze. Sounded like the sensual swoosh of a well-dressed woman in the dark.

I slid the key into the front door lock and let Gabe and myself into the building.

Up at the end of Narragansett, the usual collection of mystics and maniacs had figured out the sunset was over and were heading back to their burrows.

We let ourselves into the apartment, pulled the lawn chairs over to the window, and rewound. We were fast-forwarding through the stuff we'd already looked at when something caught my eye. "Stop," I said. "Go back to the part where Pemberton or whoever the fuck he is comes out and gets into it with the security guy. The part where he gets rid of him and puts another guy in his place."

Took us a couple of minutes, but eventually we found the spot I was looking for. We watched Pemberton's face twist with annoyance as he stood on the front steps and watched the guy pretend to garden the pair of flower boxes. We watched as he told the first guy to get lost. When the banished guy disappeared between the house and the nearest shed, Pemberton stuck his head back into the doorjamb and said something. A minute later another security type came out the front door to take his place.

"Where'd he go?" I asked.

"Who?"

"The first guy. The one who went between the buildings." I pointed at the screen. "He didn't come back out."

"So," Gabe began, "unless they've got a Star Trek transporter room back there, there's gotta be a way into either the house or the shed."

"Yep," I said.

"Assuming we were regular renters, what are we supposed to do about garbage?"

"Dumpsters in the basement. Blue for recyclables, black for trash," I said.

"You ever been down there?"

"Nope."

Gabe tapped the screen. Pointing to the single metal garage door at the rear of our building. "That's gotta be the door where the super rolls the dumpsters out into the alley."

As usual Gabe had a point. Unless the super for some perverted reason chose to roll a half a dozen fly-encrusted dumpsters out through the front of the building and then down the alley, that door had to be where he set the trash out for the garbage trucks.

"It's only twenty or thirty feet from our back door to the alley between the house and the building," I said.

"They'll make us in an instant," Gabe pointed out. "And even if we make it to the alley, they'll have us on tape trespassing."

When somebody knocked on the door, I assumed it was Carolyn Saunders come to join the party. Since I always like it when I'm right about something, I was wearing a big shit-eating grin as I pulled the door open, thinking she just couldn't stand not knowing what was going on. I had an "I told ya so" at the ready, right up to the moment when I turned the knob and the door exploded inward, flattening my nose, bouncing hard off my forehead, sending me stumbling backward into the room, with my knees turned to rubber and my vision a Technicolor kaleidoscope spiraling through my skull.

I remember catching sight of Gabe coming out of the lawn chair in Duchamp sections. The sounds of feet scuffling along the floor and a series of guttural straining noises. I brought both hands up to my shattered nose and they came away slick and thick and bloody.

Behind me somebody bounced off a wall with a thud. A low keening sound, rhythmic and mournful, began to fill the room. With my vision all haywire, I aimed a fist at what appeared to a black hooded head, made solid contact, heard him grunt. As I spun toward Gabe, somebody bear-hugged my knees, trying to pull my feet out from under me. I jerked one leg free and pistoned up a knee with all the power I could muster. The sound of his teeth pulverizing each other ricocheted off the walls like castanets. He began to make noises as if he were grubbing for roots. I kicked the air out in front of me but missed everything and nearly fell on my ass.

My vision was beginning to clear as I felt hands on my shoulders, swung an elbow back, and connected with something solid. Hooded figures were all over Gabe like wasps at a picnic. Something stung my shoulder. I lashed out in that direction but again drew thin air. The movement brought my head around in time to see the needle jammed deep into my right shoulder. I reached for it, yanked it out just as my already fractured vision began to shrink, moving inward, getting smaller one line at a time, until my last vision was a pinhole of Ronald Reeves stepping into the room wearing one of his mechanic's shirts. EARLE, it said. My head felt as if it were about to explode.

"Nice and easy. No marks," he said. "Just so they're not around on Thursday night. Anybody finds what's left of them after that . . . don't matter, 'cause ain't none of us gonna be around after that."

Almost immediately, my vision sorted itself the rest of the way out. I wasn't unconscious. Quite the opposite, I was wide awake and able to see and hear everything going on around me. It's just that I couldn't move any part of my body. I couldn't even blink my eyes or keep the stream of drool from forming at the corner of my slackened mouth.

Somebody solved my immovable eyelids problem by pulling a hood over my head. Smelled like a dirty pillowcase. Then they zip-tied me from stem to stern. Next thing I knew I was lifted from the floor by three sets of hands.

"Let's go," I heard Reeves say.

Had I been able to so much as twitch, I might have smiled as they carried us out through the same rear door Gabe and I had just been talking about and dumped us into the back of some kind of truck. Rough wooden floor. Roll-up door on the back. The door rolled down with a bang. The latch was set from outside. It was deep-space dark. A minute later the truck started to roll.

I told myself to pay attention. To keep track of what direction we were traveling. How long the trip took. What kind of roads we were driving on. Sounds. Anything that might be of use to us later. Unless, of course, there wasn't gonna be a later, which was the gruesome possibility I was trying like hell not to think about.

I knew the O.B. area well enough to tell that the truck was moving north along Sunset Cliffs Boulevard and then onto Interstate 8 up past Nimitz. After that, I started counting, trying to measure out the minutes and the miles. My head felt as if it must have been bright red and visibly throbbing.

We passed the southbound I-5 ramp and then Hotel Circle and the 163. East . . . we were headed due east on the 8 toward El Centro and the desert beyond.

I was pretty much inert matter but managed to stay focused for the better part of an hour. When I lost count, I went back to listening, trying to store it all away.

In what I estimated to be about another hour, we slowed down and swung in a wide arc to the right. Like we were getting off the freeway. Forcing myself to listen. Trying to form in my mind a picture of the world outside. The new road was rougher and sounded different under the tires, and . . . yeah, the swoosh of cars passing had all but disappeared. A pothole bounced my head off the floor. I wanted to scream in pain but couldn't for the life of me find the scream button.

In another forty-five minutes or so the pavement ended for good, and the dirt roads began. Miles and miles of them, ticking and tocking beneath the truck bed as we seesawed our way forward over a washboard of uneven terrain.

By the time the truck bumped to a stop, I'd lost track of everything except the painful pounding in my head. The door suddenly rolled up. Judging from the feel of the rocking, three people climbed up into the truck bed with us. Someone took hold of my feet, dragging me toward the back of the truck, where four more hands took ahold and set me gently onto the ground behind the truck. I listened as they went back for Gabe.

One of them was shouting at the others in Spanish. "*Sí,*" one of the others answered back several times.

I was lying on my side when they rolled me over onto my face, cut the zip ties from my body, and pulled off the hood. From the sound of it they did the same for Gabe.

Wasn't a half minute later when I heard the truck start. I tried to raise my head, but it felt like it was the size of a bus tire, so I just relaxed and listened to the sounds of the truck till it faded into the general hum of the universe.

I don't know how many times I drifted off to neverland before the desert sun came peeping over the horizon, fluttering my eyelids enough to drag me back to consciousness again. In the near darkness, I could see Gabe about six feet away, lying motionless on the ground. I tried to say something but couldn't force anything out. That's when I realized I could now see Gabe because, sometime during my fitful periods of unconsciousness, I'd somehow turned my head in that direction. My mouth was full of dirt and pebbles. I managed to pucker up enough to spit some of it out, but it seemed like an acre and a half of desert floor was still stuck to the inside of my mouth. That's the moment when I realized that whatever drug they'd injected us with was beginning to wear off.

By the time I could muster sufficient muscle to sit up, the sun was fully visible above the horizon and I was sweating like a racehorse. I looked over at Gabe, who was on all fours doing a stoned-out grizzly bear impression.

I swallowed air and tried to force a sound from my throat, but the only thing that came out of my mouth was sand and gravel. I sputtered, spit, and looked around.

They'd dumped us at the base of a big-ass desert mountain, somewhere out in the middle of nowhere. To the east—hard to tell how far away—but way out there beneath that nuclear sun, giant white wind turbines did battle with the hot breeze blowing through the bone-dry canyons . . . looked like a million giant white pinwheels. To the west, nothing much at all . . . far as the eye could see, nothing but sand and scrub mesquite. A single rough track heading north marked the route the truck had taken after dumping us.

I got up on one knee first, then the other. Felt like I was standing on the edge of a cliff, so I waited awhile before I attempted a full Homo erectus. Made it on the first try but just barely. Stood there on the desert floor, waving like a willow in the wind.

I took two tentative steps toward Gabe and then stopped and waited for my equilibrium to reboot. I wiped my right hand on my shirt and then stuck a couple of fingers in my mouth, scraping along between my lips and gums, trying to get all the sand and gravel out of my mouth. Got most of it. What was left ground between my teeth when I closed my mouth. I winced but couldn't work up enough saliva to wash it out.

"You got any idea where the hell we are?" Gabe slurred.

"None."

"We can't just stay where we are," Gabe said. "Not unless we can find some shade and water."

I nodded. "Sun's gonna kill us if we stay here."

"That's what's supposed to happen."

"Whatta you mean?" I asked.

"You remember all that yammering when they were handling us?"

"Yeah."

"They were saying they should handle us gently so there wouldn't be any marks on our bodies in case anybody ever found us."

I thought it over. "Smart," I said finally. "Couple of bodies found out in the desert. No visible marks. Cause of death, dehydration. Sure, there's gonna be questions—you know, how we got way the fuck out here and such—but nobody's gonna put a lot of energy into getting the details unless there's some hint of foul play."

Gabe tottered around in a tight circle. "Which way?"

"I say we follow the truck."

"We need shade," Gabe said again.

I shrugged. "We can't stay here."

"You know anything about desert survival?"

"From French Foreign Legion movies," I said.

"This is a death march, man," Gabe said. "We choose wrong and we die out here."

"Seems to me that all we know for sure is that the truck went that way, so sooner or later we're gonna run into another road if we follow the truck."

"We came a long way on the dirt," Gabe pointed out. "How far, you figure?"

"Fifteen, maybe twenty miles."

"We ain't gonna make it that far."

"Let's go," was the best thing I could come up with.

All this stroll was missing was the fife and drum. We hiked for most of an hour over the featureless landscape. Following the tire tracks, losing them once in a while, and then finding them again. Moving steadily toward the northwest.

Sometime around noon, I stopped and pointed at an uneven bump on the edge of my field of vision. "What's that?" I asked.

"Looks like a tree or a bush," Gabe said.

That's all it took. Something was better than nothing. We began trudging in that direction. Ten minutes later we were gazing at some kind of short, thick desert greenery replete with beautiful purple flowers.

"I think it's called a smoke tree," Gabe said.

"We can crawl down under it and get out of the sun," I said.

"I'm thinkin' maybe we ought to check it for snakes first," Gabe rasped.

I reached down and lifted the nearest low-hanging branch. The molten sun lit the shaded space at the bottom of the tree. It took my senses a second to put the picture together. Straight lines. Something rounded at the other end. Boat shoes. Shoes? I looked over the top of the tree at Gabe. I swallowed hard. "You maybe ought to see this," I said.

Gabe walked around and squatted at my side. I lifted the branch higher, allowing more light into the space beneath the foliage. Gabe flinched. Almost fell over backward.

Looked like he was asleep. Fully dressed, brown cargo shorts and the remains of a blue-and-white Hawaiian shirt. He was lying in the fetal position. His skin had shrunken brown and wrinkled like a deflated football. His lips had retreated from his mouth, allowing me to see the pink upper denture that had fallen down onto his lolling brown tongue. Looked like a set of those chattering joke teeth.

I couldn't resist. I bent forward and touched his nearest arm with my index finger. Felt like old leather. The desert had petrified his corpse. Dried him out like an apricot.

Gabe crawled back up beside me. "Can you lift it higher?"

I stood up and put my legs into it. Gabe carefully went through the dead man's pockets but came up with nothing. Whatever it was that held a person's skeleton together had loosened up. When Gabe carefully rolled what was left of him up onto his side, his remains started to come apart. Looked like maybe one of his legs had come loose from the hip socket. On the other leg, the foot flopped deeper into the hole. For reasons unknown, we took the time to put him back in the same position we'd found him in. Almost like we owed it to him. No matter what.

"You thinking what I'm thinking?" I asked when we had all the pieces more or less back in place.

"The missing Mr. Pickett. The old guy who insisted on seeing Mrs. Haller, called social services, and then did a disappearing act."

"Yeah . . ." I pointed at the body. Made a motion to suggest that we maybe could remove the remains from their final resting spot and take it over ourselves.

"Should we?" I asked.

"I'm not getting in there," Gabe said. "I'll die somewhere else."

So we left him in peace and followed our own footprints back to the road. Musta been one, one thirty by that time. The sun was a golden hammer, and we were rusty nails. Sometime around three o'clock in the afternoon, I stopped sweating. The inside of my mouth was so stuck together I had to reach up and give my lower jaw a hand in order to pry it open. My toes started catching parts of the desert floor as we stumbled along. Neither of us said much of anything other than to offer an occasional encouraging word. We kept pushing forward, slower now, a bit of loose-kneed wobble in our strides as we followed the tire tracks west.

We walked until the moon began to rise in the east. It wasn't like we ever decided to stop walking either. At some point we simply sat down on the ground, right in the middle of a small circle of mesquite. We looked over at one another and then flopped over onto the sand. Last thing I recall was Gabe saying, "We ain't gonna make it, Leo."

Gabe might have said something else, but by that time I was engulfed in torrid dreams. Dreams of the ocean and of fire. I saw myself rising from the rippling waves like some god come to earth, and then a minute later my thighs rubbed together and I spontaneously burst into blue flame. Next thing I remembered I could feel myself swimming on the desert floor; part of me knew it was absurd, but I couldn't stop myself. I was drowning in a sea of sand.

And then Gabe was shaking my shoulders. Took me a while to get my eyes to focus. "Maybe we ought to walk while it's cooler out," Gabe said.

I came up off the ground in sections. Took a hand from Gabe and a couple of tries to stand upright.

I looked around. In the distance the wind generators spun languidly in the night air. Some twirling one way, some the other, creating a strobe-like sensory disruption, kinda like one of those old TENSION signs. Overhead the Milky Way glittered like a flaming carpet. The moon was . . . was . . . I lost my train of thought . . . something about a ghostly galleon flitted through my head as we collected what remained of our wits and stumbled on.

# Chapter 12

Carolyn Saunders had banged on the security door three separate times before she bothered to try the handle. When the door opened to her touch, she checked the surrounding area to see if anybody'd seen her little exercise in stupidity.

Unfortunately the big blue door wasn't nearly so accommodating. She banged on it, waited, and then closed the security door and started back for the stairs.

She was a couple of risers from the bottom when the voice stopped her in her tracks. "Hey." She looked up. It was the guy in the ground-floor apartment on the alley side of the complex. She thought his name was Kevin and that Leo and Gabe were friendly with him. "You lookin' for Leon?" he asked.

"Yeah," she said.

"They didn't come back last night," he said. "Neither of them."

"You're sure?"

"I hear everybody comin' and goin'. That's why my apartment's so cheap."

"Maybe they—" she began.

"I went up to tell them I got my truck back—you know, like it got stolen the other day—and Gabe always stays up real late . . . but last night there wasn't nobody home. No lights, no nothing. Real weird."

Saunders opened her mouth.

He cut her off. "Their car's out back."

"Maybe they went—"

He interrupted again.

"They been here six or eight months, and far as I know, they ain't ever gone anywhere before. Sure as hell not on foot."

He wanted to talk. She could tell. That made one of them.

"Thanks," was all she said before turning hard left and walking back out to Del Monte Ave. She'd been trying to call Leo for the better part of an hour before she'd decided to drive over. Hot and frustrated, she'd jammed her car into the handicapped spot across the street and thrown the OFFICIAL POLICE VEHICLE sign on the dashboard.

Now she unlocked the door, leaned in, and rummaged through her purse until she found the key to the new apartment that Leo had given her the other day. She shouldered the bag, locked the car, and then checked the doors individually by hand. Cop sign on the dash or no cop sign, you left your car unlocked around here and there'd be a family of four living in it by the time you got back.

Saunders walked a long Z over to Narragansett and let herself into the new building. The foyer and stairs had one of those floral-print carpets that was so visually busy you could slaughter livestock on it and nobody would have noticed. Someone was playing Fleetwood Mac. "Go Your Own Way." A muffled NPR station rumbled from another apartment.

She mounted the stairs and found number eight at the back of the building. She let herself in, checked the hallway behind her, and then closed the door. The minute she turned toward the room her breath caught in her throat like a fish bone. She pulled her gun from her right hip and used two hands to raise it to shoulder level as she sidestepped inside, swinging the weapon from side to side as she moved. A pair of lawn chairs lay on their sides on the carpet, one of which had been completely broken in two. The window on the alley side yawned wide open. A silver piece of duct tape fluttered in the ocean breeze. A series of paint scars on the lower corner of the window casing said something had been violently torn from its moorings.

"Musta been the camera," she whispered to herself as she began to move around the space in combat stance. Didn't take long. The chairs and the dinged-up window frame were all there was. Other than that, the place was empty.

She clipped her weapon back into its plastic holster and reached for her phone. Stopped and just stood there, mouth breathing. To call whom? What would she say?

. . .

"I think you better take this call, Mr. Pemberton."

Pemberton set the *Architectural Digest* facedown on the end table and looked across the room toward Hector. "A call from whom?" he asked.

"The Department of Health and Human Services."

Pemberton held out his hand. Hector walked over and handed him the phone.

"Pemberton here," he said.

"Mr. Pemberton . . . my name is Marcia Grant. I am a senior officer in the San Diego County Human Services Investigation Bureau. We have been informed that you are the legal executor for Florence Haller. Is that so?"

"Yes it is," he confirmed.

"Human Services has received a complaint regarding the welfare of Mrs. Haller."

"From whom?"

"I'm afraid we are not at liberty to share that information, sir."

Pemberton sighed loud enough for Marcia Grant to hear.

"What can I do for you, Ms. Grant?" he asked.

"Pursuant to California law 15610.23, after such a complaint is filed, our personnel are required to meet with Mrs. Haller personally in order to assure her continuing welfare."

Pemberton pulled his feet from the leather ottoman and sat up straight in the chair.

"Mrs. Haller is quite ill," he said. "Her doctor—"

She cut him off. "We will be arriving with our own doctor," she said.

"I'm afraid—" Pemberton began.

"And a bench warrant," she went on. "Ten thirty this Friday."

"I'll have to consult with her physician. I'm not sure he'll—"

"Ten thirty this Friday," she said again. More forcefully this time. Click.

Pemberton sat bolt upright in the wing chair for several minutes before he pushed the call button on the underside of the end table. Hector appeared thirty seconds later.

"Yes sir."

"I need Mrs. Cisneros, Mr. Reeves, and Dr. Trager immediately. No excuses. Tell them we need to discuss a major change in plans."

"Yes sir." Hector turned and hurried for the door.

"Hector?" He turned back. "Are you prepared? Have you got your personal arrangements in place?" Pemberton asked.

"Yes sir. For some time now."

"When we walk out of here, we won't be coming back."

Chapter 13

A thin silver line on the eastern horizon said morning was on the way. Problem was we both knew this could well be the last sunrise either of us saw, a thought that tended to put a damper on conversation. You know things are going badly when you look over at your traveling companion, someone you genuinely care about, and your first thought is, "Jesus . . . hope I look better than that."

Whoever said that death was the only real enemy had a point. You want something to make your other problems look trivial, a mental picture of your sun-bleached bones decorating the desert floor will sure as hell do the trick for you.

Add a coyote gnawing on the bones to the picture, and you've arrived at full-scale terror.

We looked like death. We smelled like death. But somehow the word never came up between us. Like maybe, at this point, neither one of us particularly gave a shit. Or neither of us wanted to be the one to first to say it out loud. I chided myself for hoping I looked better than Gabe.

I'd rummaged through the annals of my life several times as we'd staggered on through the darkness. Some good, some bad, some moments to be proud of, others conjuring nothing but the hot face of shame. Such is life, I decided.

I'd wondered why it was so easy to forget the good and dwell on the bad. Somewhere in the middle of the night, I'd come to the conclusion it was nothing more than part of our genetic survival package. Funny thing about life on earth, you could find eternity in a flower one minute and then eat bad chili in the next. When that happened, your *will to live* yelled in your ear: "Fuck the flower; remember the chili."

We kept walking . . . slower now . . . My right knee felt as if somebody'd driven nails into it. I'd have limped except I couldn't figure out how to limp on both legs at the same time. As morning crept over the horizon, it felt like we were marching in deep sand. My legs were screaming at me. The impressions of the truck's tires had disappeared sometime during the night. All we had to go on was the fact that the sun rose in the east. Not that it mattered much. We weren't going to make it to another day without water. Watching *Beau Geste* thirty-five times hadn't made me much of a desert survival expert, but I knew that much for sure. We might live for a week without food—it had been done before—but without water, we'd be dead before the sun winked at the darkness again.

The sun was halfway over the eastern horizon when it began to prick at my skin like nettles. Felt as if insects were crawling over me. I bowed my neck and trudged on. I have no idea how much ground we'd covered by the time I next looked at anything but my own scuffling feet.

When I finally looked up again, my first thought was that it had to be a mirage. Some trick my mind was playing on me. What looked like a mound of boulders spread out over the desert floor like dice. Or more likely something pushed to the surface by geothermal forces eons ago and left to bake in the desert sun.

I stopped walking. Gabe kept going for half a dozen steps before grinding to a halt and looking back my way. I tried to wet my throat to speak, but wet was out to lunch, so I pointed. Gabe's eyes swung that way.

"You see it?" I finally managed to rasp. Felt like I was gargling gravel.

Gabe nodded and then turned and led the way forward.

The boulders were bigger than they appeared from a distance. On the side opposite the rising sun, about six feet of shade soothed the desert floor. We plopped down onto the sand and leaned back against the nearest boulder. Must have been ten degrees cooler in the shade. A sudden shudder ripped through my body. I shivered violently. Hugged myself for a long time before it finally stopped. When I dropped my hands back into my lap, I noticed how the skin on the backs of my hands was suddenly loose and sloppy. Almost as if my hide had somehow separated itself and was now merely the bag my body came in. Another series of shudders racked me.

Took an intense effort to swallow. Felt sharp and dry, like I was swallowing pushpins. My head felt enormous, like if I didn't pay attention to keeping it straight, it might fall off and go rolling across the sand. I looked over at Gabe.

Gabe hawked several times. Managed a swallow or two. "This is it, man," Gabe growled. "This is as far as I go. My legs are done."

I started to say something, but Gabe waved me off. "We pulled off a lot of shit together, man . . . but this . . . this . . ." At which point Gabe ran out of words. I waited and allowed the silence of the desert morning to engulf me.

Gabe's throat rippled again. Looked to be swallowing barbed wire. "If I'm gonna die, I'm gonna die in the shade," Gabe said.

"I'm glad we were together," I croaked.

Gabe looked over. "Wouldn't have it any other way."

All I could do was to nod my agreement.

I closed my eyes and leaned my head back on the rock. I couldn't tell you how long it was before I heard the buzz for the first time. All I knew for sure was that, by that time, the lower half of my body was in the sun. That's when the first whirring sound bored its way into my skull. Sounded like a giant bug was stuck in my ear. I suddenly recalled summer nights long ago when Joey Ortega and I had used BIC lighters and aerosol cans to fashion makeshift flamethrowers with which we had terrorized the local june bug population. My most vivid sensory recollection was the ungodly smell they emitted as they curled into ashes.

I cracked open my burning eyes. My vision was crisp but twirling like a merry-go-round. My first thought was that a dragonfly was buzzing around in front of my face. My second thought was that the damn fly ought to show a little respect for the dying, so I swatted at it. Missed by an acre or so.

That's when I realized I was no longer operating in real time. That there was a serious lag in my responses to sound and movement. The bug rose straight up into the ruthless sky. Took me a minute to haul my eyes up and find it again. Hovering there, staring at us with its buggy eyes . . . and those wings . . . no . . . no . . . not wings. I blinked several times. Four wings. Wailing away at the sky . . . propellers . . . four propellers. The bug dropped down to the level of my face and hovered there. And then, for a moment, my vision reassembled itself and I could see it was a drone, not a bug. Black and plastic.

I looked over at Gabe. "Hey," I croaked. "Hey. You see this?"

But nothing. Gabe was out of the office.

Instinctively I reached out toward the sound. The bug backed off a bit. The whirring filled my ears.

I waved hello. The drone rose straight up into the desert sky, maybe fifty feet or so off the ground, and then buzzed off in the direction we'd been walking in.

I struggled to my feet. I watched the drone for maybe half a minute before it became too small to see. I wanted to yell at it. To tell it not to go, but I just couldn't hack anything out in time. I stood there with my arms atop the nearest rock. I locked my knees so I wouldn't sink back to the ground. The sun was sautéing the top of my head.

Just as I started to sink back into the remaining shade, I saw what I first took to be a dust devil, twirling a ringlet of sand and dirt into the molten sky. I ran a hand over my burning face and looked again. It was closer. I closed my eyes and started over. Even closer now . . . no doubt about it.

It's difficult to describe the degree of exultation that washed over me like a rogue wave. I wanted to run toward it, squealing like a *Jeopardy!* winner, but I wasn't up to the task. Wanted to call out but wasn't able to do that either, so I just stood there waving my arm like a signal flag as the brown swirling cloud moved steadily in our direction.

Wasn't till the dust settled back to the desert floor that I could make out that it was a pickup truck. Mostly army green except for the passenger door and the right front fender, both of which were the color of flat red primer. Something old, the make and model of which I didn't recognize.

There were two of them—a man and a boy of about ten. Dressed alike. Jeans; loose, once-white linen shirts; and big straw hats. The man was carrying a gallon jug filled with water. If I'd been able to muster the moisture, I think I may have broken into tears right then and there. The man stopped at my side. The kid ran over to Gabe. From the corner of my eye I could see the boy shaking Gabe's shoulder.

"You guys all right?" he asked.

I shook my head.

The boy yelled, "Papa." Called with his arm.

The man looked at me. I gestured with my head for him to go and tend to Gabe. He got the message. I watched that jug of water leave the way a rottweiler watches a dropped rump roast. I spit but nothing came out.

Took both of them to roll Gabe over and prop the wide back against the nearest rock. I watched as the guy unscrewed the top and poured some of the water over Gabe's head. When Gabe coughed twice and then reached up to wipe away the water, it felt like a Subaru had been lifted from my chest. At that point I must have made some noise or other, because all three of them looked over at me.

I slid down the rough side of the boulder and plopped on the ground. Turned out Bobby and Carlos were father and son, although it was hard to see how. The kid was of obvious Hispanic descent. The guy was about as Hispanic as I was, but I wasn't in any position to ask questions at that point, so I just let it go.

Bobby went back and forth to the truck a couple of times. Came back with a big blue plastic tarp, a bunch of old rope, and a pair of metal fence posts from whence he rigged us up a rudimentary shelter from the elements. In the meantime, the boy kept ferrying the jug back and forth between Gabe and me, letting us have a little at a time, pulling it away before either of us could guzzle more water than our systems could handle. When the first jug was empty, the kid ran back to the truck and came back with a fresh one.

Once we were able to at least partially walk, they manhandled us one at a time over to the shelter and made us comfortable.

"Whatchu doin' out here wid no water?" Bobby asked us after we'd begun to come around a bit.

"It's a long story," Gabe said.

"You could die out here," Carlos added.

"Darn near did," Bobby said.

"Where are we?" I asked.

"This is the Mojave National Preserve."

"Where's the nearest town?" Gabe asked.

"Baker," Carlos chirped. "That's where we live."

"What day is it?" I asked.

"Tuesday," Bobby said. "Had them a teacher's in-service day at his school today, so we figured we'd come out here and fly the drone a bit."

For some reason, knowing what day it was made me feel better. I closed my eyes. Felt like there was sand in them. *I'll just rest them for a couple of minutes,* I told myself. Next thing I remember was waking up just before nightfall, needing to take a bladder buster of a leak. I crawled out from under the tarp and pushed myself to my feet. Either the world was still spinning or I was. It was hard to tell. I had a headache that would have stopped a rhino. My legs were weak and wobbly as I shuffled around the far edge of the rock pile to relieve myself. My throat felt like I'd swallowed a handful of thumbtacks. Other than that, things were just peachy.

When I turned around to leave, Bobby was standing behind me.

"You guys ready to leave?" he asked. "We gotta get back. Carlos got school tomorrow."

In the semidarkness, Gabe limped around both of us, all the way to the far side of the rock formation. Then Carlos walked fifty feet out into the desert and relieved himself onto the desert floor.

Took us a half an hour to take down the makeshift tent and stow everything back in the truck. Bobby got the motor started. Gabe and I crawled up into the bed and settled in and around the rest of the cargo.

Carlos went back to the campsite to make sure we'd left no sign that we'd ever been there. I was pulling a fence post out from under my ass and thinking about what a nice sense of preserving nature Carlos had, when a high-pitched scream filled the air.

Some noises don't require interpretation or translation. They're just the wordless expressions of disaster. Of terror. Of fear. The three of us were out of the truck in a flash. I felt like I was going to come apart at the joints. On my right Gabe was stiff-legging forward like Boris Karloff playing the Mummy.

"Carlos!" Bobby cried as he broke into a full sprint.

When I rounded the corner of the rock pile, the first thing my eyes lit upon was Carlos. Bug-eyed, writhing on the ground. Scooting along on one hip while holding his ankle and screaming his head off. That's when I saw the snake. Worse yet, that's when I heard the dry rattle of its tail hissing in the air. It stopped me cold.

"Oh Jesus," fell out of my mouth unbidden. The snake, having detected the presence of Gabe and me, suddenly was heading back toward Carlos. I started forward to intervene somehow, but Bobby streaked in front of me in a full sprint.

He grabbed his son by the ankles and started to drag him out of harm's way. Carlos was still shrieking like a jay when Bobby tripped over a rock and went down in a twisted heap. I watched as he hopped back up to his knees and threw a hand out onto the ground to help lever himself to his feet.

The snake ran his tongue in and out several times and then struck at the hand. My mouth was hanging open as the rattler recoiled from the bite and turned and swerved off in the other direction. Bobby was cradling his hand and rocking on his butt like a hobbyhorse. Carlos was starting to hyperventilate.

Gabe and I got there at the same time. Gabe grabbed Bobby by the shoulders and hoisted him to his feet. "Where's the nearest hospital?"

"We got us an urgent care facility in Baker," Bobby said through clenched teeth.

I had Carlos in my arms and was hurrying toward the truck. As I passed Gabe and Bobby I said, "Gabe, you drive. Bobby, ride up front with Gabe. Show him the way outta here." I stumbled but kept loping along with the boy in my arms. When I looked back over my shoulder, Bobby was cradling his arm like a baby as Gabe hurried him across the sand.

The truck was still running as Gabe climbed into the driver's seat. I lifted Carlos into the truck bed and climbed in after him. I grabbed the blue tarp, fluffed it up as much as I could, and put Carlos down onto it. He was breathing like a freight train. I leaned down and put my face right up into his. "Carlos . . . listen to me," I said. "I need you to calm down. The more excited you are, the more of that snake juice you're going to pump into your system. What you need to do is get real quiet here. Inside and out. Just real quiet. You understand what I'm saying to you?"

He nodded and started to cry.

"Close your eyes and count your breaths."

When he did it, I leaned out over the edge of the truck bed and shouted in Gabe's ear. "Take it easy, man. Nothing crazy," I said. "We break an axle out here and all of us are dead. Just get us there in one piece."

Gabe grunted. "Long time since I drove a stick."

The clutch chattered like hell at first, but we swung in a wide arc, a rooster tail of dust following in our wake like a filthy cape.

I had Carlos's head in my lap as we bounced across the jagged terrain. His ankle was starting to swell and turn the color of an eggplant. I kept telling him to take it easy, to relax as much as he could. I hugged the boy close to me, trying to cushion him from the bumps. I could feel his breathing getting shallow. Feel his body having contractions. I hugged him harder.

The deeply ribbed bed of the truck was pureeing my tailbone as we raced along. Bobby kept leaning out the passenger window screaming into the wind, wanting to know how Carlos was doing. At least that's what I imagined he was asking. Frankly, I couldn't make out a word he was saying. I kept nodding at him like a bobblehead doll. Finally, I bent my head down onto Carlos's chest and ignored him.

My senses came alive again the second we bounced up onto the paved road. I craned up and looked around. Two-lane blacktop. Yellow line down the middle.

Gabe had the shifting thing down. We were making some time now. More wind generators out in the distance; their massive white blades seemed to be motioning us forward, as if to say *hurry up, c'mon, man, move your ass.*

I looked through the dust-streaked back window of the truck. Gabe was holding the steering wheel like it was a life ring. Looked like Bobby had finally run out of gas. His snake-bitten hand was the size of a shovel. It hung loose, bumping against the front of the seat as the truck rocketed along. He'd keeled over onto Gabe's shoulder, his limp body rocking slightly to the tune of the truck.

I was about to sit back down when a sudden jolt shook the truck like we'd run over a boulder or something. I saw Gabe flinch hard.

Flinching was one thing. The flames licking out from the engine compartment were something else. Gabe looked back at me through the window. Jaw set like a bass, eyes hard as bullets.

I leaned out around the corner of the cab and shouted in Gabe's ear. "Drive till the fucker dies!"

Gabe nodded. Readjusted the hands on the wheel and stomped the gas pedal hard.

I told myself we'd get there, no doubt about it, yes sir, not to worry, and sat down next to Carlos. I picked him up by the shoulders and put the top half of him in my lap. Two things immediately became apparent. The boy was shaking like a palsy patient, and the truck was, little by little, slowing down. I took a deep breath and held it.

Chapter 14

"Sergeant Saunders, I assure you we're doing everything we are able to do. The law is clear. We are obliged to give seventy-two hours' notice prior to entering anyone's house. We've given official notice and are scheduled to arrive for an interview on Friday morning."

She'd said her name was Marcia Grant. She was the honcho for elder abuse complaints. "Couldn't we . . ." Carolyn stopped herself. Blew out a chestful of air.

Marcia Grant seemed to feel her frustration. "The only other recourse would be a search warrant executed by the police. Perhaps you should discuss your concerns with your own department. Assuming you have probable cause, or as I'm sure you are aware, if there's exigent circumstances—"

"Yes," Carolyn stammered. "Thank you . . . I . . . thank you."

Carolyn broke the connection. She snatched her keys from her kitchen table and hurried for the door. She didn't have a plan. Nobody was giving her a search warrant for Florence Haller's home without a truckload of probable cause. That wasn't going to happen. Besides which she was presently on administrative leave and not assigned to anything remotely connected to the case.

She backed her car out onto Rosecrans and rolled south all the way to Cañon, veered right at the light, and started up over the hill to Ocean Beach. All she could think of was to run by both apartments and see if maybe they'd come back sometime during the night.

She stopped at the new apartment first. Let herself in. Everything was just as she'd left it yesterday. Broken chair and all. She went through the rest of the apartment in a combat stance. Nothing. She returned her weapon to its holster, silently cursed, and headed downstairs to her car.

As usual there was no place to park on Del Monte Avenue, so she swung around into the alley behind the building, slid the car as far to the right as possible, threw the OFFICIAL POLICE VEHICLE sign on the dash, and got out.

She hustled up the concrete stairs two at a time. Same deal here. Everything as it had been the day before. Nobody around. She kicked the security door in frustration.

Back in the narrow courtyard, she walked to the back and knocked hard on Kevin's door. Once. Twice. Before the inner door opened.

He was wearing a pair of sweatpants and a gray sports jersey of some kind. Number twenty-three. It was 11:20 in the morning. The guy looked like he'd gone to bed about an hour ago.

"You seen either of those two?" she blurted before he'd stopped blinking.

"Nah," he said, running a hand over his yawning face. "They ain't been back." He scratched his belly. "You wanna get in?" he asked around another yawn.

"How we gonna do that?" she asked.

He unlocked the door and stepped out into the courtyard. "The slider's open and the screens don't lock." When he saw her hesitation, he started across the space and climbed the stairs about two-thirds of the way up, at which point he climbed up onto the wrought-iron handrail and balanced for a moment before reaching out, grabbing the railing on the balcony, and pulling himself up.

Carolyn watched as he climbed onto the balcony, slid the screen door aside, and stepped into the apartment. She hurried up the stairs. By the time she reached the landing, Kevin had the door open. She stepped inside.

He woke up in a hurry when she pulled her gun from her hip.

"Why don't you step outside while I check the place," she said.

"You a cop?"

"Outside," she said again. "Please."

He stepped onto the landing. She closed the door and went through the apartment room by room. Nothing seemed amiss. Both beds were made. No keys or phones or anything that somebody would have left behind had they been abducted.

She returned the gun to her hip and stepped outside. Kevin was assuming the position against the wall of the neighbor's apartment. A cop had Kevin's face pressed against the wall. Another was aiming his weapon directly at Carolyn's forehead. "Hands on your head," he yelled. "Now."

When she complied, he jammed her hard against the wall right next to Kevin and began to pat her down. She could feel his gun grind against the back of her head as he relieved her of her weapon. "My name is—" she began.

He lifted a knee and jammed her harder into the wall. She felt him slip a cuff on to one of her wrists and then pull it down behind her, just like they taught you at the academy.

She told him who she was.

"Where's your shield?" he asked.

"Well . . . at the moment I'm on leave," she started, "so I—"

"She's a cop," his partner threw in. "I've seen her at the West Precinct. I think she partners with Reynolds."

"We'll sort this out down at the station," the other cop said.

. . .

"*En inglés, por favor,*" Garrett said.

"*Un momento, señor.*"

It was more like four *momentos* before a new voice came on the line.

"Good morning, sir. What can I do for you?"

"I'd like to arrange a wire transfer."

"Certainly, sir. I'll need your account number and a routing number for whatever account you'd like the money transferred to."

Garrett read her both numbers.

"Just a moment, sir."

This time *un momento* morphed into five or six before she clicked back into his ear. "Sir?" she asked. "Are you still there, sir?"

"Yes," Garrett said.

"Sorry for the delay," she said. "Sir, we don't seem to have any record of that account number. Could you give it to me again? Perhaps I transcribed it wrong."

He did and added, "I checked the account yesterday morning and was assured the money had been deposited."

"Yes, sir. Just a minute, sir."

He waited.

"Sorry, sir. We have no record for such an account or any such confirmation number. Would you like me to connect you with security?"

"Yes. Please," Garret said.

The line clicked several times.

"Security . . . Romero," the gruff voice said.

Chapter 15

Towns like Baker don't have outskirts. One minute you're out in the desert, next minute you're in the middle of town. The green-and-white sign at the edge of town claimed a residency of 736 parched souls.

By that time we couldn't have been doing more than thirty miles an hour. The truck engine was sputtering and backfiring, sounding like it was gonna blow to pieces any second. The paint on the hood had been blistered by the fire in the engine compartment. Heat waves and smoke rose from under the hood like ghostly dancers. Looked like you could fry a pork chop on the damn thing.

Bobby was sitting up now, his snake-bitten hand as far out in front of himself as he could manage, as if he thought keeping it at a distance were maybe therapeutic. He used the other to point to the left. Gabe swung the wheel in that direction. He started yelling out the window, wanting to know how Carlos was doing. I went into another fit of head nodding, trying to tell him the boy was hanging in there.

We arrived at Desert Medical Services in a cloud of smoke and dust. Must have been a slow day for the local doc in the box. We'd barely stopped rolling when three people in blue scrubs were out the front door, hurrying in our direction. Two women and a man.

Over the top of the cab I shouted, "Got two snakebites here."

"What kind of snake?" the taller of the two women shouted back.

"Rattler," I said.

"You sure?" she wanted to know.

"Absolutely."

She said something to the guy, who turned and sprinted back toward the building.

I hustled to the back of the truck, opened the tailgate, then leaned in and grabbed Carlos by the feet. His eyes popped open when I picked him up.

"We're at the clinic," I told him. "Everything's gonna be all right."

Bobby had managed to climb out of the truck. He took two steps in our direction and then collapsed in sections. The second woman ran to his side. Gabe slid out of the driver's seat and limped around the front to help.

With a violent shudder and a single cannon shot from the tailpipe, the truck engine shook, rattled, and died. It was hissing like a nuclear teakettle. Steam was rising into the sky. Next thing I heard was the rattle of the gurney as the guy rolled it toward the truck. Gabe and the male nurse hoisted Bobby aboard. I followed along, Carlos in my arms, staggering a bit under the load but willing myself forward.

The woman in charge pointed at me. "In there," she said, indicating the room on the right. I lumbered in and laid Carlos on the examination table. I stood by his side, trying to catch my breath, willing my vision to stay still and my legs to keep moving. Mostly it was the other way around.

"How long ago did this happen?" she asked. "What time?"

I shrugged. "Two, three hours ago—something like that."

She looked at me as if to say, *"Come on, man."*

"We've got no phones or watches," I explained. "No nothing."

She raised an eyebrow as she snapped on the overhead lights.

"It's a real long story," I tried.

I watched her unlock the cabinet over the double sink and find the bottle she was looking for. She walked over and put a hand on Carlos's heaving chest.

"It's gonna be fine," she told him.

"It really hurts," Carlos whined.

She looked over at me and whistled. "You got any idea how burnt up you are?"

"Been afraid to look," I admitted.

"Carlos . . . do you know how much you weigh?" she asked the boy.

"Eighty-four pounds," the kid said.

I leaned against the wall and watched as she carefully prepared a syringe and then injected Carlos with the antivenom. The kid was brave. He flinched at the needle but otherwise gritted through it.

"Am I gonna die?" he wanted to know when she'd finished putting a Band-Aid over the injection site and another gauze bandage over the bite marks on his leg.

She patted his head. "Nope," she said, smiling. "You're going to be with us for a good long time, son."

"How's my dad?" he asked.

"He's gonna be all right too," she told him.

When I wandered out into the reception area, Bobby had been wheeled off to another room. Gabe was sitting in one of the plastic chairs, hooked up to an IV. Looked like saline solution in the bag. Two minutes later I was sitting in the chair beside Gabe, likewise hooked up to an overhead bag. Sometime during the second bag, I could feel my cells coming back to life. It felt warm—like crawling under the covers on a cold night. I closed my eyes. I was just about asleep when Gabe spoke.

"You know, I've been going over this in my head," Gabe said. "Those motherfuckers just left us out there to die. Like we were a couple of stray dogs or something. That's a real no-class move, man."

"That fucking Reeves," I said.

"Yeah . . . I saw him."

The drip drip drip of saline solution.

"This ain't over," Gabe growled. "I don't know about you, man, but I'm taking this shit seriously. I'm handing somebody his ass over this. I mean . . . yeah, we were poking our noses into their business. We weren't exactly keeping a low profile. But, man, we don't know shit. We're no threat to these guys, and they decide to off us anyway. Cold."

I looked over at Gabe. They'd slathered zinc oxide all over our sunburned parts. We looked like a pair of greasy, oversize mimes.

"We're probably gonna need to shower first," I said, trying to lighten things a tad.

Gabe wasn't going for the levity. "Like we were a pair of kitties stuffed into a bag of rocks and thrown into the river," Gabe said. "That's cold, man—cold."

I closed my eyes. They felt like they were full of sand. I rubbed at them and leaned my head back against the wall. Tears began to roll down my chapped cheeks. If Gabe said anything after that, I wasn't awake to hear it.

• • •

Marshall had been expecting unwanted visitors and thus had planned to be gone by the time they showed up. The rumor mill had been chirping for weeks. Insurrection was in the air. Paulie K. wasn't in his beloved Fresno right now. He was in Oregon, looking for Marshall. Marshall knew it wouldn't be long before he showed up. The Brotherhood had more leaks and cliques than a woven basket, and all of them said that Marshall was about to either offer up a scapegoat or become one. No middle ground.

Marshall had just loaded the last of his gear into his car and then returned to the office for a final check. He was about to leave the storefront he'd been using for an office since he'd been forced to flee the Conway mess, when they arrived like a thunderstorm. A low roar in the distance at first, then the unmistakable crack of chain lightning. The rumble of Harleys still hung heavy in the air when the door banged open.

Paulie K. burst into the room wearing a World War II German helmet and a full-length leather duster, right out of the friggin' movies, followed by a couple of morons replete with long goatish chin whiskers and enough German insignia to rattle when they moved. Not exactly keeping it low-key, as Marshall's directive had demanded.

"Goin' someplace?" Paulie sneered. "That why you ain't been taking my calls?"

Marshall thought about lecturing Paulie on the need to maintain a low profile but decided against it. These were not reasonable men.

"I'm taking your suggestion," Marshall said evenly. "I'm going to take care of Waterman myself."

"Where?"

"San Diego."

Paulie K. laughed out loud. "You think you still got it in you?" he scoffed.

"Sometimes one must lead from the front."

"Do your leading real quick, Marshall." He jerked a thumb back over his shoulder, toward the pair of Aryan assholes plugging up the doorway. "At this point, lotta these boys just as soon take it out on you personally."

"I'll handle it," Marshall assured him.

"You better," Paulie said.

Marshall pushed his way past Paulie's minions, walked out to the car, got in, and drove off. It had started to rain. He watched in the bleary mirror as they turned and disappeared back into the storefront.

Marshall had the wipers on high and had nearly reached the paved road when he came upon a blue Ford Focus sitting unoccupied in the middle of the driveway. Facing out toward the street. Blocking his way. He tapped the horn. Waited. Nothing. Tapped it again. Still nothing. He got out of the car and walked over to the other vehicle. The rain hammered the surrounding forest. The sharp snap of a twig jerked Marshall's head around. His lungs turned to stone.

For a nanosecond he didn't recognize the man. Looked like a monk or something. Marshall thought the man standing at the edge of the forest wearing a hooded plastic poncho was pointing a green plastic pop bottle at him. Wasn't until the figure spoke that it all snapped into place, and Marshall's insides caught fire.

"That's the trouble with fanatics like you, Mr. Marshall. Somewhere inside, you really believe that everybody feels like you do but is too scared to say it out loud."

"Garrett," leaked from Marshall's lips as the shrouded figure began to move his way. "Is there—"

"You just can't help thinking everyone else is as incompetent and dishonest as you are. It's what gets you out of bed in the morning. That feeling that you're somehow better than other people. That somehow you've been cheated by fate."

"I don't understand," Marshall muttered.

"Yes you do," Garrett said. "It's all tied up in that stupid master-race shit of yours."

Marshall began to blubber. "I've got money," he said.

"Show me," Garrett said.

Marshall put his hand on the door handle. Garrett stepped closer. Using only his fingers, Marshall pulled his briefcase from behind the seat and set it on the roof of the car. He slipped the latch, reached inside, and pulled out the blue bank bag containing the Brotherhood's last sixty-three thousand bucks.

"You can have it."

"You shouldn't have tried to cheat me," Garrett said.

"We've got a holy mission here. Sometimes one must—" was as far as he got before the first bullet hit him about an inch and a half below his navel. With the pop bottle taped over the muzzle, the little automatic was nearly silent. Both the report and Marshall's frantic scream were swallowed by the relentless drumming of the Northwest rain.

Marshall dropped to his knees, holding his belly like a child, rocking it as if to put the burning pain to sleep.

Garrett walked over and stood directly over him. When Marshall turned his rain-beaded face upward, Garrett shot him in the forehead. Marshall flopped over onto his side, still holding his belly. His glasses were covered with raindrops, but his sightless blue eyes still seemed to be searching the horizon for relief.

Garrett dropped the gun onto Marshall's lifeless body, picked up the bank bag, turned, walked back to the rental Focus, and got in.

He used his final disposable phone to call the Oregon State Police and report the body. After a quick stop at a FedEx outlet, he was back in the car.

He stopped at the first rest area he came to on the interstate, found the public pay phone, and called his wife.

"It's me," he said as soon as she picked up.

"Hi, honey," she cooed.

"I'll be home in the morning."

"Ooooh, great," she said. "Don't forget. We've got Robert's middle school parent-teacher conference tomorrow night. He'd be so disappointed if you missed it."

"I'll Uber it from the airport."

"Oooooh . . . what about the carpenters? Aren't they coming tomorrow?"

"Yes," he said. "But it's all been planned out. By this time tomorrow we'll have a new toolshed just like you wanted. We'll finally be able to put all that stuff in the garage someplace else."

"Can't wait. Wish you were here already," she said.

"Bye, baby," she said.

Fifty minutes later he was reminded how much he disliked the carpet in the Portland International Airport.

. . .

"Come in," the voice boomed from behind the door.

San Diego PD Captain Charles Nailor always wore his full dress uniform. Along with every medal and citation he'd ever won over thirty-five years on the force. Carolyn had always figured he was going for a military look. Problem was, he had so overdone it, he looked more like a fancy hotel doorman.

Carolyn stepped into the room and closed the door behind herself.

Nailor was behind his desk with his hands clasped behind his back, pacing up and down in front of the flag stand.

The two people sitting at the conference table—they had to be Internal Affairs. White man. African American woman. They had that look. That withering of the soul that comes with trading in human misery on a day-to-day basis.

Nailor wasted no time. "Sergeant Saunders, would you prefer to have your union representative present?" he asked.

First off, Carolyn had met with Helen Buffington, her union rep, the day before and thus knew that Helen and her husband had driven up to Big Bear last evening in order to attend some sort of family outing. Secondly, Carolyn had no intention of telling IA anything more newsworthy than the current weather, so it didn't much matter.

"No," she said as she took a seat across from the IA contingent.

He handled the introduction. Sergeants George Dovel and Lauren Edlund. Saunders made it a point not to acknowledge either of them. Instead, she simply rested her elbows on the table.

"How can I help you?" she asked.

From the look of the squirming, they'd expected quite a bit more rigmarole before actually getting started. Sergeant Edlund picked up a handful of paperwork and began tapping it on the table, as if to get it nice and square. Her partner clicked his pen a couple of times.

"You were detained by patrol officers earlier today." Dovel made it a statement rather than a question.

"Yes I was," Carolyn said.

"You were apprehended illegally entering an apartment on Del Monte Ave, in Ocean Beach. Is that so?"

"If you say so," Carolyn said.

"Your failure to cooperate with our—"

Carolyn cut her off. "I'm sitting here, aren't I? I'm answering your questions. You want me to dance for you or what?"

"I want you to tell us what you were doing in that apartment," she snapped.

"Did you have a warrant?" her partner added before Carolyn could answer.

"No," Carolyn said. "I did not."

"Are you presently on administrative leave?"

"Yes I am."

"Prior to going on administrative leave, were you in some way assigned to a case that was in any manner attached to that apartment?"

Carolyn thought about it. A big part of her was inclined to tell them the truth, claim exigent circumstances, and hope for the best, maybe reduce it to a suspension rather than a firing offense, but that would surely be the end of Leo and Gabe's unofficial witness protection program. Another, bigger part of her said they deserved better than that. So all she said was, "No. I was not."

"Did you have the residents' permission to be in their domicile?"

"No," she said.

Dovel and Edlund eyed each other and then stood up in unison. Edlund spoke directly to the captain. "We'll be scheduling a disciplinary hearing for next week," she said. "We will require that the union rep be present." She turned Carolyn's way. "Also, you might—Sergeant Saunders—you might consider hiring outside counsel to represent you."

With that, they gathered up their stuff and grimaced their way out the door.

Nailor sat down in his upholstered chair and rocked back as far as it would go.

"You know, Sergeant, I'm real old school. Watched a lot of departmental politics in my time, and I'm tellin' you, this doesn't bode well for you. It may be time to consider other employment options."

Without another word, Carolyn got to her feet, pushed her chair back under the table, and walked out.

Chapter 16

Bobby and Carlos were in good hands, so we started looking for a way back to San Diego. His name was Frank Feeney. Maybe forty. Denim everything. Tall and skinny as a fence post. Looked like his hide had turned to leather after a lifetime in the desert. He ran a small cattle ranch about thirty miles outside of Baker. A hundred head or so. He'd come into the clinic first thing in the morning to get a flu shot. He was on his way to Barstow to see his sister, who'd just had her third child.

I can't imagine what he must have thought of a pair of greased-up, white-faced strangers trying to hitch a ride with him as far as Barstow, but somewhere beneath the *strong silent type* exterior beat a good heart—something noble that said if a stranger needs help, you pitch in if you can. Almost restored my faith in humanity, he did.

That's how Gabe and I managed to hitch a ride out of Baker. He dropped us off at the Barstow Marine Credit Union on Main Street. What the word *marine* had to do with this arid little community was anybody's guess, but if it worked for them, it worked for me. We said our goodbyes and got the hell out of the sun as quick as we could.

You know what they say about money. How it's not important unless you don't have any. Well . . . we didn't have any. No credit cards either. No ID. No nothing. All I knew was my account number from the Point Loma Credit Union and the last four digits of my Social Security number, and half a dozen phone calls later, I had a couple of grand in my hip pocket and was signing for a rental car from Enterprise.

Three hours later, we left the rental car at the airport and took a cab back to Ocean Beach. First stop in O.B. was at the property management company to borrow a spare key to the apartment. We walked home from there, let ourselves in, and were in the process of taking inventory when a knock sounded on the security door.

Without discussion, Gabe grabbed the chrome automatic and then flattened against the wall behind the door. I pulled it open. Kevin. I snapped the lock and pulled open the inner door.

"Guess what," he said.

"What?"

"That friend of yours—the cop lady."

"What about her?" I asked.

He told us the story about breaking into the apartment.

"They arrested her?"

"Arrested me too."

"Where is she now?"

"No idea. When they found out who she was, they let me go."

"Thanks, man," I said. When he didn't move, I said, "We got a bunch of shit to do here, Kevin. See you later. Thanks again."

I closed the door and hustled into the bedroom, found the bag of burner phones, and dialed her number.

"Yeah."

"It's me," I said.

I heard a big release of breath.

"I was worried about you guys."

"You had every reason to be," I said and told her the story. "What about you?" I asked when I finished.

"I'm gonna get fired."

"Yeah . . . Kevin stopped by," I said.

"I was just about to sign up for LinkedIn," she said.

"We've got a better idea."

"What's that?"

"We're gonna start kicking over rocks and see what slithers out."

"Oh . . . ," she stuttered. "I don't . . . I couldn't . . ."

"What have you got to lose?" I said quickly.

Pin-drop silence.

"I'm in," she said after a moment.

. . .

We used the keys I'd given Carolyn to let ourselves into our overpriced and ill-fated surveillance apartment and then went through it like we were expecting a terrorist attack. I don't know about anybody else, but combat stancing my way through an empty apartment and not finding a damn thing always makes me feel like some special kind of idiot. Sadly, everything was as we'd left it, broken chair and all, except, of course, the camera and recording equipment were long gone. Gabe walked over and looked out the window.

"Where's all the security assholes?" Gabe asked.

I slid in beside Gabe and looked down at the alley behind the cliff house. The alley was empty.

"Nobody in sight," I said. "That's weird."

"Always been at least one guy out there," Gabe added.

"Which means what?" Carolyn prodded.

"Maybe they all went to the movies," I tossed in.

Gabe wagged an angry finger at me. "You remember what Reeves said when they were trussing us up like turkeys?"

"No bruises?"

"Yep, but he also said that what he needed was for us to be gone until Thursday—that's today—and how after that it wasn't going to matter 'cause none of them were gonna be around."

"So whatever the hell they got going on is coming down tonight."

"Not here," Carolyn added. "This is way too public."

Gabe and I nodded in unison. "Lemon Grove," I said.

"Gotta be."

"Sure would explain all that security out in the middle of nowhere."

"Then why have all the security here?" Carolyn asked.

"Maybe we ought to go out to Lemon Grove and find out," Gabe said.

I looked over at Carolyn. She grinned.

"It's like you said, Leo. What have we got to lose?"

Gabe pulled the shiny automatic from the holster and checked the load.

Carolyn did the same with her piece. So as not to be left out, I checked mine too.

As we walked around the block to get to the entrance to the alley, the wind had freshened, and the onshore flow carried water in its pockets. My cheeks were wet after half a block. As we walked, I wondered how history would describe this little scene that was about to play out. The one where the retired PI, the professional leg breaker, and the suspended cop break into the house of one of the richest women in the city and . . . and . . . what?

Fortunately, by the time I'd thought it through that far, we'd reached the Niagara side of the alleyway. The three-story apartment building on the corner blocked the wind from the Pacific. It was suddenly much quieter and somehow far more ominous.

We took our time, moving deliberately, expecting at every step that somebody would pop out the front door or from one of the alleys. Nobody's hand was far from their weapon. About a third of the way there, one of the garage doors on the far side of the alley began to rise in a series of rumbles and squeaks.

We froze as a white Mercedes backed out of the garage, closed the door, and headed down the alley in our direction. God knows what it must have looked like to the driver. Three deer in the headlights, hands poised at their belts, looking about as furtive as humanly possible. Instinctively, we turned our faces away until the Mercedes rolled out of sight. Nothing to hide here. No sir.

We were within camera range now. That much was for sure, and yet nobody came out of the house to confront us. Our pace got less leisurely. More of a dog trot as we neared the front door. When Gabe and Carolyn paused at the bottom of the stairs, I shouldered my way between them and gave the front door several hard raps. Nothing. Not a peep.

I looked up at our rental apartment. The window was blank and bare. I checked all the windows facing the alley. I couldn't swear nobody was lurking in the darkness, but, superficially at least, we seemed to have the alley to ourselves.

I knocked again. Harder and longer this time. Still nothing.

I leaned on the door. First with my shoulder. Then with my hip, right before I dug my feet in and gave it some serious effort. The door began to groan and pop. The minute Gabe put a shoulder into it, a ripping sound slashed through the alley like a whiplash as the door frame was torn asunder and peeled inward.

We had another Maalox moment as we waited for an alarm to begin clanging. When it didn't, we cringed away from the daggerlike splinters sticking out from the door frame and followed one another over the threshold into a dark entrance hall. My first thought after looking around was that all this place was missing was a suit of armor and maybe a stuffed wildebeest or two. Very stodgy, mahogany paneling, dark box ceiling, lots of heavy oak doors. Your classic haunted house.

Carolyn headed for the nearest closet, pulled the door open, and stepped partially inside. Ten seconds passed before her head poked out.

"The alarm system's turned off," she announced.

I snapped on the hall lights.

"Probably means they ain't coming back," Gabe offered.

"Also means the only people they want to see less than us are the cops. You want the cops to show, you leave the system turned on."

The ocean side of the house was one large frilly front parlor looking out over the frothy Pacific Ocean. Whoever'd picked the wall art really liked flowers. A swinging door at the north end led to an industrial-strength kitchen, then a formal dining room and an office area up by the street that looked like it got a bit more use than the rest of the house. Across the hall was a rather luxurious study. Plush leather sofa, couple of Eames chairs, and a solid wood desk that looked like it must have weighed five hundred pounds. Snakelike tangles of wires said the phones and computers had been hastily removed.

We were on our way upstairs when Carolyn noticed the six-panel door under the stairs. "Where's this go to?" she asked as much to herself as to one of us.

I grabbed the knob. Locked. I didn't hesitate. Just stepped back a pace, turned my back to the door, and put a size 13 mule kick into the middle of the damn thing. It swung inward, bounced off the wall so hard it reclosed itself. I pushed it open again and peered inside. Dark as hell. Old wooden stairs going down.

"Basement," I announced.

On my left a light switch was attached to the stone foundation wall. I flipped it. That's when I saw the feet. Barely visible in the circle of light at the bottom of the stairs. A pair of brown brogans. Scuffed and unmoving.

I grabbed the wooden rail in my right hand and started down the narrow treads. Halfway to the bottom I could make out the outline of the person wearing the shoes. When I saw another light switch, I flipped it too. And there he was. Tweed coat and all. Would have appeared to be sleeping except that his head was completely turned around backward. Maybe two hundred degrees off straight ahead. The sight stopped me in my tracks. I shivered. Carolyn bumped into my back and then Gabe into hers.

"Heads don't do that," Gabe said.

"It's Trager," I said. "Looks like the doc's made his last house call."

I let myself wander down the last five stairs. Carolyn and Gabe spread out on the concrete floor on either side of me. The doctor's gladstone bag was lying open on the floor, its contents fallen this way and that. Vials and needles and bandages and whatever a defrocked doctor carried around with him.

I bent at the waist.

"Don't touch anything," Carolyn hissed.

I pulled my hand back.

Gabe squatted and looked closely at the doctor's neck. "Snapped his neck in two. Gotta be Reeves, showing off how strong he is."

Carolyn piped in. "Getting rid of Trager was not the worst idea they ever had either. He was definitely the weak link."

We turned off the lights as we made our way upstairs and closed the basement door. The central staircase was wide enough for the three of us to climb abreast of one another. Three doors on either side of the hall and another at the far end.

We moved down the hall, checking the rooms as we came to them. Each side of the carpeted corridor had two bedrooms with a shared bathroom between. All of them were dusty and empty and smelling like nobody'd opened a window in years.

The door at the far end was locked but not for long. I mule kicked it open on the first try. The minute the door blew open, all three of us froze in our tracks. Flowers everywhere. The wallpaper, the curtains, the bedspread, the weave of the carpet. Flowers. And yet that's not what drew our eyes. What commanded our attention was the full-size freezer whirring away at the foot of the empty bed. I nearly burst out laughing.

"Gotta be," Gabe said with a cynical remnant of a smile.

"Yeah," I said. "That would explain a lot of things."

"You think . . . ?" Carolyn asked.

"Have a look," Gabe suggested.

We stayed where we were as Carolyn crossed the room and stood for a moment staring down at the freezer. For the second time today, it occurred to me that this whole thing had a horror-movie quality to it. I imagined some scaly hand coming out of the frozen mist, grabbing her by the throat and then pulling her inside.

Carolyn reached down and flicked the chrome latch, then used both hands to pry the iced-up lid open. A cloud of frozen vapor rose from the freezer. Carolyn swooshed it away from her face, waited for the cloud to clear, and bent her head toward the interior.

She immediately recoiled. She looked over at the two of us with hard eyes, then gestured with her head that maybe we should bring ourselves over there.

"Jesus," she breathed. "They didn't even wrap her up or anything."

As I'd never met, nor so much as seen a picture of, Mrs. Haller, I could only assume that the old lady lying there in the fetal position was her. The only thing I was sure of was that whoever was lying there scrunched up was the poster child for freezer burn. The body itself was iced over solid. Looked like it had been in there for eons. Nearly petrified at this point. Like those steaks I would occasionally lose in the family freezer and find years later looking like old wooden shingles. Only the frosty, medium-length gray hair and the brightly flowered dressing gown said it was an older woman. The rest of it was nearly unrecognizable.

"We've gotta call this in," Carolyn said.

"No hurry. She and the doc ain't goin' anywhere," Gabe muttered.

"Forensics has to—"

"Let's check the rest of the place first," I suggested.

I wiped the handle and the top of the freezer clean of prints and closed it, and we carefully closed the broken door behind us, as if to leave her in icy peace.

Took us a few tries to figure out how to get into the sheds on either side of the house. At either end of the front parlor, doors I had assumed to be closets opened out into the alleys between buildings and thus into the sheds. Funny thing was, they were completely empty. Not a net or a buoy or anything vaguely nautically related. Even the floors were swept clean.

"So where's all that fishing stuff they supposedly been bringing across the border?" I asked. "Twenty loads or so. That's a big pile of stuff we're talking about. These things ought to be full up to the rafters."

"Charity said the only parts of the Haller trust that hadn't been sold off in the past year and a half were this property here and the one out in Lemon Grove, which, if we're to believe Mrs. Haller's son, they don't have clear title to, because his trust fund says he gets a share."

We let ourselves back into the front parlor and then followed the wide hall back to the front of the house.

"They left in a big damn hurry," Gabe noted as we walked by the study and what must have been an office for the second time. Things had literally been ripped from the walls. Drawers had been hastily emptied. Wastebaskets overturned. Nothing personal anywhere.

"Social services was coming tomorrow on an elder abuse complaint," Carolyn said. "Friday morning at ten thirty."

"How do you know that?" I asked.

"Because *I'm* the one who filed the complaint, and because I spoke with them on the phone. You know, trying to hurry their asses up. They were showing up with their own doctor and a court order allowing them to see Mrs. Haller in person. They'd already notified Pemberton. He wasn't a bit happy about it."

"So the party was over," Gabe said. "Whatever the hell it is they got going on is over the minute social services gets here on Friday."

"If Charity's right, they been selling things off for quite a while now. I'm thinkin' maybe we just accelerated their schedule all of a sudden."

"What about the dead kid?" I asked. "Remember him? Isn't that how this whole thing started?"

"What about Pope and Greenway? Who offed them?" Gabe asked. "Eagen said somebody popped John Henry Marshall yesterday. Who did that? All we really got is that Reeves works for both places and could

HEAVY ON THE DEAD

probably, with a little help, get that kid's body to the spot where it was found, and that whatever scam these people are running makes them real paranoid about people stickin' their noses into their business. Other than the fact that they're a bunch of murderous bastards, we don't know one damn thing for sure.

"Seems like either they outsmarted us and got outta Dodge in the nick of time, or they've still got the final act to play out," Gabe said.

"It's not much," Carolyn said. "Nothing we can take to the authorities."

"Let's take a ride instead," I suggested.

"Where?" Carolyn looked grim.

"Lemon Grove," Gabe and I said in unison.

Chapter 17

The porch light snapped on. I watched as the knob turned, and then the door cracked open as far as the brass chain would allow. Her eyes were nearly black. At least the one I could see through the narrow opening. I was about to ask if she remembered us, but she beat me to the punch.

"You two sure been workin' on your tans," she said.

"After a fashion," Gabe muttered.

The door closed. I heard the chain rattle and then watched as the door swung open. She gave Carolyn a curt nod and then turned her attention back to Gabe and me.

"What brings you back to these parts?"

"We've got a serious bone to pick with Mr. Reeves," I said.

"You do look a bit overcooked," she said, stifling a smile.

"That's what the bone's about," I told her.

"Reeves and his friends left us out in the desert to die," Gabe said.

She thought it over. "You two seem to have a nose for trouble," she said after a while. She gestured at the house at the bottom of the hill. The yard lights were on, casting long, interlaced shadows across the ground. "You mean to cause trouble for Reeves?"

"As much as we're able," Gabe assured her.

"Good," she said. "Big doings down there today. Several big rigs pulled in earlier. Had cars coming and going ever since sun up. Bunch of 'em."

The deep rumble of a diesel engine caught everyone's attention. As the smoke-spewing stacks appeared at the top of the hill, she said,

"Another one." We watched as the rest of the cab and then the trailer rolled over the rise and into view.

The driver took one look at the steep hill and began feathering the air brakes. Squeaking and hissing his way down at about one mile an hour.

I looked over at the woman. "If all hell breaks loose, call the cops," I said.

Some things don't require discussion. We instinctively knew we were never going to get a better chance than this. Without a word, all three of us crossed to the south side of the street and began inching our way downhill, moving furtively among the cactus and shrubbery, from house to house, yard to yard, watching the eighteen-wheeler, brakes screaming and steaming and whining, until it turned right at the bottom and rolled slowly toward the gate over on the side of the grove. We trotted alongside, with the trailer between us and the cameras, too close to the trailer to show up in his mirrors.

When the truck turned left onto the gateway, we hurried over to the south side of the dirt road and threw ourselves over the edge. By the time I belly crawled back up to where I could see again, somebody had pulled open the gate and was using a flashlight to direct the truck through the opening.

I reached out and grabbed Carolyn by the shoulder and started scooting along the embankment until the truck was once again between us and the guy with the flashlight, then crawled up onto the dirt road and scampered over to the far side of the truck, staying even with the trailer wheels so our feet wouldn't be visible from the other side.

That's how we got through the gate. Tiptoeing along in lockstep with the trailer until the gate started to close behind us, at which point we all took off running toward the long metal shed at the back of the property.

We stood shoulder to shoulder, backs plastered against the corrugated metal siding, huffing and puffing from the exertion, listening hard for any indication that we might have been seen. None came. Just the steady rattle of the diesel creeping along.

I stepped around Gabe and peeked around the corner. The semi was backing up toward what appeared to be the largest building on the property. Two eighteen wheelers were still backed into the brightly lit opening, as the guy with the flashlight kept walking and urging the driver backward with the light.

Out at the front gate, a car was easing out onto Santa Rosa Street. They'd gotten about a third of the way to the top of the hill when another car, coming in the other direction, lit 'em up like a ballgame. Two adults in front. Biggest one driving. Looked like the silhouette of a kid in the back. The car coming our way nosed up to the gate, which slid out of the way, allowing the car to drive into the yard and around the circle.

I levitated about a foot and a half off the ground when Gabe tapped my shoulder and pointed at the short chain-link fence behind us. I walked over and looked down into the canyon on the far side of the fence. Took my eyes a while to sort out the huge tangle. Lobster traps, big purse seiner nets, ropes, pulleys, buoys, floats, several old wooden dories bottoms up. Coupla metal net tenders. All the fishing equipment they were supposedly bringing back to the States for sale, dumped in a huge pile down at the bottom of the ravine.

"Pssst," Carolyn hissed, pointing around the corner. I hurried back over and snuck a peek. The driver was out of the truck. Smoking a cigarette. Pemberton was standing in the yard, talking to him.

"If they're not running fishing gear, what's in the trucks?" Gabe asked.

"Dope," I suggested.

Carolyn shook her head. "It's not like you can just start up a large-scale drug business in Mexico. You start moving any real weight, one of the cartels is going to be up your butt so far you'll be able to smell hair gel. And once they get involved, what you're most likely to end up is dead." She made a throat-slashing gesture. "You and everybody you know. Those people don't give a shit."

I had an idea, pulled my burner phone out of my pocket, and scrolled back through the numbers I'd called in the past week until I came to the one Gabe had gotten from the woman at the Tijuana dump. The one she called when she had a kid to deliver. I dialed it and then peeked around the corner.

My eyes found Pemberton in the semidarkness. I watched as he reached into his pocket and pulled out his oversize phone. Looked like he was holding a piece of toast in his hand. He stared at the screen and then poked a finger at it. I hung up. He stuffed the phone back into his pocket, said something to the driver, and walked quickly out of sight.

"Kids," I said. "They're selling kids."

Carolyn looked over my shoulder at the screen. "That's the same restricted number we tried to look up the other day."

"Yep," I said.

Gabe: "We gotta have a look inside the building there."

I knew what Gabe was thinking. This was the point where things were about to get hairy. We were trespassing. Carrying unregistered firearms with a suspended police sergeant covering our backs. Under normal circumstances, if anybody got shot, all three of us were looking at hard time. San Quentin. Some sketchy shit like that.

If, on the other hand, these guys were running a human-trafficking ring and we could bring the heat down on their heads and save some of these kids from fates I didn't even want to think about, then all bets were probably off. We could kill all of them and most likely walk away. Hard time vs. heroism. No middle ground.

I pointed down the narrow space between the chain-link fence and the back of the building. Gabe began moving that way. Carolyn fell in behind as they edged their way through the thick, waist-high field grass, sidestepping along the corrugated metal, until Gabe went down with a thud. Gone in a whoosh. Carolyn and I hurried to the spot where Gabe had disappeared. An eight-foot section of the embankment had eroded itself down into the canyon, leaving a gaping hole between the building and the fence. Gabe was folded up in the bottom of the pit, looking up at me and shaking that big head in disgust.

"You okay?" I whispered.

"Other than the heartbreak of psoriasis," Gabe growled and struggled to one knee.

"Moderate to severe?" I asked.

"Of course."

Gabe raised a hand. I took ahold and heaved for all I was worth. From there on, we moved more carefully, pawing like blind horses, making certain of our footing as we inched down toward the end of the building. I dropped to one knee and peered around the corner.

The big building had four windows on the back side, throwing bright-white chevrons of light across the browned-out grass. Carolyn didn't hesitate; she took off running, covering the distance in about five seconds and then sitting down with her back to the building, motioning us forward. Gabe and I lumbered over.

All three of us duckwalked under the first window, getting out of the light and into the deep shadows. Gabe kept going down to the next window. Carolyn moved on to the next.

I flattened myself against the building and peeped around the corner of the window as if Methuselah himself were probably going to be staring back at me.

Big, huge room. Probably where they used to store the grove's farm equipment. Except now . . . it was . . . I was at a loss for words . . . couldn't decide whether it looked like a room full of storage units or the biggest dog kennel I'd ever seen. I looked over at Gabe, who was, not coincidentally, looking at me. Gabe's face bent into a question. *Are you shitting me?* it said.

They were chain-link enclosures. Maybe forty of them. Eight by eight by eight. About two-thirds of which were filled with kids. My eyes took it in. I had a ready-made label for everything I was looking at, but on some deeper level, a part of me refused to process the sight into a coherent whole. *Selling kids,* some voice kept screaming at me. *Are you fucking kidding me . . . you can't be serious . . . you can't be . . .*

That's the point where the door on the far side opened up and five people came into the room. What looked like a couple of the security types leading the way, Reeves, Pemberton or whoever the hell he was, and some fat little rat-faced guy I'd never seen before.

Reeves and the two security mopes walked halfway down the front row of cages. The taller of the two security types walked over to the wall, opened the door of the gray electrical box, checked the box, checked the cage number, and threw the switch up. Wasn't till the other guy frog-walked her kicking and screaming out into the aisle that I could get an unobstructed view. Somewhere between ten and twelve years old, wearing what looked like a long white nightshirt. Reeves grabbed her around the middle, hoisted her up onto his hip, and carried her out into the middle of the space. She was screeching as he carried her along and then finally set her on her bare feet in front of the fat guy.

I wasn't prepared for what happened next. As the new guy stepped up close to her, Reeves reached down, put his hands on her shoulders, and pulled the nightshirt up over her head and off. She was standing there naked, sobbing so loud I could hear her hiccupping hysteria through the closed window.

It was all I could do not to lose it and kill somebody right then and there. My head felt like it was going to explode as I forced myself to watch the guy reach into his pants pocket and pull out a thick envelope. He handed it to Pemberton, who opened it up and fingered his way through the contents.

With a nod from Pemberton, Reeves stuffed her back into the nightshirt in the moment before the security duo lifted her from the ground by the elbows and began carrying her toward the door at the front of the building.

I made a *stay where you are* gesture with my hand. Carolyn and Gabe nodded in the semidarkness. Then I turned my back and hurried back to the south corner. I peeked around. The three semis were still lined up there. I trotted over to the first truck, ducked around the front, then around the second one, and finally around the third.

I got there just in time to see the two security slugs force the girl into the back seat of a new Cadillac Escalade. I had to clamp a hand over my mouth while I watched the Cadillac drive across the yard and out the gate. I wanted to scream at the taillights to stop as they bounced over the top of the hill and winked from view.

When my lungs remembered how to work, I hurried back around the trucks. Gabe and Carolyn had moved down to my end of the building. I slid to a halt and knelt down beside them. "This is a fucking drive-up window. People are showing up and taking kids with them," I said. "We gotta keep that from happening. God knows where they might end up. We'll never be able to find them again." I swung my arm in a short arc. "I mean . . . I don't see these motherfuckers keeping any kind of records about where they send these kids."

"Nobody else leaves this place," Gabe said. "Not one fucking kid."

"Did you see what that asshole did?" Carolyn asked.

"Don't remind me," I snapped.

"When he . . ."

At that point I gave up any pretense of adult behavior and clamped both hands over my ears. If she hadn't shut up, I'd have started yammering like a monkey.

Might have been better if we'd talked about it. Gotten it out of our systems. As it was, each of us was left with nothing but the psycho conjuring of our own minds, where unwelcome images looked a lot like unseemly desires—where black-and-white nudie pictures boiled up from some steamy caldron we'd never admit to putting on the stove.

I had just pushed myself to my feet when the lights in the big room suddenly went out. I peeked inside. A single mercury-vapor light high on the metal wall cast a ghostly purple shadow over the interior.

I was still figuring out what to do next when headlights swept over the yard. I heard the gate clatter closed. Heard a car door slam shut and muffled chitchat.

Carolyn crawled to my side. "Kids first," she whispered. "We need to get the kids out of harm's way before we do anything else."

I looked at her hard. "This is where the rubber meets the road," I said. "I'll understand if you don't want any part of this." When she didn't say anything, I kept talking. "I only know two things here. One, I'm not letting these assholes take any of these kids anywhere. And two, I'm not letting anybody shoot me if I can help it—and I can help it." I pulled my weapon out of my waistband.

She was shaking her head as if she were having an argument with herself—and losing. "I wanted to be a cop since I was ten. I can't imagine doing anything else for a living." She pulled her weapon from her waist. "And I'm not leaving these kids here either," she said. "Let's go."

I turned toward Gabe. "I'll get to the panel and unlock everybody. You tell 'em we're the good guys and that we're gonna get them out of here."

"How we gonna get 'em outta here?" Gabe growled. "Ain't like we can do a Pied Piper routine with 'em."

I thought about it. "One of the trucks, maybe," was the best I could come up with.

Gabe opened the door of the nearest truck and heaved up into the cab. A second later Gabe hit the ground with both feet. "No keys."

Carolyn took the cue and climbed up into the truck in the middle. "Keys are in it," she stage whispered.

"Can you drive one of these?" I asked Gabe, who laughed in my face. "I could barely shift that damn pickup truck."

"I can drive it," Carolyn said.

The look on our faces gave her the urge to explain. "I drove a garbage truck when I was an undergrad. Three years. Paying off those damn loans. I can drive the damn thing." She pointed at Gabe and wagged a finger. "And you, of all people—you really ought to lose that *but you're a girl* look on your face."

Gabe managed a grudging grunt and headed for the back of the truck, where we opened the overhead as quietly as we were able and then slid the built-in ramp out onto the concrete floor.

I duckwalked around the front of the first truck and peered down the space between it and the next trailer. Gabe was close enough that I could hear a round jacked into the chamber as I crawled along. Once I made it to the back of the trailer, I got to my feet. Gabe was hard by my right elbow.

"You ready?" I asked. When nobody answered, I took that for a yes. Rather than crawl or attempt to hide us from any cameras that might be filming, I took off for the far side of the room at a lope, keeping my gun up by my right shoulder and my eyes glued to the door at the north end of the building.

I skidded to a stop in front of the electrical box, jerked open the door, and used my left palm to flip every damn switch in sight. The air filled with the clatter of electric locks snapping open. Somewhere in the semidarkness several children began to cry out.

Gabe was talking to the kids in Spanish now. Moving down the rows of cages, repeating the message over and over, moving slowly, making sure everybody heard.

Most of the kids seemed paralyzed, but three or four of the older ones opened their unlocked doors themselves and started moving our way, an action that seemed to embolden many of the others to do the same thing.

They looked like angels in that faltering light. A line of white cherubs first walking and then running headlong toward the rear of the building, Gabe jogging alongside encouraging them in Spanish.

That's when the door popped open. I can't tell you whose head it was, but I can say I definitely used my gun to make a serious dent in the top of the head. He must have been holding the knob at the moment of impact because the door slammed closed as the slug drove him backward, a series of actions that seemed to seriously discourage further peeping.

Out in the middle of the cage compound, two of the kids were frozen in place by fear. I ran that way, stuffing my gun back into my waistband on the way. I grabbed a little girl around the waist and hauled her up onto my hip. She was screaming like a thousand seagulls and wiggling like a beached eel when I heaved the other kid up onto my other hip and started running toward the rear exit.

My vision was bouncing up and down like a tennis ball as I covered the distance. I caught a glimpse of children running up the ramp like angels ascending to heaven in the nanosecond before I saw Gabe lift that shiny automatic and let loose with three rounds. Behind me someone began making noises like a gored matador. I had no idea what was going on behind me or what Gabe was shooting at, but I was real glad it wasn't me.

I heard the sound of Carolyn starting the engine, watched the smoke blowing out the pipes as the revving truck rocked on its springs. Gabe was launching kids up into the trailer as I arrived. One of the older boys reached down and, with the aid of a friend, took one of the little kids from me. Gabe grabbed the other and hoisted him up.

I jumped and grabbed the door, using both hands and all my body weight to roll it closed. Gabe snapped the latch. We jammed the ramp back into the back of the trailer and then I started sprinting up the side of the truck.

"Go, go," I was screaming. "Go, go . . ."

Carolyn didn't require further encouragement. The cab's tires chattered and then burned serious rubber as the engine strained to get the trailer in motion. I watched the big rig bounce across the yard, shifting up, gaining speed as it approached the side gate. The prospect of a closed gate failed to dim Carolyn's ardor. She not only took out the gate but about six feet of adobe wall on either side of the opening. Damn thing exploded like it had taken a mortar shell.

I watched, breathless, as she crimped the wheel hard to the right and skidded the cab around the corner. The trailer swung wildly one way and then the other, looked maybe like it was going to roll up onto its side but straightened itself in the last second and roared off, trailer's ass end shimmying like a hula dancer.

In my peripheral vision, a running figure bolted into view. Must have been the guy from the front gate. I snapped a shot off in that direction but missed. The guy dropped to one knee and returned fire. So close to my face, I felt the buzz on my cheek as it passed.

A loud report numbed my right ear. The guy out in the yard went down in an irregular heap. I looked left. Gabe was reloading. When I snapped my eyes back to the yard, the front gate guy was back up. Moving in slow motion, dragging one leg behind him like a stubborn puppy as he inched back out of view.

Carolyn had downshifted into granny gear and was roaring up the hill at all of three miles an hour. A sudden fuselage of fire erupted from the other end of the building. I hit the deck as the garage door frame began to come apart. Pieces of wood and metal filled the air around my head. I crawled out the entrance, keeping the trucks between me and the yawning garage door. Another volley sent me diving to the ground, hands covering my head like some caveman ducking a shillelagh.

The gatekeeper limped back into view. I rested my arm on the dirt, took a deep breath, and touched off a round. He went down again. This time he stayed there.

Gabe crawled out from under the other semi and stood up. Carolyn was about two-thirds of the way up the hill when suddenly the brake lights came on. The trailer stopped moving. Then the white backup lights. And then that fucking beeping they do when they're backing up. I could hear it all the way from down here.

She was backing the truck into somebody's driveway. That was as far as I got before Gabe sidestepped over, grabbed me by the collar, and started dragging me toward the front yard. Shouts echoed in the night air. The sound of an engine starting. Another volley. More shouts and shots rang from the darkness.

I twisted loose, ran over, and knelt by the gatekeeper's side. I rolled him over and separated him from the big black automatic he'd been carrying.

"How many you got left?" I asked Gabe.

"Two."

I tossed Gabe the gatekeeper's gun. "Let's get the fuck outta here," I said.

We took off running for the front gate. Halfway across the yard, the lights hissed on. We were lit up like a birthday cake. Not only that, but the gate was closed. Bullets buzzed through the air like angry wasps as we hurled ourselves forward, running past the front gate, over to the enormous ficus tree at the front corner of the yard.

The base of the tree must have been five feet across. No bark. Smooth as a baby's ass. I lay on my stomach as they began pouring ammo in our direction. I steadied myself and touched off a round at the next muzzle flash I saw. And then another.

Must have hit something, because the second one sure pissed somebody off. A few seconds later they started throwing enough fire our way to start a military coup. I rolled over behind the tree trunk and let them exercise their trigger fingers. The tree was *très* stout. You could have worked it over with a howitzer and it wouldn't have given an inch. I felt like apologizing to all the ficus plants I'd mistreated over the years.

Leaves were floating down upon us like green hail. A sudden flash of headlights swung across the yard. Looked like a prison break. The shattered gate yawned as a pair of cars came sweeping out from behind the house. Two of them. One behind the other, coming hard in our direction. A gleaming burgundy Jag was leading the way across the yard. Backlit by the second car's headlights, the driver's thick silhouette told me it hadda be Reeves behind the wheel.

I used the tree to steady my hand and put two through the Jag's windshield. Passenger side. Both of them. Damn. The phalanx veered sharp right, starting a wide circle of the front yard, swinging around so's they could have a straight run at the gate.

I stepped out from behind the tree. I only had four rounds left in the gun. I looked over my shoulder, out through the jagged gate. A line of white caught my eye.

Carolyn was unloading the kids. Probably at the gardening lady's house. Way in the distance, the wail of a siren began. I saw Carolyn run along the side of the trailer and hop up into the driver's seat. Heard the roar of the big diesel.

The screeching of tires pulled my eyes back to the yard. The cars were negotiating a one-eighty, dodging among the dead trees and concrete planters as they swung back this way. The last car didn't quite make it. It hit one of the planters head-on. Blew the planter to pieces but really fucked up the car. They lurched forward another six feet and then got lodged on a concrete shard. The Toyota wagon was billowing steam and smoke like a calliope. I watched as all four doors swung open and a quartet of long shadows began hightailing it for the darkness of the side gate.

That was the good news. The bad news was that the other vehicle had successfully slalomed through the grove, gotten itself lined up on the gate, and was now rolling at it like a ground-to-ground missile.

Gabe stepped around me. Feet planted wide. Weapon pointing straight up at the sky. The Mount Rushmore facial expression told me all I needed to know.

"Let 'em go," I said. "Sounds like the cops are on the way."

"Motherfucker tried to kill us," Gabe said.

"Ain't worth dying over," I said through clenched teeth.

The scream of shredding metal jerked my attention back up the hill. If the agonized grinding sound were not sufficient, then the eight-foot fountain of sparks following the truck down the hill erased all doubt.

Carolyn was barreling down the hill. She hadn't bothered to slide the ramp back into the truck, creating a tongue of sparks and fire lapping at the ass of the trailer as it roared down the slope. When I heard her shift into high gear, I grabbed Gabe by the belt and began struggling back toward the ficus tree. Gabe dug in and turned fierce eyes on me. For a second, I thought I might get shot, but the fountain of sparks and fire rocketing our way kidnapped Gabe's attention. I watched Gabe's head swing from the hill to the yard and back. A small crooked smile showed itself.

"Crazy bitch is gonna kill 'em all," Gabe said.

We ran like hell and threw ourselves behind the tree trunk about five seconds before the eighteen-wheeler met the Jag about six feet outside the gate. Sounded like a bomb went off. The impact catapulted the Jag into the air, somersaulting it backward, crushing the roof in the second before the oncoming truck smashed into it again, driving it back into the yard like waste before the wind, rolling the car over longwise a couple of times. The yard was filled with torn metal, swirling dust, and the maniacal glinting safety glass.

The front half of the Jag was crushed flat. What remained was wedged under the front bumper of the truck, which showed no signs of losing momentum. I caught a glimpse of Carolyn in the driver's seat as she roared by. The set of her jaw told me she still had the pedal to the metal.

Gabe and I stepped out from behind the tree and began trotting along behind the screeching pile of moving magma. The car's carcass was shedding wheels and plastic and pieces of metal, forcing Gabe and me to bob and weave to avoid getting clipped by a piece of flying debris.

When the big rig drove the car completely through the corrugated front wall of the building, the truck finally began to slow. The nearest section of the building's roof collapsed; the truck slammed into the pile of broken debris and finally bumped to a halt. The air brakes heaved a hissy sigh. Something metal fell to the floor with a clang. And then it went quiet.

We were running now. The symphony of sirens filled my head. The hill was ablaze with red-and-blue light bars. All the cops in the world. At least two fire trucks. I turned back and began to pull twisted metal siding out of my way. Pitching things aside as we worked our way up the cab of the truck. Gabe squatted beneath a fallen roof beam, lifting it high enough for me to sneak beneath on my hands and knees. I crawled along the side of the trailer until I came to the cab step, then stood up and grabbed the door handle. Locked.

I climbed up onto the step, pulled off my shirt, wrapped it around my arm, and slammed it into the glass. Hurt like hell. On the third blow, the window disintegrated. I reached through and opened the door from the inside. I grabbed the steering wheel and pulled myself up into the cab.

She was still strapped in. Out cold. Big bruised knot glowing purple on her forehead. Broken nose hosing thick blood down her shirtfront. I put my hand on her chest. She was breathing evenly. I unsnapped her seat belt harness and laid her down on the seat. I slid her over and sat down on the seat next to her.

I heaved a sigh and tried to compose myself. I was doing pretty well. Breathing deep and massaging the back of my neck, until I looked out through the truck's cracked windshield. The scene was like a crimson jigsaw puzzle—fragmented—some assembly required.

The Jag's roof had been torn off sometime during the crash. What looked like two bags of stew meat were seeping their bloody way through the back seats. The only thing recognizable inside the Jag was sitting behind the wheel. Looked like the initial impact had driven the steering column completely through Reeves's chest, pinning him to the seat like an insect specimen. The horrified look on his face told the tale. He'd seen it coming. He'd had one of those *come to Jesus* moments right before he got kabobbed. Probably didn't say much about me as a person, but I was glad.

■ ■ ■

Garrett paid the cab driver and was waving bye-bye when his wife came bouncing down the front steps. She threw an arm around his waist as they watched the driver back out into the street and motor off.

The lawn was a carpet of fallen leaves. He made a mental note to call the gardener first thing in the morning.

"The kids?" Garrett asked.

"At my mom's."

"Did the . . ."

"FedEx brought the package this morning. It's in your office."

"Good."

"Quite a bit more than we anticipated," she commented.

"Things got a little hinky," he told her. "A service charge became necessary."

Garrett had his suitcase in one hand and his wife in the other as they climbed the front stairs and went into the house. He stopped by the master bedroom and put his suitcase on the padded leather bench at the end of the bed, then headed across the hall to his office.

"What time is the parent-teacher conference?" he asked as he snapped on the overhead light. She told him it was at seven.

"Great. Plenty of time."

He pulled the office chair back from the desk and peeled back the clear plastic runner that kept the chair from ruining the carpet. He used his fingertips to take hold of the carpet pile and lift a square section of carpet, revealing a small safe built into the concrete floor. He sat in the chair, twisted the knob left and right, and pulled open the door. A flat pile of documents covered the bottom of the space; the overnight envelope was wedged in diagonally. He wiggled it out.

He dropped the overnight delivery envelope onto the desktop.

"Sixty-three thousand and fifteen dollars," his wife said.

"There won't be any more calls from Mr. Marshall," he said as he thumbed through the contents without removing them from the envelope.

"Was he dissatisfied with the service?"

"He was just another guy who wanted something for nothing," Garrett said. "Like most of the people in the country these days."

"The world is becoming so uncaring. It's like nobody gives a darn about doing a good job anymore," she said. "If there were more men like you . . ."

He chuckled, replaced the runner and the carpet, and crossed the hall back to the bedroom. "If there were more men like me, there wouldn't be a rush hour anymore."

His wife followed. "Oh . . . stop it," she tittered.

He began removing his clothes and arranging them geometrically on the foot of the bed.

"Run it through your internet company a little bit at a time. Make it disappear."

"I've already started," she assured him.

"I'm going to hop in the shower."

"I got your blue suit back from the cleaners."

"Thanks."

"No place like home," she trilled.

"No toilet like your own," he sighed as he padded off to the en suite.

Chapter 18

Took the better part of two weeks for the dust to settle. In the end, what saved our asses is that it involved little kids. Seems like rescuing twenty-three children from probable sexual slavery more or less absolves a body from any random felonies they may have committed along the way. Also, for once, there was no other side of the argument. Even white supremacists hated baby rapers. Turned out half the people who lived on the Lemon Grove street with Reeves had security cameras, so the cops ended up with the license numbers of everybody who'd picked up a kid and were presently in the process of running them down.

The problem for Gabe and me revolved around that same lack of middle ground. In a case like this, only heroes or villains need apply. There was no door number three. It was the kind of unsophisticated story arc that made for good TV but was a number of nuances short of a meaningful existence. Seemed like the only choices we had were to circle the wagons and try to fade into the background or to accept the white hat accolades of the news media, who were all over us like a cheap suit as soon as the cops released our names, claiming that under the astute direction of one of their own, the erstwhile and heroically gallant Sergeant Carolyn Saunders, we had minimally aided in the rescue of twenty-three children and in the destruction of a human trafficking ring.

And then, of course, there was the fact that nobody in charge had a clue. Despite assurances that they'd get to the bottom of things and the constant refusal to answer specific questions because it was an *open investigation*. Truth was, nobody was exactly sure what in hell had happened. And nobody had any idea how to get those children home either, but there was no way they could say that out loud.

From what we gathered from Carolyn and the squad of assistant district attorneys they'd unleashed on us, in addition to the kabobbed Mr. Reeves, the other two piles of meat in the Jaguar belonged to a guy named Hector Pometta, a small-time armed robber who, not coincidentally, had also served time at Brushy Mountain, and to an unidentified mangled male wearing an expensive pair of Valentino trousers. A man whose DNA profile was not on file anywhere and whose hands, at some point, must have been pulled under the body of the skidding car, rendering them a pair of ragged mittens unfit for the taking of fingerprints.

So we squinted knowingly into the cameras, stuck out our chins, and did our best impression of humble heroes. Took the newshounds about a week to move on to other things. By that time, the cops had figured out that they were probably never going to get definitive answers because the only people who knew them for sure were no longer on the same side of the turf as the rest of us—that and the fact that they found the unfortunate Mr. Pickett's withered corpse right where we'd told them they would. Seemed like finding bodies did wonders for our credibility.

The only one of the conspirators unaccounted for was Corinna Cisneros, who'd crossed the border and then dropped completely out of sight. The Federales claimed they were giving chase, but nobody was holding their collective breath.

The forensic accounting geeks reported that early returns from their digital bean counting suggested that Jack Haller's description of the situation had more or less been on point. That the guy known as Pemberton had, in some nefarious manner or another, managed to wrest control of Allied Investments from Mrs. Haller's grasp and into his own, at which point he'd begun to liquidate all of the estate's assets, transferring the proceeds into a Caribbean bank account that the forensics squad had subsequently located, only to learn that the account had been frozen by Jack Haller's legal team the year before.

They theorized that when Pemberton's ill-gotten gains suddenly became unavailable to them, and the golden opportunity to clean out the Haller trust seemed to be slipping from their grasp, they hit upon the idea of using the trucks supposedly containing fishing gear to traffic children across the border.

U.S. Immigration Services confirmed that because the return of the supposed fishing gear was part of a multinational agreement between Mexico and the U.S.—an agreement that quite generously had allowed Mexico to collect sales tax on the sale of the Haller fleet—the trucks had been exempted from normal border inspections and issued Global Entry status.

As far as the Feds could determine, this had been going on for about a year and a half. How many kids they'd sold, to whom, and where the kids were now was anybody's guess, but, as might have been expected, authorities vowed to neither eat nor sleep until every one of these children had been accounted for and returned to his or her rightful family. Something that Gabe and I knew wasn't going to happen.

As also might have been expected, every Hispanic rights organization within a hundred miles—people already pissed off by the "zero tolerance" border policy—these folks were marching, rallying, and blocking freeways nearly every day somewhere in San Diego County. Any pretense of international civility was out the window at this point.

As for the unfortunate Mrs. Haller, around whom this whole maelstrom swirled, forensics said the old lady'd been dead and frozen solid for at least fourteen months or so, thus making it impossible to determine a precise cause of death. It came out a few days later that all of the suspects who were either found dead at the scene or rounded up from the surrounding hills later in the day had served hard time somewhere and had been granted a second chance by Mrs. Haller's philanthropic largesse. I figured that, you know, in some ways maybe it was better the old girl wasn't around to find out that no good deed ever goes unpunished. We got enough cynics already.

If there was any good news at all, it came in the form of another message from Eagen. The burner phone I'd left on the kitchen counter was blinking like a pinball machine. I picked it up and pushed the button. Eagen on my voicemail. He was amused. I could tell right away.

"Listen, man, I got no idea at all what any of this has to do with what you two got going on, but . . . first off, and you probably know this already, those two idiots they sent down to Mexico looking for you got their buttons pushed right there in hippie-dippy Ocean Beach. What you probably don't know is that guy John Henry Marshall—the little runt we been looking for—the one who did all the talking for those Aryan assholes . . ." I thought I heard Eagen swallow a chuckle. "Well, the Oregon State Police found him in the woods south of Portland—shot to death. They also picked up four more of those white-power types. Found 'em searching an old abandoned storefront that Marshall'd been using for a base of operations. Buncha white-power rectums from Fresno. Claim they don't know nothing about what happened to Marshall. OSP's got 'em under lock and key down in Salem and plans on keepin' 'em for the foreseeable future. I asked a bunch of questions, but OSP really don't know what in hell's going on neither. I find out anything else, I'll drop a dime on you."

I was about to hang up when his voice crackled over the line. "And by the way, man. The surveillance task force is picking up a lot of chatter to the effect that the white-boy membership figures Marshall got what he deserved for what happened up in Conway. Sounds like you and Gabe are pretty much off the hook. Nobody's looking for you guys anymore. So I'm guessing you can, if you feel like it, go back to being Leo instead of Leon. Okay . . . that's it. Later."

• • •

And so, it was two o'clock on a Tuesday afternoon. The only good thing I could say about the ceremony was that cops, unlike politicians, tended to be short-winded. Carolyn was getting the SDPD Medal of Valor, a raise in pay grade, another week off to recover from her injuries, and her name added to the list for the lieutenant's exam in February. That and the fact that she looked real good in her full dress uniform.

Gabe and I took in the proceedings while leaning against the rear wall of the downtown conference room. Four local TV stations were recording the gala.

We stayed put while Carolyn was congratulated by most every public figure in San Diego County, each of whom wanted a picture with their hero du jour. Office wall material, I figured.

When the mayor's press secretary finally left, only the three of us were in the room. Carolyn walked to the back to where we were standing.

The bump on her forehead was shrinking, and she'd painted a lot of foundation makeup over her blackened eyes. She didn't look nearly as much like a raccoon as she had a few days back. Her nose, however, was a mite more crooked than it used to be.

"You have your car keys?" she asked me.

I fished around in my pants pocket and came up with them. She took them from my hand and tossed them at Gabe, who snatched them from the air like a fly.

"I'll bring him home when I'm done with him," she told Gabe.

She grabbed me by the elbow and began pulling me toward the door. As we stepped through the doorway, she turned and said to Gabe, "If he's any good, I may keep him for a few days."

Gabe grinned and pocketed the keys.

"See ya later tonight," Gabe deadpanned at me.

. . .

A few days turned out to be Sunday morning. Early. The onshore flow was thick as chowder when Carolyn let me out on Del Monte. I walked around to the driver's side. She rolled down the window. This was the awkward point where people usually said things in the short run that they didn't mean for the long term. We'd both been to enough rodeos not to make that mistake.

"Thanks," I said.

"Thank you," was her amused reply.

"We'll have to do this again sometime," I ventured with a smile. Mr. Tentative.

"You have my number."

I managed to swallow the overwhelming urge to profess undying love.

"Later," was all I said instead.

She rolled up the window and eased out into the street.

I watched her taillights turn left on Sunset Cliffs Boulevard and fade into the mist. I was lost in remembered lust when an unexpected voice pulled me from my bliss.

"Hey, Leo," it said. I turned toward the street.

Brandon stepped out from behind a parked car and started my way. From the look of the trash scattered on the grassy divider, he'd been there all night.

"What's up?" I asked as he crossed to my side.

He fidgeted, ran a hand over his face, then spit it out.

"You know . . . I was thinkin' . . . you know, about what you said about having this thing maybe taken off my head."

He was wearing his camo outfit with the hat pulled down over his bar code.

"The offer still stands," I said. "From what I understand, they can laser that thing off like it never was there."

"Yeah," he said. "I'm thinkin' maybe I'd like to give it a try."

I threw an arm around his shoulders. "What say we hoof it over to Jake and Eggs and have breakfast. After that maybe we can make some calls."

"Yeah. That sounds good."

As we strolled along Del Monte Avenue, he said, "I'm kinda scared—you know what I mean? That tat's kind of been my brand for a long time."

"That's the fun part," I said.

"What?"

"Reinventing yourself. I'm thinkin' I've done it four or five times in my life. I always go into it assuming I've got a pretty good idea of who I'm going to be afterward . . ." I laughed out loud as we turned the corner. "And then I turn out to be somebody else entirely. Always freaks me out."

ABOUT THE AUTHOR

 G.M. Ford is the author of eleven other novels in the Leo Waterman series: *Who in Hell Is Wanda Fuca?*, *Cast in Stone*, *The Bum's Rush*, *Slow Burn*, *Last Ditch*, *The Deader the Better*, *Thicker Than Water*, *Chump Change*, *Salvation Lake*, *Family Values*, and *Soul Survivor*. He has also penned the Frank Corso mystery series and the stand-alone thrillers *Threshold*, *The Nature of the Beast*, and *Nameless Night*. He has been nominated for the Shamus, Anthony, and Lefty Awards, among others. He lives and writes in Ocean Beach, California.